ROGUE ORDER

(A TROY STARK THRILLER—BOOK 7)

JACK MARS

Jack Mars

Jack Mars is the USA Today bestselling author of the LUKE STONE thriller series, which includes seven books. He is also the author of the new FORGING OF LUKE STONE prequel series, comprising six books; of the AGENT ZERO spy thriller series, comprising twelve books; of the TROY STARK thriller series, comprising eight books; of the SPY GAME thriller series, comprising ten books; of the JAKE MERCER thriller series, comprising seven books (and counting); of the TYLER WOLF thriller series, comprising seven books (and counting); and of the new LARA KING thriller series, comprising seven books (and counting).

Jack loves to hear from you, so please feel free to visit www.Jackmarsauthor.com to join the email list, receive a free book, receive free giveaways, connect on Facebook and Twitter, and stay in touch!

ISBN: 978-1-0943-8690-4

BOOKS BY JACK MARS

LARA KING THRILLER SERIES
ASSET ONE (Book #1)
ASSET TWO (Book #2)
ASSET THREE (Book #3)
ASSET FOUR (Book #4)
ASSET FIVE (Book #5)
ASSET SIX (Book #6)
ASSET SEVEN (Book #7)

TYLER WOLF THRILLER SERIES
DOUBLE AGENT (Book #1)
DOUBLE CROSS (Book #2)
DOUBLE ASSET (Book #3)
DOUBLE DOCTRINE (Book #4)
DOUBLE JEOPARDY (Book #5)
DOUBLE THREAT (Book #6)
DOUBLE TARGET (Book #7)

JAKE MERCER THRILLER SERIES
ABSOLUTE THREAT (Book #1)
ABSOLUTE DAMAGE (Book #2)
ABSOLUTE FORCE (Book #3)
ABSOLUTE PERIL (Book #4)
ABSOLUTE TREASON (Book #5)
ABSOLUTE VENGEANCE (Book #6)
ABSOLUTE TARGET (Book #7)

THE SPY GAME
TARGET ONE (Book #1)
TARGET TWO (Book #2)
TARGET THREE (Book #3)
TARGET FOUR (Book #4)
TARGET FIVE (Book #5)
TARGET SIX (Book #6)
TARGET SEVEN (Book #7)
TARGET EIGHT (Book #8)
TARGET NINE (Book #9)
TARGET TEN (Book #10)

TROY STARK THRILLER SERIES
ROGUE FORCE (Book #1)
ROGUE COMMAND (Book #2)
ROGUE TARGET (Book #3)
ROGUE MISSION (Book #4)
ROGUE SHOT (Book #5)
ROGUE STRIKE (Book #6)
ROGUE ORDER (Book #7)
ROGUE ATTACK (Book #8)

LUKE STONE THRILLER SERIES
ANY MEANS NECESSARY (Book #1)
OATH OF OFFICE (Book #2)
SITUATION ROOM (Book #3)
OPPOSE ANY FOE (Book #4)
PRESIDENT ELECT (Book #5)
OUR SACRED HONOR (Book #6)
HOUSE DIVIDED (Book #7)

FORGING OF LUKE STONE PREQUEL SERIES
PRIMARY TARGET (Book #1)
PRIMARY COMMAND (Book #2)
PRIMARY THREAT (Book #3)
PRIMARY GLORY (Book #4)
PRIMARY VALOR (Book #5)
PRIMARY DUTY (Book #6)

AN AGENT ZERO SPY THRILLER SERIES
AGENT ZERO (Book #1)
TARGET ZERO (Book #2)
HUNTING ZERO (Book #3)
TRAPPING ZERO (Book #4)
FILE ZERO (Book #5)
RECALL ZERO (Book #6)
ASSASSIN ZERO (Book #7)
DECOY ZERO (Book #8)
CHASING ZERO (Book #9)
VENGEANCE ZERO (Book #10)
ZERO ZERO (Book #11)
ABSOLUTE ZERO (Book #12)

CHAPTER ONE

February 13
4:15 pm Central European Time
Musee Poitier (the Poitier Museum)
Rue de Monceau, 8th Arrondissement
Paris, France

"Paris is worth a mass," the man said under his breath.

The day was cold and gray. It had rained earlier, but now it had stopped. The streets were still wet. Overhead, the late day sun was trying to do something behind the heavy clouds, but it was hard to say what.

The man went by Richard Tickler. It wasn't his name. He wore dark blue maintenance coveralls that were identical to the ones worn by the men who worked for the Musee Poitier. He carried a back pack that was also dark blue, as if it had been issued as part of the uniform.

He had a dark blue American-style baseball cap with the bill pulled down, covering his eyes. He wore a black KN-95 mask on his face. There had been a vicious cholera outbreak in Romania and Moldova, the result of a terrorist attack. Another attack in Croatia was thwarted by the secret police.

The outbreak was ongoing, though getting better. Two million people were still displaced. An unknown number had died, possibly tens of thousands. But everyone, all across Europe, was waiting for the next shoe to drop. Who would be next? Given the situation, it was perfectly natural to wear a mask like this. Also, it disguised his identity.

He walked down the street along the outside of museum. It was a long building, white stone, with steep, gabled roofs made of blue slate. It had once been the mansion of a wealthy merchant family known as Poitier, now a museum that housed their classic art collection, gemstones, items of interest from the early 1800s, and some modern exhibits acquired or borrowed by the family trust that owned the place.

Inside the grounds, at the center of the building, were sprawling gardens that lay mostly fallow this time of year.

Tickler had been in town for two weeks. He had visited the museum three times, in different disguises. He had the layout more or less memorized. He knew exactly where he was going and what he was doing.

He went to a tall, green metal door that concealed an alleyway inside the building grounds. There were ornate spikes at the top of the door. Tickler took out a large key ring with about a dozen keys on it. Crowds of bundled-up winter tourists swirled past without paying him any attention.

Just a workman with all his keys, nothing to see here.

One of the keys was a metal pick. He slid it into the simple lock mechanism, felt as it raised the tumblers, jimmied it a tiny amount, and then turned it.

"Voila!" he said, as the lock turned easily.

Musee Poitier had security, of course it did. There were tens of millions of Euros worth of exhibits inside, possibly more. Invaluable exhibits, in fact. At least one would be hard to put a price on. But the security here was the kind that kept honest people honest. It couldn't keep out people like Richard Tickler.

He closed the heavy door behind him and moved up the alleyway. He kept his head tilted down. There were cameras here, it was difficult to say how many.

He glanced at his digital watch. 4:19.

One more minute. The timing had to be perfect, and so far, it was.

There was another steel door here, grayish white, and flush with the back of the building. This one had a serious lock with multiple bolts and sensors wed to the interior alarm system. Tickler didn't approach the door, not just yet. A maintenance man wouldn't go through that door from the outside.

He checked the watch again. It blinked from 4:19 to 4:20.

His heart skipped a beat. He took a labored breath behind his mask. The cameras, everywhere in this building, and in many places in this neighborhood and across the city, should have just gone down. The ticket-issuing computers, accounting software, and all manner of other digital equipment, should have all stopped working.

He had no way of knowing if that had happened or not. Up until this moment, he had taken very minimal risks. He was about to cross the threshold.

"Here goes nothing," he said.

From the pocket of his coveralls, he took a small incendiary charge. With black-gloved hands, he ripped open the plastic seal and slipped it out of its cardboard package. He stuffed all the packing back into his pockets.

The charge was a circular disk with a sticky backing. He affixed it directly to the lock mechanism, set the timer for 0:10, pressed the tiny red button, and walked away up the alley. There was a rusting green dumpster here, and he ducked behind it.

BOOM.

The noise was loud, but not deafening.

Smoke rose from the door. Tickler got up and walked to it. A hole had been blown clear through the locking mechanism and right through the door. The hole was all jagged and shredded metal. He poked two gloved fingers through the hole, hooked them on the sharp metal and pulled.

The door swung open easily. No audible alarm sounded.

He poked his head inside. It was a back hallway, piled with boxes, tools of various kinds, and cleaning equipment. He smiled behind his mask.

He was in.

***

When the riot broke out, Yves Saint L'Orange was in the lobby of the museum.

It was a silly alias, not his real name. He and his partners tended to take on names like this. They were fun-loving, or tried to be.

"Welcome to the new Paris," a man next to him said, as a surge of young immigrants, screaming and yelling and laughing, pushed and shoved their way through the wide open double doors. Security guards attempted to push them back out, or at least close the doors, but it was no use.

The lobby was an elegant atrium with marble floors, the ticketing desk and bag check along one curved wall. The computer system had gone down a moment ago, and within seconds of that, a flash mob had flooded in from the street outside. Seconds after that, a loud BANG had come from deep inside the museum.

Everyone ducked at the sound, paused, then continued what they were doing. It might have been an explosion. It might have been a heavy book dropping to the floor.

Yves had been standing in line when the system went down. Now, he had drifted into the center of the atrium, dressed as a typical 30-something tourist. He wore a dark green pullover, corduroy pants, and warm, comfortable boots with a fur lining. He had a dark beard, wool hat, sunglasses, and a light blue surgical mask.

He watched as the young migrants, most dressed in black or other dark colors, pushed through the doors. They were North Africans, or possibly Middle-Easterners, with some Sub-Saharan Africans thrown in. They looked like they were high-school age, or a little older. Most were young men, but there was a smattering of young women.

In seconds, the atrium became dense with them. The ones in the lead pressed further into the museum, then took off running down the wide halls, still laughing and shouting. The crowd nearly filled the atrium now, shoving and jostling. Yves laughed, but then he was pushed, lost his feet, and fell to the floor with about five of the migrants.

"Okay. That's enough of that."

He had lost his bag in the fall. It didn't matter. There was nothing in it but decoy generic tourist stuff - a water bottle, an energy bar, a pair of cheap binoculars - in case anyone in authority actually took a look inside. He had never touched the bag, or anything in it, without gloves on.

He got up and worked his way out of the chaos. In one exhibit room, the kids had taken out spray paint cans and were defacing priceless paintings on the walls.

Yves had no feelings about that.

Quickly, he darted up a broad spiral staircase. It was perfectly normal to do so. Several people were on the stairs with him - the tourists were moving away from the riots downstairs. Everywhere, people were shouting. A trio of security guards ran past, plunging down the stairs. A second later, another one came, a straggler. He had removed a nightstick from his belt.

Good. The violence was about to begin. Violence, havoc, confusion. That's what they needed here, at least for several more minutes.

Yves moved down a wide hallway with parquet floors. The walls on either side were hung with large paintings. Yves barely glanced at them. He'd seen them already. They were those very realistic paintings of things that artists made in the centuries before photography. Yves preferred 20th century art - Pablo Picasso, Salvador Dali, Paul Klee. This museum didn't have that kind of thing.

He made a right turn, then a left. He was moving deeper into the museum. Up ahead, in the center of the hall, in fact at the confluences of two hallways, was a large glass box with a light shining on it from overhead.

Yves walked right to it. No one was around. The security that would normally be here must have abandoned their posts to deal with the riot downstairs.

There were cameras on two of the walls, but they didn't work. The computers that ran the cameras, and where the video footage went, were down.

Inside the box was a large, green gemstone. It must be nearly the size of a man's fist. It glimmered under the spotlight above. The light seemed to play on endless grooves and striations in the stone. It wasn't the most breathtaking gem that Yves had ever seen. It certainly wasn't perfect.

It was worth a lot of money because it was comparatively rare. It was worth more than money.

Anyway, none of that mattered.

Richard Tickler appeared, approaching up the crossed hall from Yves's right. He looked somewhat ridiculous in his blue maintenance uniform and his baseball cap pulled down over his face.

Tickler looked at Yves.

"Yves," he said.

He pronounced it, "Yuh-vez."

He kept a straight face as he did so. Deadpan humor, that was Richard Tickler's stock-in-trade.

"Dick," Yves said.

"Richard," Tickler corrected him.

They both gazed down into the box now.

"Quite a thing," Tickler said.

Yves nodded. "Yes."

Dick kneeled, unslung his knapsack, and opened it. He handed a small pair of bolt cutters up to Yves. Yves instantly went to the small lock on the side of the glass box and cut it. The lock was strong, but Yves was stronger.

It took a little application of effort to break it, but that was part of Yves's role on these jobs. He could break stuff, smash stuff, and carry stuff. He was rugged.

The lock broke and fell to the floor. It echoed through the empty halls. Yves kneeled, picked up the broken lock, and put it in his pocket.

He handed the bolt cutters back to Dick. Dick had already removed a dark wooden box from his bag and placed it on the floor.

He took the cutters from Yves and slid them back into the bag.

Yves glanced around. There was nothing to see. The lights here were dim in order to enhance the effect of the spotlight shining on the gemstone. The hallways were empty. Shouts and screams floated up to them from downstairs.

Dick took a large gemstone, seemingly identical to the one in the glass box, from the wooden case on the floor.

He glanced at Yves. Yves nodded and opened the glass case, pulling the whole thing back and tilting it on an angle.

Dick stood. He stared down at the exhibit for a moment. It was almost like he was taking a break. Yves didn't say anything.

In one fluid movement, Dick snatched up the real gemstone and replaced it with the fake, both things happening nearly simultaneously. He placed the fake one in a position that perfectly, or nearly perfectly, matched the position of the original.

Yves slowly let the lid close.

Dick had already disappeared the gemstone somewhere, slid the wooden box into his bag, and was walking away back the way he had come.

From another pocket, Yves pulled a lock identical to the one he cut, and he locked the case closed again.

He turned and headed back the way he came, toward the circular stairs down to the atrium. He moved quickly to re-enter the surging chaos as soon he could, though the security cameras weren't working, and he was carrying nothing incriminating on his person.

He was an innocent man.

***

"Another day, another euro."

Outside, Richard Tickler walked down the service alley, between the outside of the mansion, and the high walls of the interior gardens.

He was moving away from the blown-out back door. Destroying a door had been a risk, but gemstones and other valuable items sometimes had embedded security features that made them impossible to leave with through regular entryways. Also, two men entering from different directions were less noticeably together than two men coming through the front entrance. Finally, a getaway vehicle was less noticeable when it was parked on a lesser side street.

In any event, no one had come to investigate that door. All of the guards must still be occupied with the sudden invasion of migrants. And with the cameras down, it was possible, maybe even likely, that no one knew the door was blown.

None of that was his affair any longer.

He approached the tall, green steel door to the street. The bag on his back seemed heavy, much heavier than when he came in. He knew that was wrong. The real Star of Versailles, which he was carrying now, and the fake one, weighed the exact same amount. The added heaviness was the danger.

There was a lot of sound outside - shouts, screams, wild laughter, intermittent whoops and wails of sirens. He tried to picture the scene, but he couldn't imagine it. He would just have to see it for himself.

On this side of the door, the deadbolt was a simple mechanism he could turn with his gloved fingers. He did so, and pulled the door toward him.

A small police car was parked at the curb, directly in front of him. The blue light on its roof was on and circling, but the siren was off. A mob of young black and brown kids was running down the street, streaming by in two and threes and fours, sneakers and boots slapping the pavement. They were fleeing the front entrance of the museum, which was around the corner from here.

They had served their purpose, though they had no idea what it really was. Now they were attempting their getaway.

Tourists pressed themselves against the walls of surrounding buildings so as not to be run over in the melee.

Richard glanced to his left. Up at the corner, there were four or five more police vehicles blocking off the narrow streets.

He went to the police car in front of him, opened the door, and slid into the passenger seat. A blonde-haired woman, her hair pulled into a tight ponytail, sat behind the wheel. She was dressed in a police uniform that hugged the curves of her body. She wore a black mask on her face and black driving gloves on her hands. All that showed of her face was her pretty blue eyes.

She wasn't a policewoman. She called herself Holly Danger, though that wasn't her real name. She had once driven race cars on a low-level professional circuit, one of the first women to break into that field. She had done a lot of things before now.

"Nice outfit," Richard said. "It becomes you."

Holly put the car in gear, and pulled slowly away from the curb, watching her mirrors, mindful not to hit any of the running children. She drove for a few blocks, then made a left turn onto a wide boulevard.

Richard slipped his backpack off and placed it at his feet. Then he settled back into the seat and pulled his seatbelt across his chest. He closed his eyes, content to let Holly navigate the City of Paris traffic. He sighed.

"How did it go?" she said.

"Fine. About what I expected."

"Yves?"

Richard shrugged. "Right where he needed to be, when he needed to be there."

"So everything went…"

He nodded. "Smoothly, yes."

He opened his eyes and looked at her.

"The car?"

Everything, every single thing, had to be right. They needed to ditch this cop car as soon as possible.

"It's in an underground car park in the 11th Arrondissement," Holly said. "The security cameras there are disabled as of an hour ago. I disabled them. We should arrive in a few moments. I have a showroom drape in the boot of this car. It will take five minutes to wrap this one so it's hidden, then off we go."

Richard nodded. "Good."

A new car, new identities, and soon, a large amount of money.

A fabulous new life awaited.

***

"A very exciting day," Jacques Trudeau said.

He was returning to his post 20 minutes later.

Sweeping the invaders out of the museum had been an all-hands call. Jacques was a big man, who at the age of 42 years, was perhaps 20 pounds overweight. Even now, he was still breathing heavily, and his uniform felt a bit stretched and askew.

He had corralled three of the young people himself, and dragged them out to the street by their collars, well before the gendarmes arrived.

Jacques's post was at the confluence of two hallways, and right where they met, the infamous Star of Versailles made its home. There were paintings all along both corridors, and two other lesser gemstones down the line. But the Star of Versailles was the main attraction.

He took up his post. Nothing seemed amiss.

This was where he had stood all day, five days a week, for the past six years. It was generally a very boring job. Truth be told, while he disapproved of immigrant flash mobs and immigrants in general, he was glad for a little excitement.

Some of the rioters had been detained by the police. Many more were pushed back out to the street. A couple of priceless paintings in the lobby area were defaced with spray paint. They would have to be sent away to be carefully cleaned.

It's wasn't the first time something like this had happened to a Paris museum. It wasn't even the first time it had happened at Musee Poitier, though this was the first time something on this scale had taken place.

The newcomers to France were barbarians, many of them. They would gleefully destroy the culture of the place that offered them sanctuary from the troubles in their own countries. Jacques shook his head.

"Send them home. See how they like that."

He glanced to his right and noticed his mobile phone on the floor, propped up against the wall. He had nearly forgotten that he placed it there.

Before he left, he had laid his phone down, facing the Star of Versailles. Then he had turned on his video camera, and let it run. This is because a few minutes before the riot began, the desk had alerted him that the security cameras were down.

Leaving his phone behind was a little stop-gap strategy until he returned. The phone was barely noticeable against the wall. In the dim light, you'd almost have to know it was there to see it.

Not that anything was going to happen. Nothing ever happened on this hallway.

He picked up the phone, stopped the recording, and began the playback.

He watched the video, expecting to see nothing. So far, he was right - there was nothing. There wasn't going to be anything. He began to fast-forward the video, first 2x normal speed, then 4x times, just to get it over with.

He was watching it with one eye, the other eye watching the hall, his mind wandering back to, and savoring, the fighting and craziness downstairs.

He caught a glimpse of two men in the video.

He stopped the footage and went back to before they appeared.

His heart skipped, just a tiny amount.

Now he watched the video on normal speed again as the two men entered the frame from different directions. They were masked and wearing hats. One man, the taller and broader of the two, was wearing dark glasses despite being indoors.

It was difficult to see their faces. Jacques suspected it would be nearly impossible to identify them.

Now he watched them break open the glass case just a few meters from where Jacques was standing, then steal and replace the Star of Versailles, taking less than a full minute to do so. Seconds later, they were both gone, out of the video frame.

Inside Jacques's mind, a whole set of assumptions began to fall away.

The nihilistic invasion by migrants was…

A ruse.

It was a decoy. Far from being the disordered chaos typical of inferior peoples, it was a well-organized plot to lure the security guards downstairs, and away from the most valuable exhibits in the museum.

It was a plot, specifically, to pull Jacques away from his post. And it worked perfectly.

"Oh… my… God."

An instant later, he was on his radio to the front desk.

CHAPTER TWO

6:55 pm Central European Time
Madrid Atocha Train Station
Madrid, Spain

"Ya lo tengo," Troy Stark said into the tiny microphone hidden behind his collar.

In English, it meant "I already have him."

Months in Spain had done wonders for Troy's Spanish language skills. He still spoke in simple, declarative sentences, but his vocabulary had expanded, and the words were readily available to him.

The long delays while he thought something in English, translated it into Spanish in his mind, and then said it out loud, were mostly gone. He didn't always understand what was said back to him, but even that was coming along.

He stood in the wide concourse of the Atocha Train Station, eyes scanning the bustling station, as a crowd of people flowed in from the train platform. Most of the people wore masks. Some stopped at the various gourmet food shops that lined the station, others simply kept moving along, maybe eager to get home.

They had all just exited the afternoon train from Marbella, on the southern Mediterranean coast, what the Spanish called the "Costa del Sol."

Far above Troy's head, the late 1800s arched iron and glass roof soared, showing the dark sky. Closer, there was the tropical garden of banana, coconut, and breadfruit trees. Troy could see why Miquel was obsessed with this place. Beyond the 2004 terrorist attack that killed 193 people, this must be the most beautiful train station in the world.

Certainly, Troy had never seen one that rivaled it.

The man Troy already had was a tall, pudgy, balding white guy. Perhaps he was an athlete at one time, but that was 20 years and countless hours in pubs ago. The guy had big shoulders and strong hands and that big belly that was probably as hard as a plate of steel. Troy had punched a few of those in his time.

The man wore a green Chelsea football jersey under an open brown leather jacket. He wore the black plastic tracksuit pants typical of guys like him.

The fashion disaster alone was enough to make Troy dislike him.

The guy trailed a red, beat-up rolling suitcase behind him, and carried a blue gym bag with a white stripe over his shoulder. The bags were what interested Troy and about a dozen undercover Madrid cops and Guardia Civil that were salted all over the station right now.

Troy blended in seamlessly among the throngs of travelers. He wore blue jeans, a black jacket, and comfortable leather boots sprung in all the right places. A pair of Ray-Ban sunglasses were perched on top of his head. He had a two-day growth of beard, and was wearing a white KN-95 mask, like most people here. He had a blue and green striped overnight bag at his feet.

He could be just another tourist passing through. He could be waiting for someone to get off a train. He could be anybody.

He was on loan to the Madrid Police from El Grupo Especial for this operation, courtesy of his boss. It worked because the last thing on Earth that Troy looked like was a Madrid cop. This fact was confirmed as the mark walked right past him, and barely glanced Troy's way at all.

Troy watched the guy from the corner of his eye, waited several seconds, then began to follow him. He didn't bother picking up the overnight bag. He wanted his hands free, and the bag was a decoy, with nothing useful inside. Someone else would retrieve it.

It had only been a week since they stopped the cholera attack. Dubois was still recuperating from her kidnapping ordeal, El Grupo Especial was in limbo once again, and Troy was working with the local cops against drug traffickers moving hash and possibly heroin or cocaine into Madrid.

Troy had a phantom feeling that was hard to shake. His throat was still sore from the Serbian professional killer nearly choking him to death.

It was worse than sore. After all, a little soreness might linger from something like that a week or more later. This was different. It was as if the man's hands were still clamped around Troy's throat. It was almost like he was hallucinating.

Troy had taken to wearing open collars to limit the effect of it. He couldn't imagine putting on a necktie right now. It was interesting, this feeling he had, and he tried to see it that way, cold and clinical, as though he was the subject of his own science experiment.

A few minutes before the guy nearly strangled him, Troy had been shot in the arm, straight through, with a small caliber weapon. The wound had been cleaned and treated, and was healing nicely. It was swollen and sore, he could feel it throbbing and probably would for the next month, but it was nothing like the feeling in his throat.

He shook his head to clear it. He was on the job here. He could wonder about all this at a later time.

As the suspect wove his way through the crowds, Troy followed with practiced ease, maintaining a safe distance, never quite looking directly at the target, and yet never losing sight of him. The guy wasn't hard to follow. He was nearly Troy's height, thick-bodied, lumbering along through the crowds like the Frankenstein monster.

An image flashed through Troy's mind of going toe-to-toe with this guy. The adrenaline began to course through Troy's veins. If he was being honest, this was what he lived for - the thrill of the chase. He was one of the good guys, yes, but the chemicals in his bloodstream didn't care which side he was on.

On the most basic animal level, he just craved excitement. He liked to mix it up. He had started as an amateur boxer when he was 15 years old. He had joined the US Navy at 18, and began SEAL training at 19. Now, at 32, he had been on one mission or adventure after another for nearly half his life.

"Steady," he whispered to himself. "Stay focused."

Now wasn't the time for a trip down memory lane.

He slowed as the suspect stopped abruptly to check a departure board. While the heavyset man studied the board, Troy turned and feigned interest in a nearby magazine rack outside a store, discreetly observing the man from the corner of his eye.

The magazines flashed bright colors, big, carefully airbrushed celebrity faces, and voluptuous, near naked bodies. They were nearly identical to the consumer magazines that would jump out at you in an American airport or train station, except with different names and in a different language.

“Hola! Como estas?" a woman said to Troy as she walked past, clearly mistaking him for someone else. She was tall and blonde, in high heels and a long coat, wearing a colorful mask with what appeared to be toucans embroidered on it, and carrying several packages. It looked like she had gone somewhere on a shopping trip.

“Bien,” Troy said. “Gracias. Y usted?”

“Tu sabes!” she said, and laughed, gesturing with her store packages.

Troy laughed, too. She was perfect. She couldn't have given him better cover if she tried. She continued up the concourse, and Troy watched after her, as though he was checking out her form. She passed the suspect, and neither one noticed the other. They were living in two separate realities, close in space and time, and yet galaxies apart.

The man in the football jersey and leather jacket turned away from the departure board. A men's room was directly behind him, and he disappeared into it. He moved quickly for a big man loaded down with two bags. In fact, he was gone in a flash.

Now you see me, now you don’t.

“El esta en el bano," Troy said into the microphone. The Madrid cops tended not to speak or understand much English.

“He’s in the bathroom.”

Troy started moving toward the entry where the man had just gone.

“En el bano de hombres.”

“In the men’s room,” he clarified, in case there was any question.

“Me voy alli.”

“I’m going there.”

Troy paused and counted under his breath, allowing a few seconds to pass.

“Uno… dos… three… four…”

He went in.

Upon entering the gleaming men's room, the familiar scent of disinfectant met Troy's nose. He scanned the area, spotting the suspect standing with his bags at a row of urinals. Troy fought the urge to act prematurely. There might be dope in those bags, there might not. But the money man had not yet appeared.

Patience. Take your time.

Troy moved to the line of sinks and began to wash his hands as if that was the whole reason he'd come in here. Automatic motion-sensored water, automatic motion-sensored liquefied soap, nothing to touch, ever. In a minute, Troy would wave his hand under a paper towel dispenser, and a sheet of coarse brown paper would slide out all by itself.

Germs, man. Germs will kill you.

As a child, Troy had been taught that germs were good for you because they helped keep your immune system strong. Events of recent times seemed to stand that bit of old-school wisdom on its head. It turned out that lab-grown, weaponized cholera was NOT good for you. It did not keep your immune system strong.

Troy went through the motions of washing his hands three times, all the while watching his prey, far to the right, out of the corner of his eye. This was going to become awkward in another moment. The hunted was parked too long at a urinal, and the hunter was parked too long at the sink. Pretty soon, the hunted was going to catch on.

“Esta jabón es terrible,” grumbled an elderly gentleman next to Troy.

This soap is terrible.

Troy had no idea what the old man was talking about. The soap was fine. It was like any other bright pink, mass-produced, greasy liquid chemical that stunk like the Exxon Valdez disaster. The hot water could barely burn the stuff off his hands. Troy could picture helpless seabirds caked in large pink balls of it.

"Si," Troy said. "El peor.”

Yes. The worst.

People were very chatty in Madrid. It made for great cover. Nothing to see here. Just a couple of random guys talking about soap.

Troy watched as the suspect zipped up and turned toward the stalls. He pulled his rolling suitcase behind him and left it leaning against the cold tile wall. Then he opened the stall door at the far end, cast a furtive glance around the bathroom, and disappeared inside with the gym bag. The light above the stall turned from green to red.

Occupado. The light next to it was already red.

"Here we go," Troy said, his voice low. He took a breath.

“Que?” said the old man, now drying his hands with a paper towel.

Troy waved his hand in the air. “Nada. Soy loco, siempre hablando.”

Nothing. I'm crazy. Always talking.

"Ah." The old man nodded, but his eyes said he wasn't sure. He seemed to force a smile on his face. Then he walked away. It was probably better not to talk to insane people in public toilets.

The meeting could very well be taking place inside those two stalls.

Suddenly, another man entered the restroom, carrying a gym bag identical to the one the first suspect had carried. Blue, with a narrow white stripe. The man was smaller than the first, younger, and darker, with black hair. He wore a black t-shirt and blue jeans, no jacket. He had black sneakers on. He looked like a guy who could run far and fast if he needed to.

The newcomer made his way down the row of stalls. He stopped, opened the door next to the one the big man has gone into, and disappeared himself. That was it, for sure. Identical bags, and someone had gone to the trouble of making the Occupied light malfunction. It was always red, so no one would go in there.

This was the meeting. This was where the exchange would take place.

“Ambos estan aqui,” Troy said into his microphone.

They're both here.

Troy moved slowly down the row of stalls. Another man turned from the urinals, a middle-aged guy in glasses. He saw Troy and knew something was amiss. His eyes went wide. Troy put his index finger to his own lips, then gestured toward the men's room exit with his thumb. The man nodded and went.

The soft scuffle of fabric against the tiled floor reached Troy's ears, and he knew the exchange was happening. He crouched down and peeked under the stall barriers. Two sets of feet were there. One gym bag slid under the barrier. Then the second one slid under, going the other way.

“Aqui!" Troy shouted. "Ahora!”

Here! Now!

Troy lifted his right leg and kicked in the door to the stall in front of him. He planted the bottom of his foot on the door and just savagely blew through the lock.

The startled face of the young man perched on the toilet, still fully dressed, stared back at him in shock.

Troy lost his Spanish. He pointed at the guy.

“Don't you move a muscle?"

Troy moved to the next door, the one on the end. He took another breath. The door swung open without him kicking it. The big guy stood there. He had removed his leather jacket. His shoulders were broad enough that he could barely fit in the stall.

“Oi, what the hell are you doing, mate?”

The man's British accent was thick, and a hint of surprise lingered beneath his anger. Troy wouldn't call it fear, just the unpleasant sense that things hadn't gone according to plan. The cramped bathroom stall reeked of sweat and stale cigarette smoke. The guy's personal hygiene was not the best.

“You're under arrest,” Troy said.

“For what?”

Troy gestured at the floor. "For whatever's in that bag."

The man smiled. One of his front teeth was missing.

“Ain’t my bag. It was already here."

Where were those Madrid cops? On siesta?

"Look, you were filmed getting off the train. I'm a cop. I didn't end up here by accident. It's simple. We can do this the hard way or the easy way."

The man shrugged.

“Hard way, then.”

Troy shook his head. He stepped back to let the man out of the stall.

The younger man, seeing an opening, suddenly burst out of his stall and ran for the exit. He left his bag behind. He made it to the wide open doorway before half a dozen uniformed cops ran into him coming the other way. The group ended up on the floor, in a squirming, shouting mass. For a second, it looked almost like an octopus.

The Madrid cops were here, finally.

“Listen, you still want to do this the…”

Troy turned back to the big guy just in time to catch a punch in the face. The guy had big stone hands. Troy's head snapped back. His bell rang. For a second, everything in the bathroom seemed to go fuzzy and indistinct.

The hard way, indeed.

Troy backed and took a fighter’s stance, right leg back, left forward, hands up.

"Mate, I'll be out in the morning. And I relish the chance to hit a copper."

The room swans back into focus. Troy punched him, hands like lightning. Left, left, right. Solid right. The guy's head turned this way and that, absorbing the punches.

Somewhere in the distant past, his old white-haired Irish trainer Declan shouted:

"One two, Troy! One two!"

Now, the big guy's blue eyes were hard. He wasn't smiling anymore.

Troy hit him again.

Left, left… BANG!

Right.

The guy was tough, but he wasn't going to last. His face was bloodied. His eyes were starting to lose focus. His hands were drifting below his chest.

BANG!

Right again.

The light in the man's eyes went out. He lost his footing and slid down along the wall. Troy's blood was up. The guy had sucker punched him. That was nice. Troy held his left hand out and raised his right for one more shot.

“Agent Stark!”

He turned and the lead Madrid cop was there, in street clothes. He held up his badge to Troy as if Troy didn't know who he was. Captain Cruz. Clean-shaven dude in jeans and a tight black t-shirt, a guy who hit the gym a lot. He smelled like he had gone swimming in a pool of cologne. He was the only one in this group who seemed to speak English fluently.

He shook his head. "No more. That was plenty."

Troy nodded. "Got it. He hit me first."

Cruz nodded. "Okay. We'll note it. Resisting arrest. Assault on an officer. Did you identify yourself?"

“Yes.”

“It'll be on the recording then.”

Troy blinked to clear the cobwebs. The guy had tagged him pretty good.

“Yes, it will.”

Now, the bathroom was flooded with cops in uniform. Already they were pushing into the stalls, and pulling the bags out, hands gloved in plastic. Already, they had cuffed the Englishman and were pulling him to his feet.

Troy watched as one bag was unzipped. Bricks of a brown powdered substance were wrapped in plastic baggies and stacked inside. The next bag was opened, and of course there were bricks of euros in that one.

Troy turned and stepped away, his head still a bit foggy. It would be nice to get out of this crowded restroom.

“Good work, Stark,” Cruz said.

Troy raised a hand in acknowledgment, and slipped his way through the crowd of police. He walked out onto the concourse, and immediately there was a sense of space and clean air. The glass ceiling soared high above his head again, as did the trees. It helped to clear his head.

The shops were still open, just as they had been moments ago. Very little had changed, really. Maybe Troy would buy a sandwich and a soda, and just sit and let the travelers flow by, no agenda, no surveillance, just a guy out people watching.

His mobile phone began to vibrate in his pocket. He took it out and looked at the screen. Miquel Castro-Ruiz.

Troy sighed and answered it.

“Stark.”

"Hello, Agent Stark," Miquel said, his voice tinny over the connection.

“Hello Director Castro,” Troy said.

“What are you doing right now?”

Troy shrugged. "Just hanging around a train station, like you asked me to do."

“Is the operation over?” Miquel said.

Troy had the sense that Miquel knew the operation was over. That's why he was calling now. Someone had alerted him the moment it ended.

Troy smiled. "Good question."

“I need you to come in,” Miquel said.

CHAPTER THREE

9:05 pm Central European Time
Headquarters of El Grupo Especial
Outskirts of Madrid
Spain

"Agent Stark," said Miquel Castro-Ruiz, the director of Interpol's European Rapid Response Investigation Unit. Among themselves, they referred to the place as El Grupo Especial, or El Grupo for short.

"Thank you for coming."

Miquel stood like a guard at his office door in the darkened upstairs hallway. He was dressed in a blue dress shirt (open at the collar, Troy noted, and immediately felt strong hands grip his throat again), khaki pants, and soft leather shoes.

Miquel's hair was short and slicked back. His face was lined with years of chronic worry, and his goatee was nearly entirely white. His eyes were sharp and alert. He held a Styrofoam cup of what was probably coffee in one hand. He was a good-looking man in late middle age.

It was after hours at their strange, isolated, office park headquarters in suburban Madrid. There were hardly any cars in the lot outside. The trees on the grounds were thin and bare. Headlights from the nearby highway flashed across the windows of the nondescript building.

Troy nodded. "I couldn't have done it without you."

It was true, as far as it went. Miquel had used the El Grupo budget to replace Troy's previous lime-green Smart Car, which had been firebombed by the southern Italian mafia, the 'Ndrangheta.

Now Troy had a sky blue Smart Car, a two-seater a little newer but just as tiny as the previous one. It was also just as silly-looking, with the same incredible fuel-efficiency, and ease of parking. He had the same problems as before, getting up to speed on highway on-ramps. The Smart Car was probably the most un-Troy Stark car in the world. But he liked it.

What would be the most Troy Stark car in the world? Probably one of those Toyota pickups with the .50-caliber machine gun mounted in the back, which African gangs and militias used in places like Somalia and Liberia. If not that, then perhaps a perfectly restored 1965 Chevy Chevelle, an old-school American muscle car with a 350 horsepower V8 engine.

"How was Atocha?" Miquel said.

The question was loaded with meaning.

In his policeman days, Miquel had been among the first emergency personnel to arrive at the train station after the bombing. The carnage he witnessed there was what turned Miquel into the man he was today - obsessed with terrorists and terrorist atrocities, obsessed with capturing or killing them, but more than anything, obsessed with anticipating their moves and stopping them before they could attack.

Troy knew that Atocha wasn't just a train station to Miquel. It wasn't where Troy had just done some undercover work with the Madrid police. It was like a state of mind, a place of dread, and a symbol of safety or innocence that had long ago been lost.

But that wasn't how Troy experienced it. To him, it was a really pretty station, beautiful even, perhaps the nicest in the world.

He shrugged. "It was fine. We rolled up a couple of guys. There was a bag with dope in it, maybe brown heroin, and another with cash. One guy tried to resist, but you know..."

Troy smiled.

"It didn't work."

Miquel didn't smile. If anything, he seemed disturbed. Maybe he was hoping that Troy had gone back in time 20 years and changed the outcome of the bombing. But that wasn't in the cards. The destroyed platform, the shredded steel of the train, the corpses, the office lady who was gone below the torso - Troy had heard the entire story. Those things couldn't be taken back and were always going to be there.

"You weren't brutal with him, were you?" Miquel said.

Troy shook his head. "I subdued him, nothing more. I know we are walking a fine line these days."

Miquel nodded. "Good." He held an arm out toward the conference room, which was brightly lit down the corridor from them.

"After you."

The conference room was dominated by a long, high-tech table, its surface alive with a series of monitors, a keyboard in front of each. The large monitor on the wall, at the far end of the room, was dark. A line of black CPUs were stuffed under the table.

At some point in the recent past, Jan Bakker, the lead intelligence analyst at El Grupo, had decided that the original design of the conference room just didn't support his need for huge amounts of data, so he had moved a bunch of extra computers in here.

Jan was here, hunched over a computer screen, staring at what appeared to be an interior map of a building. He wore an ugly, orange-brown sweater and jeans. He wore open-toed sandals on his bare feet. He was a hulking figure, tall, broad, with big shoulders and a great big perfectly bald head. He wore thin steel-rimmed glasses, which looked incongruously fragile compared to his wide face and massive body.

When Troy first met him, he thought Jan was going to be his partner, and he welcomed the idea of having this much muscle beside him.

But it wasn't to be. Jan was a gentle soul, gigantically intelligent, who was comfortable hijacking satellites remotely, breaching secure technology systems, and poring over endless streams of information, then deciphering their secrets. Falling out of airplanes and shooting it out with hardened criminals just wasn't his place in life.

"Hi, Jan," Troy said.

Jan nodded, without looking up. "Agent Stark. How was your evening?"

"Very nice," Troy said, and almost laughed. He supposed it had been nice.

Troy glanced at two of the screens that were on. One showed a green gemstone that almost seemed to glow and had hints of blue and other colors. Another was that schematic map of a building interior. Another was a topographical map of a region in Central Africa.

Jan's large hands moved deftly over one of the keyboards, pulling up a long series of numbers in a spreadsheet format.

Along one wall was a table with a coffee maker. Someone had recently made a fresh pot of coffee. Steam was still rising from the top. Troy moved toward the table. He grabbed a white Styrofoam cup off the top of the stack. He and Miquel were two peas in a pod in this way. They both downed a lot of caffeine.

“Hello, Agent Stark,” said a deeply musical female voice.

Agent Dubois sat, or perhaps sprawled, at the far end of the conference table.

Troy had seen her there the whole time. Indeed, she was the first thing he noticed when he walked in. He'd been deliberately ignoring her presence. She wasn't supposed to be here. She was on injury leave.

He'd last seen her around noon today, and she'd said nothing about coming into the office.

She wore a form-fitting bodysuit. The bodysuit was dark, maybe a deep blue. He had trouble determining the color. There was a bright red belt around her waist that looked like it was made of plastic. She had chunky black combat boots on her feet. Her hair was up in a tall Afro, a red sash to match the belt wrapped around it.

She looked like a cartoon version of a superhero. She was, in a word, beautiful.

In this bright light, the swelling and bruises on her face, though fading, were still visible. They ruined the superhero effect to some extent.

Troy met her dark eyes. Everything was there between them, unspoken. She stared at him, but she did not smile.

"Hello, Agent Dubois," Troy said. "I must say I'm a bit surprised to see you here."

She shrugged. "Director Castro personally asked me to come in."

"It must be something important, in that case," Troy said. "In all likelihood, something dangerous, even life threatening."

He turned to Miquel. It was more than a little annoying that Miquel had called Dubois in. As far as Troy knew, he and Dubois had successfully kept their little thing a secret, but even so… Dubois had been captured by a Serbian gang just a week ago, had been beaten and nearly executed.

Troy had rescued her in a desperate operation that killed an unknown number of gang members and caused an entire row of warehouses and buildings in central Belgrade to go up in flames. From the helicopter they flew in to escape, the thing looked like the Apocalypse. All of this after they had just come from the northeast of Romania, where a deadly manufactured cholera outbreak was killing people by the thousands.

Dubois could use a little break, maybe.

"What's going on?" Troy said.

Miquel's face was deeply lined. He was serious, probably still ruminating on the Atocha situation.

"It shouldn't be dangerous," he said. "Almost certainly not life-threatening."

"What is it?"

"A jewel heist in Paris," Jan said from behind them.

“The Star of Versailles,” Miquel said. "It's a gem of unknown origin, part diamond, and partly made of a very rare stone called tanzanite, which is usually only found in a small corner of Tanzania. It's a striking green in color, but there's a heavy streak of cobalt inside that also makes it seem to glow blue. It is unique in the world, and its rarity is thought to make it priceless."

“If it seems to come from Tanzania, why do they call it the Star of Versailles?”

"It's just a marketing ploy," Jan said. "The Palace at Versailles tends to make people think of opulence, beauty, unrivaled elegance. The name lends those qualities to the gem, even though the two are unrelated."

“Where was it stolen from?” Troy said.

“A smaller museum called Musee Poitier. This afternoon, several events happened at once. A widespread computer outage affected much of Paris, including the museum. Their systems, including video monitoring, went down. Moments later, a flash mob of possible North African and sub-Saharan migrants stormed the lobby and much of the lower floor. During the confusion, two men entered the museum from different directions, met at the Star of Versailles, stole it, and replaced it with a fake.”

“I hadn’t heard anything about this,” Troy said.

Not that he would have had any time to hear of it. Troy had been tied up with train surveillance since this afternoon and hadn't checked the newspapers.

"You wouldn't," Jan said. "They've kept it out of the news."

“Who has?”

“The Poitier Family Trust,” Miquel said. “They’re the ones who have asked us to investigate the theft.”

Troy stared at Miquel. A private entity had asked El Grupo to step in and investigate? How did that work? El Grupo was part of Interpol, who collaborated with police forces throughout the world, not the private trusts of wealthy families.

“Why would they do that?”

“Why would they ask us to investigate, or why would they suppress the fact of the theft?”

Troy shrugged. "All of it."

“They called us because the secret of El Grupo is out. People know the work we've done as an organization, accomplished to a great degree by the bravery of you and Agent Dubois here. We agreed to take it on because Interpol isn't assigning us any new projects while our status is under review. In any case, where our investigations take us is entirely up to us to decide."

"And the reason they're keeping the theft under wraps?"

"A couple of reasons," Miquel said. "One is that the thieves were clever about replacing the gem with a replica. The Museum wants them to think they got away with it. They believe this makes it more likely the thieves will slip up and make a mistake."

Troy could see that. A bit unusual for a museum to be savvy about criminals and their ways, but okay. Maybe they were hit by jewel and art heists on a regular basis.

"The other is the museum itself," Dubois said from her seat at the end of the table. "They want to avoid controversy and bad publicity."

Troy turned to look at Dubois. When he faced her, she could barely repress a smile.

"The origin of the diamond has been obscured. It's almost certainly a so-called blood diamond, mined by slave labor under the control of a violent militia, warlord, government or foreign corporation in Central Africa. The Poitier Museum has never divulged where it's from, how old it is, or how they came to possess it. Moreover, the Poitier Family's vast wealth stemmed from the West African slave trade, beginning in the 1600s up through the American Civil War. They were slave traders, with their own trans-Atlantic shipping, and they also owned plantations in Haiti, the Bahamas, and the area around New Orleans."

"An early example of vertical integration," Jan said.

"The modern generations of the family like to stay out of the public eye, and even the Poitier Museum itself, while a lovely museum, prefers to avoid publicity. The Star of Versailles may not be the only exhibit that was obtained by questionable means. Rumors suggest that there are artworks and treasures held by the museum that have never been announced or put on public display."

"They collaborated with the Nazis," Troy said.

Dubois shrugged. "There's no proof of that."

Troy turned back to Miquel.

"You want to work for these people?"

Miquel shook his head. "We work in the public interest. We have no new cases at the moment. Until Interpol determines our permanent status, we are open to suggestions. The Poitier Family Trust wants to give us an inside look at a successful jewel heist. We may learn something, not just about this theft, but about the networks that move stolen art, gems and antiquities across Europe and the world."

"We get to go to Paris," Dubois said. "I can show you the city."

Now Troy's head was on a swivel.

"Are you back on the job, Agent Dubois?"

Troy didn't like the sound of that. He and Dubois hadn't talked this through, and in fact he had been dancing around the issue. But after what happened in Belgrade, he did not like the idea of Dubois being put in harm's way.

Moreover, she was on leave. She had been injured in the line of duty, and there was no way she was completely healed yet.

"It's good for her to get right back on that horse," Miquel said.

"I can still see the lumps on her face," Troy said. "Is that going to be her new nickname around here, Lumpy?"

"Paris is my hometown," Dubois said. "You'll need an expert to guide you."

"I've found my way around strange cities before," Troy said.

Dubois gestured with her chin. "How's your arm?"

"It's fixed."

She shook her head. "No, it isn't. Gunshot wounds don't heal that quickly."

Of course, she saw him changing the dressing where the bullet went through every day. She saw the angry red and purple swelling and the raw entry and exit wounds. She saw it just this morning.

"No one died here," Miquel said. "And no one is going to. No one is even going to get hurt. Jewel thieves are not violent criminals. They're smart, they're innovative, they like to get in, get out, and disappear."

"The thieves caused both a widespread tech system outage and a flash mob of young migrants, happening simultaneously," Jan said. "From what I'm hearing, several of the mob members who were detained by police said they were paid 15 euros in cash each to participate. And they claim they don't know where the money came from."

Troy nodded. "Very clever," he said.

"Enjoy yourselves," Miquel said. "It's a fascinating case. Very little risk, unlikely anything bad will happen. The thieves have probably moved on, or maybe you'll catch them before they do. Either way, you and Agent Dubois can go to Paris in the morning and snoop around a little, as you Americans would say."

"We wouldn't say that," Troy said. "Not since the 1950s."
Miquel smiled. "Consider it a working holiday."

CHAPTER FOUR

February 14
3:15 am Central European Time
A flat
Neighborhood of La Latina
Madrid, Spain

"Happy Valentine's Day," Dubois said behind him.

Troy was standing in his bedroom, to the left side of the window that overlooked the street. He enjoyed looking out that window, but in recent days, he had taken to positioning himself at hard angles to the left and to the right.

A shooter was likely to face the window straight on and try to hit someone directly in his line of sight. Troy no longer gave the shooter that option.

Below his window, the dark early morning streets were empty. In the daytime, the narrow winding streets were lined with colorful buildings, painted in greens and blues and yellows and reds, that had intricate balconies and windows, each one unique from all the others. But this time of day, the vibrant colors were muted and hard to see.

The apartments on this street were taken by regular people. Troy knew all, or nearly all, of them by sight. A sniper would have to set up on a rooftop. Troy gave this theoretical sniper nothing to hit.

Just across the street from his flat was a postage stamp-sized, fenced in space that less than two weeks ago was still the parking lot for this building. It had exactly five spaces, and one of them had belonged to Troy Stark. He used to put his lovely lime green Smart car in there.

Now, the lot was walled off with tall wooden boards, two of them hinged like a sort of gate, except the gate was shut with a heavy chain and padlock. Handbills and advertisements for plays and bands had begun to appear on the walls. Troy knew that on the other side, the space was charred by fire, the once-colorful stone of the surrounding buildings blackened with soot.

Troy was wearing a pair of boxer briefs and nothing else. It was a cold night, and the heat wouldn't come up into the radiators until around dawn. The chill in the apartment brought gooseflesh up on his legs and arms. His feet were on the polished hardwood floor, and the surface was like ice. He liked that about living here. They didn't waste heat on people who were sleeping.

"Happy Valentine's Day, Agent Stark," she said again.

Troy turned to face her. Valentine's Day. It was brutal. He had lost track of time, and this oh-so-special day had slipped his mind. Here in Europe, they didn't tend to ram holidays down your throat in the same way as the United States. The economies here were smaller and not as desperately dependent on consumers buying useless stuff.

Some flowers would probably save him, and maybe dinner out.

Dubois was staring at him.

The bed was rumpled, the sheets and blankets twisted. A pillow had fallen onto the floor. She had extricated a heavy comforter from the mess and was under it. Her eyes were poking over the top of it. There seemed to be a gleam in those eyes, a hint of trouble. She was tiny. She was pretty. She was sexy.

He forced on a smile.

"Happy Valentine's Day, Agent Dubois."

They did this weird thing where they addressed each other formally, as though they had just been assigned to each other. It was kind of cute, he supposed.

The closer he grew to her, the more he hated the idea of her doing this job. She had nearly died a week ago. There was no way around that fact. They were on a mission, and she had been captured by a Serbian mafia clan. It happened right in front of his eyes, and there was nothing he could do about, not in that moment.

And that wasn't even the worst of it. The long-term fallout from these operations was worse. They had mostly destroyed an Albanian human trafficking gang, the Baruti clan. Troy had killed Mateos Baruti. Baruti had been allies with the Italian 'Ndrangheta. They had blown up his car just over a week ago in a botched attempt to murder him.

In his short time here, he and Dubois, and by extension El Grupo Especial, had made powerful enemies. The Baruti. 'Ndrangheta. Possibly the Serbians. Possibly Serbian and Russian intelligence. And Lucien Mebarak was still out there somewhere.

Even if they left Europe right now, this coming morning, it wouldn't matter. Even if he and Dubois retired from this, went off the grid, and opened a beachfront sandwich shop on the Pacific coast of Nicaragua, somewhere their enemies would never find them, it was already too late.

Dubois's mom, and Troy's entire family, would still be at risk.

The thought of that made him deeply sad. He couldn't see a way out of this situation. He couldn't kill entire mafias. He couldn't wipe out entire intelligence agencies. He had gone all the way in on this work, had approached it with the cowboy mentality he'd had for much of his life, and hadn't given enough thought to the consequences.

Colonel Missing Persons had people watching over his family. The one-eyed spymaster Persons had been Troy's commander in the Navy SEALs, then later recruited Troy for missions with Joint Special Operations Command. After Troy was drummed out of the SEALs for insubordination, Persons had recruited him to this new life, working for Interpol, and whatever unnamed American intelligence entity Persons represented. Persons had promised to keep Troy's family safe.

But how effective was that going to be, and how long would it last? Persons could retire, or die. Would the next spookmaster in line honor the agreements that Persons had?

Meanwhile, no one was protecting Dubois's mom. Dubois had herself, and her mom, microchipped with GPS trackers. In fact, it's what had saved Dubois's life a week ago. Troy knew where to go to get her back.

But what if someone abducted Dubois's mom or simply killed her?

Troy was plagued with problems that had no clear solutions, questions that had no good answers. It was a horrible place to be.

“Why so sad, Agent Stark?”

"I'm not sad, Agent Dubois. I'm happy."

Her eyes glinted in the darkness, and the half light steaming in from outside.

“You could have fooled me.”

He shook his head. A new thought occurred to him, a better one, more positive, even mischievous. Now, the smile felt a little more real.

“What are you thinking?” she said.

"Remember," Troy said. "In the early days, you used to claim that you liked girls."

Her eyes narrowed.

“I do like girls.”

“Then what happened?”

She shrugged. "An opportunity arose that I couldn't pass up."

“What opportunity?” he said.

"The opportunity to get my hands on a body like the one in front of me right now. No lady in her right mind would let that go by."

Troy nearly laughed. "Are you a lady?"

“Come here, and I’ll show you what I am.”

He moved toward the bed. There were still a few hours before they needed to get up.

Now Dubois was grinning nearly ear-to-ear. Troy climbed onto the bed and slid under the big heavy comforter.

"We're going to Paris today," Dubois said. "On Saint Valentine's Day, of all the days in the year.

"The city of romance," Troy said. "And the special day of romance."

Dubois nodded, and slipped her small hands around Troy’s broad back.

"We make a very hot couple," she said. "Paris will be perfect for us."

“France in general,” Troy said.

Dubois looked into his eyes.

"Careful, Agent Stark. France is the country of love."

CHAPTER FIVE

5:45 am Central European Time
In the hills near the village of Eze
Cote d'Azur (the French Riviera)
France

"End of the line," Dick Tickler said. His breath fogged up the windshield.

The old Mercedes engine hummed a low, tired growl as it crested the final hill, its headlights piercing through the lingering shroud of night. Richard killed the beams as they rolled to a stop, the gravel beneath their tires crackling softly in protest. He didn't need the lights; he knew where they were.

The homestead loomed ahead, a dark silhouette against the slowly brightening horizon, keeping guard over the sleeping Mediterranean. The soft murmur of the sea far below was a stark contrast to the thundering pulse in his ears.

Holly Danger, ever the coiled spring, shifted beside him, her eyes flickering across the landscape with the wariness of a hawk. Yves Saint L'Orange had been dozing off and on during the drive, his large body stuffed into the small car's back seat. He stretched his arms wide, trying to get the stiffness out of his joints. They had been driving all night, but now, perched high above the world, there was that sense of finality, that they had pulled it off.

Tickler's hands lingered on the steering wheel, fingers tapping an anxious rhythm. He couldn't shake the feeling that his father might have gazed upon a scene just like this one before he vanished.

The old man would've loved this.

His father had been a shadow looming over his life - a thief, a mentor, and an enigma - all rolled into one. In some ways, almost every job had been an attempt to chase the specter he'd left behind, proving something to a man who was no longer there to see it.

"Dick?"

Holly's voice cut through the quiet. She was a worrier. That was one of the things he liked about her most. She was a great car thief, an incredible driver when the need arose, a wild animal in bed… and she worried a lot. Worried people checked things and re-checked them. And then checked them again.

“We good?” she said.

"Richard," he said, correcting her. He nodded, more to convince himself than anything. "We're good."

There was no room for doubt, not when they were this close. He glanced at the rearview mirror, catching a glimpse of the stubble lining his jaw and the crow's feet carved by a thousand sleepless nights. Mid-30s and already a lifetime worth of capers, misadventures, and stolen heirlooms to his name. Throw in a little bit of jail time here and there, and now THIS.

This was the score.

When he was a teenager, he had started out by breaking into the homes of rich people who were away on holiday. In the early days of giant flat panel TVs, he'd stolen and fenced about a dozen of them. They cost tens of thousands of dollars and had actual resale value in those days. It was funny to think about. You could buy a big new one these days for a few hundred bucks.

“Let’s not keep our hosts waiting,” he said.

His voice was steady despite the uncertainty that clawed at his insides. He reached for the door handle and stepped out into the dim light of dawn, ready to face whatever lay hidden within the shadows of the decrepit barn. After all, it was in his blood.

The open blue Mercedes 450 SL convertible gleamed under the moonlight,

Holly slid over into the driver’s seat.

"Nice choice, by the way," Richard said. "It was sweet rolling down here in this thing."

She smiled. "I try to steal the best."

Yves climbed out over the side.

The homestead was below them, perched on the cliff's edge. It must have been worth quite a lot in its heyday, whenever that was. The land itself, rolling hills above the cliffs, must be amazing in the daytime.

The whitewashed house stood silent, its windows like the dark eye holes of a bleached skull. It seemed like no one had been here in a good long while. Beside the house, the wooden barn was dilapidated, not sure which direction to fall. Its doors were slightly ajar, but showed no sign of life within.

“Looks like nobody’s home,” Holly said, her voice low.

Richard shrugged. "Or they're just being cautious."

He leaned over her and pressed the horn, a deep blast that cut through the silence, echoing off the cliffs and across the hillsides. He watched as a dim glow flickered to life inside the barn.

"Showtime," he said, his hand instinctively feeling for the reassuring bulge of the infamous Star of Versailles, which was hidden inside his jacket.

A million euros. But what is it actually worth?

He had a moment of doubt. Doubts like this always crept in. They were a team, and they were splitting three million euros three ways. It was a lot of money for not a lot of work. It was the score of their lives.

But they had taken all the risks here, and the thing was worth… what?

Supposedly, no one had ever put a price on it. Did that mean it was worth twenty million euros? A hundred million?

A billion?

He shook his head. There was no sense wondering now. A deal was a deal. And it would be impossible to move something worth a hundred million, or a billion, or an infinite amount of money by themselves.

"Let's not keep our employers waiting," he said.

Somewhere behind them, a rooster greeted the coming dawn - a new day, and with it, potentially a new life.

"I don't have a great feeling about this," Holly said, worrying right on cue.

Richard turned to her. "These are the people who hired us. It's going to be fine."

His thumb brushed against the mobile phone in his hand. "I'm going to call you and leave the line open. You can hear everything that goes on."

He nodded toward the idling car, its motor purring softly.

"Keep the engine running, just in case."

Side by side, he and Yves began their descent down the hill. Each step took them closer to the barn, its wooden frame a dark silhouette against the faint light of dawn creeping up over the horizon.

The Cote d'Azur was coming to life; distant villages sparkled like scattered jewels, their lights punctuating the darkness. Behind them, the city of Nice was nothing more than a distant glow.

"Beautiful night, isn't it?" Richard said.

"Yeah," Yves said. "Let's hope it stays that way."

From the pocket of his jacket, Richard could hear the muffled sound of the car's engine through the open phone line.

Keep the engine running.

A trickle of fear slid down his spine.

"Eyes open," he said.

Yves nodded. "I might never sleep again. Not after this."

"That's because you'll be up partying."

They reached the barn, the door open a crack. Yves shouldered it further, the ancient door squealing on rusted steel rollers. They stepped inside, a very faint scent of dry hay and old dung in the air. The smell was from decades ago. It never went away.

Lantern light flickered, throwing shadows across the walls. It was a real old-timey lantern, with a flame burning on a fat wick in oil.

Two young men, shorter than Richard and much shorter than Yves, stood across from them. Their hair seemed very dark. They both had thick beards, which were neatly trimmed. Their skin was light brown. One of them smoked a cigarette.

They were bagmen, expendables. They go to prison, or they could get killed, and two more just like them would pop up out of the ground like moles. But they must be trustworthy enough, or the employers wouldn't send them. There was a lot at stake.

"Hi guys," Richard said, his voice even.

There's a thousand of you but only one of me.

"Do you have it?" one of them said. He spoke English just fine, with an accent from somewhere, Richard supposed the Middle East. Arabs. Richard had the sense all along that behind the smokescreens, they were dealing with Arabs.

"Would we be here if we didn't?"

The man stuck his hand out, palm upward. Obviously, he was the one in charge.

"Let's see it."

Richard smiled. "Money first." He'd playing this game a long time, just not at this level. Minor leagues, major leagues, the way you played it was the same. The people at the top were just better at it.

Without a word, the man stooped and hoisted a satchel from the dust at his feet. It arced through the air, landing heavily near Richard's polished shoes.

"Count it."

Richard squatted, the leather of his jacket stretching taut across his back. His hands worked the clasp, unveiling stacks of currency.

"Three million euros," the Arab said. "All there."

Richard had no real sense of what three million euros ought to look like. It would be ridiculous to just crouch here, counting this. He picked up a stack bound with a rubber band. There were random hundreds and fifties, easy enough to spend, but nuts to try and count. He was going to be here until lunch.

There were stacks and stacks of it. Beside him, Yves leaned in, his attention momentarily ensnared by the sight of all that money.

It was a fatal lapse.

Richard's head snapped up, instinct flaring.

Both men across from them now brandished guns, pistols, the glint of metal harsh against the soft lantern glow.

A cascade of realizations crashed over Richard.

"Guns!" he shouted.

Too late, Yves pulled his own gun.

Their meticulous planning, their flawless execution - all of it teetered on the verge of ruin. The open phone line crackled with the sound of an idling engine.

"Holly!" Richard screamed. "Get out!"

***

The crackle of gunfire shattered the silence.

Over the phone, the muffled pops and roars mingled with static.

Holly sat motionless, her breath caught in her throat.

"It can't be," she whispered to the darkness.

She shook her head. "Dick!" Her voice was loud, almost as loud as the sound of the shots from down the hill. She shouted into the phone, lying innocently on the passenger seat. "Dick!"

Nothing. No answer.

And then, as if conjured to life by her fears, headlights blazed to life on the hillside above her, an ominous glow.

Her instincts kicked in. Everything was ruined, or maybe it wasn't. She could find out later. In the meantime, driving was what she did.

She jammed the car into gear, gravel spitting behind her as she accelerated down the dirt road, fleeing the dream that had turned into a nightmare.

The pursuing headlights came over the top, a four-wheel-drive barreling down an impossibly steep decline, intent on intercepting her.

Holly's grip on the steering wheel was white knuckled, as her foot pushed the accelerator almost to the floor.

A staccato burst of machine gun fire ripped the night.

DUNK, DUNK, DUNK, DUNK.

The gunshots punched the side of the Mercedes.

The Jeep bounced down the hill, almost on top of her.

Holly swerved, no thought now, all reflexes, avoiding the Jeep's attempt to ram her off the narrow road. The Jeep careened past and flew over an embankment, gone as fast as it came.

Holly's chest heaved, her breath caught as she rocketed forward. The road was like a dark tunnel. The arm of the speedometer was pinned to the far right.

"What the…?"

Up ahead, above her and to the right, another vehicle came bounding down the steep hill. This one was on fire. She stared at it.

It was an old wagon, burning like an inferno. It came down the hillside like a comet crashing to earth. They were trying to cut her off.

Her foot was pegged all the way to the floor.

The only thing to do was to beat that rolling fireball.

The wagon collided with the Mercedes, a flaming crash that sent her veering off course. She wrenched the steering wheel to the left, the world tilting wildly as the vehicle lurched off the road. Her car bounded over the embankment.

She was a prisoner of gravity. The hillside was a blur as the car plummeted downwards. The Mercedes sailed over a lip, then dropped off a cliff, slamming into an embankment that failed to halt its descent.

The dark water of the Mediterranean was below.

Holly spun the wheel to the right, trying to find any purchase at all. The Mercedes convertible responded with a violent twist, rolling over.

Holly felt herself go airborne. She was thrown clear, black night all around her as she somersaulted away from the tumbling car. She bounced, once, twice, down the rocks, then went airborne again.

Dimly, she realized the ground was gone. She was falling. Her body spun, and she caught a glimpse of the cliff above her, the flaming chariot to the side - right or left she didn't know - crashing down another steep hill, coming apart like a spaceship exploding on re-entry, casting jack-o-lantern shadows in the sky.

A second later she hit the water, and the world went silent, dark…

Endless.

CHAPTER SIX

9:25 am Syria Time (8:25 am Central European Time)
A ruined building
Idlib, Syria

"This is not a difficult decision," the seated man said to the group standing in front of him. "Indeed, it is not my decision at all."

To his left, there was a gaping hole where the wall of the building had been. They were five stories above the courtyard. At the far side of the courtyard, there was a steep pile of rubble where another building had been.

Concrete dust lingered in the air. Everywhere he went, he seemed to encounter this dust. It embedded itself in his lungs and made it difficult to breathe.

The man's name was Nureddine Ahmad Khan. He went by the *nom de guerre* al Shabah, which meant "the Ghost." He had earned this moniker many times over.

Twenty years ago, he had been fighting against the American invasion of the land of his birth, Iraq. He had been captured by the Americans, and subjected to unspeakable horrors in the prison they called Camp Bucca. He had emerged from that dark place a changed man. He had been burned from the inside out. He would never go back to the normal man he had once been.

Since that time, he has not been captured again. He had been in countless battles against many enemies. He welcomed death, but Allah had seen fit to keep him alive. When the enemies of God thought they had him dead, he became invisible, like a ghost, and passed through their midst unharmed. He had seen the great caliphate rise from the desert sands, only to fall apart once again.

"What do you pronounce?" a man said.

There were five men before him. Two of the men were his own fighters, dressed all in black. One man represented the community here. He wore clothes that seemed Western to al Shabah, including dress pants, shoes, a dress shirt and a dark vest. Perhaps it was all he had.

There were two more men. They were both young, and both stripped to the waist. Their wrists were bound behind their backs with lengths of rope. They were beaten and bruised. One stood with a blank stare. One was weeping quietly. These men had been brought before him because they were homosexuals, deviants, what the decadent Westerners would call "gay."

“The hadiths are clear about punishment for the acts of the people of Lot,” al Shabah said. The one who was weeping let out a loud moan. "The punishment is harsh, but these are serious transgressions. Moreover, we must command right and forbid wrong if we are to maintain a social order that is pleasing to Allah."

Now the man was howling.

Did he think this awful caterwauling would somehow save him?

“Quiet him, please.”

One of al-Shabah’s men hit the weakling across his back with the butt of an AK-47. The man immediately fell to the floor and lay there gasping.

Everything was wreckage here. Very little was left. From the great caliphate that they had been building in recent years past, with 10 million subjects inside the realm, now reduced to this tiny outpost in a mostly destroyed city. Nearly everything had been taken from them.

As if God hadn't punished them enough, a week ago he had sent a powerful earthquake. The city, a ruin after years of combat, was now a complete disaster. A catastrophe on top of a catastrophe. There was no longer any social order.

The believers of al-Nusra, once allies, were now bitter enemies. It was open warfare between them, fighting for every square meter of the city. Worse, the apostates of Assad's regime had begun their attacks again, pressing their advantage with Russian-supplied armor and Iranian-supplied rockets. The city was on the verge of collapse.

The message could not be clearer. They weren't pure. Their sacrifices were not pleasing. There was selfishness in their efforts.

“Abu Bakr, the Prophet's successor, determined that the punishment for these crimes was to be cast from a high cliff. We have no cliffs available to us, and we believe that we are following the Prophet's will when we punish the crime by casting the sinners from another high place. So my pronouncement, consistent with the teachings left to us by Abu Bakr, is to cast the guilty parties from this very building.”

"No!" the man on the floor screamed. "Noooo!”

Al-Shabah looked at the two young fighters.

"You may proceed."

The blank-faced man showed no resistance. The screaming man was dragged to his feet, and a red blindfold, little more than a rag, was tied around his eyes. The soldiers, along with the representative from the neighborhood, walked the two men through a blown-out doorway and to another destroyed exterior wall in the next room.

Al-Shabah sighed and rose from his seat. He went to the opening and looked down. At the bottom, all the way down, there were perhaps 20 or 30 people gathered around the rim of the courtyard, gazing up at them. They were at a far enough distance that there was no way the two men could land on them.

Somewhere in the middle distance, a gun battle raged. Al-Shabah could hear the pop-pop-pop of automatic weapons. Then came the louder WHUMP of a rocket finding its target. The building shook, just a bit. Bits of masonry crumbled and fell.

Al-Shabah looked along the edge of the building at the offenders. Were they guilty of these crimes? He had no way of knowing. The people of the neighborhood claimed they had been caught in the act. The evidence was slight, little more than hearsay, but community elders had vouched for the account.

Also, the two young men looked like the type. Thin, weak, effeminate.

Shabah supposed he was offended by these men. They were an affront in the eyes of Allah. But he was also plagued by what had happened at Camp Bucca, the things he'd witnessed, the things he had been forced to do himself. These things were burned into his mind, and a day hadn't passed that he didn't think about them.

He sighed again. He had seen so much death in his life. But Allah's will was Allah's will, and this was what the people wanted.

For a moment, he imagined himself as Pilate standing before the crowd of Jews. Which criminal would they spare? The murderer Barabbas. Which criminal would they crucify? The prophet Isa, Yeshua, or whom the Christians call Jesus.

"Give the people what they want."

With no fanfare, his men shoved the two deviants from the ledge where the building wall was missing. Everything went silent, and all watched as the two men fell through the air. It seemed to take a long time.

They both hit the unforgiving stone of the courtyard nearly at the same time. Their bodies folded and broke apart. Blood splattered.

A ripple of sound came from the crowd. It wasn't screams. It wasn't applause. It was more like quiet conversation, enthusiastically spoken.

Shabah turned away from the edge.

Behind him there was another man. The man was in his mid-30s perhaps, thinning hair with a deep scar just below his left eye, from a bullet that had nearly taken his life. The man called himself Ali Talib, after the cousin of Muhammad, who was among the first to accept his teachings.

Ali was a large robust, and violent man. He was Shabah's second in command and enforcer. A gun or a bomb could kill anyone, but few men could withstand Ali's strength in a physical contest.

"We can't stay here much longer," Ali said. "We can't hold it."

As young as he was, already Ali's thick beard was turning gray and white. This war would age anyone before their time.

Shabah nodded. "I know. How much do we still control?"

"Forty blocks square. Eight blocks by five blocks. No more. Much of it ruined. We are pressed by enemies on both sides. They hate each other, but somehow they hate us more. We are running out of ammunition. There is no water. There is almost no food, and we cannot send out a raiding party because of snipers at the edge of our territory."

This was it, then. Normally, this would be the time to fight to the last man. Perhaps everyone would wear a suicide vest and send as many apostates to hell as possible. The caliphate was dead.

"God has forsaken these lands," Shabah said.

The answer was to destroy all of it, not just the lands they had once held, but the lands of the people who had taken it from them. The lands of the sinners and non-believers, and the lands of the weak who believed but did not come to their aid, as well as the ones who were betrayers and enemies of God. Poison it all, and kill everyone within.

If Allah willed it, the entire landscape, and the millions across it, would soon be dead. A thousand years it would be uninhabitable, and would stand as a symbol of Allah's displeasure.

"What do you command?" Ali said.

Shabah shrugged. It was another easy answer. One of the few blessings here was Allah made the decisions for him. "We fight on. Street to street. House to house, if need be. Room to room. The key is coming, and we must hold out until then."

Ali seemed skeptical. "Is it really coming?"

Shabah was instantly annoyed. He felt it all through his body, and even to his soul. "Do you doubt what I say?"

"No."

Shabah nodded. "Good. You shouldn't doubt it. I told you the truth. It's coming. As of last night, it's in the hands of our brothers. If the corridor from Turkey stays open, it will soon be delivered to our hands."

Of course, the key was on a difficult path. The roads were demolished. Since the earthquake, one truck of international aid a day was making it through from Turkey. The Turks had lost at least 30,000 of their people. They had their own problems. The killing, the impending starvation, and the people trapped under rubble in Syria were not major priorities for them.

Ali shook his head then. He did doubt. It was obvious. He was a doubter. It was not a good way to be. It would not serve him. "Even if the key makes it through to us, how will we get from here to the weapon? The way is held by the forces of Assad."

Shabah smiled, because these questions answered themselves.

"If God wills it, we will get there."

CHAPTER SEVEN

11:10 am Central European Time
Musee Poitier (the Poitier Museum)
Rue de Monceau, 8th Arrondissement
Paris, France

"It's a complete disaster," the man said.

He was small and somewhat frail, balding, with a pair of reading glasses perched on top of his head. He wore a brown sweater and tan slacks. The sweater had orange and white zig-zag stripes across it. To Troy, this was reminiscent of the sweater the old cartoon character Charlie Brown used to wear.

Troy hadn't caught the man's name. It was too French, pronounced and delivered with too much of a flair for Troy ears to cope with it. Troy's Spanish was improving a lot. His French was stuck upside down in the mud. Luckily, the man spoke English and was willing to employ it for Troy's benefit.

Dubois probably had the guy's name. Troy glanced at her. She was wearing a bright blue bodysuit, what a person might call electric blue. She had on big black boots and a thick black belt. She was pretending to pay rapt attention to the man as he prattled on. Of course, she knew his name. Not much got by her, certainly not something like that.

This man was from the Poitier Family Trust. He was Troy and Dubois's guide through the Poitier Museum, showing them the finer pieces the place had to offer, but also demonstrating the destruction the flash mob had wreaked. The museum was closed today, to give staff a chance to regroup, and to give the decision makers of the foundation time to make a decision about the missing gem stone.

The guide, Dubois and Troy were all climbing a wide spiral staircase. Downstairs, there were blank spots on the walls where invading marauders had defaced paintings from the 1800s with black spray paint. The paintings had been taken down, and sent to be cleaned by experts in that sort of thing.

Troy was wrestling with this in his mind. It was one thing to get paid to join a flash mob and invade a museum. All in good fun, someone might say, as long as no harm was done. In this case, they had vandalized items that were worth a lot of money or were perhaps impossible to price. These were things that were probably of some cultural value, things that might be symbols of the culture that was hosting them.

“These people are filled with nihilistic rage,” the man said, answering the question in Troy’s mind as if Troy had asked it out loud, and coming down firmly on the side of “Barbarian invaders are destroying everything we hold dear.”

The man lowered his voice. He looked at Troy, and then at Dubois, as if wondering how what he was about to say would be received. His eyes showed he had made the decision to plunge ahead.

“They have low impulse control.”

He said it in a confidential tone, nearly whispering it as if he was sharing an important secret.

Dubois nodded. "Ah."

Almost certainly, her mother’s Senegalese forbears had been described in a similar manner at one time.

“What do you suppose causes that?” Dubois said.

The man shrugged his narrow shoulders. "Low intellect."

Dubois nodded again. "Mmmm.”

Troy said nothing. He was trying not to laugh.

“Perhaps I’ve said too much,” the man said.

They moved briskly up a long hallway now, the guide out in the lead, as if he was trying to put some physical distance between them and the words that he had uttered back by the staircase.

At the confluence of two hallways, they came upon a large glass box with an overhead spotlight shining down on it. Inside the box was a very large green-hued gem with flashes of blue. It was big, and to Troy's mind, kind of ugly. The size and shape of the gem made it seem almost like the world's most expensive and beautiful potato.

Troy had to remind himself that this wasn’t even the real stone.

He glanced around. No one was here. There were two security cameras facing directly at this spot.

“The cameras…” Troy said.

The man nodded. "Yes, they went down during the attack."

“The attack?”

The man turned to Troy. "Well, that's what it was, right? A cyber attack to bring down the security system, along with a sudden forcible invasion, all of which was cleverly orchestrated to allow the thieves to enter and exit unnoticed."

Troy shrugged. Whoever had taken down the security in this museum had taken down computer systems throughout Paris. In a sense, it was like killing an ant with a sledgehammer. On the other hand, it also played a diversionary role. If the security guard here at the museum hadn't filmed the theft with his phone, then it would seem like the flash mob and the security collapse were unrelated, a coincidence.

"Sure. It was an attack. It absolutely was."

"You don't think so?" the man said.

"No, I do," Troy said. "I agree with you. Our analysts, including our lead intelligence analyst, are trying to find the source of the network failure. I might have sounded surprised, because I'm used to dealing with terrorists and loss of life."

The man nodded. "We all know who you are, Agent Stark. And all of the heroic things you've done. They say you might have saved Europe, or maybe the whole world, just a week ago."

That was problematic. No one was supposed to know who Troy Stark was.

"Far-fetched," Troy said. "A very large exaggeration."

But he smiled. He looked at Dubois. "I probably just saved Croatia, and maybe Bosnia, with a major assist from Agent Dubois here."

The man turned to Dubois and stared at her. He seemed skeptical, as if something as small and easy on the eyes as Dubois, couldn't possibly assist a big violent brute like Troy Stark on his world-saving missions.

"May I ask a question?" Dubois said, mercifully changing the subject.

"Of course."

"How did the museum acquire the Star of Versailles in the first place?"

The man stared and stared.

"I mean, where did it come from? Who were the sellers? And what was the purchase price?"

"I'm afraid," the man said, "that I'm not authorized to discuss topics of a sensitive nature like that one."

***

"They stole it themselves," Carlo Gallo said.

It was a funny thing. When Troy and Dubois left the museum, they barely had any more information than when they entered. The guide made Troy think of North Korean minders, whose entire job was to help international visitors avoid seeing things the government didn't want them to see.

Troy was beginning to suspect this really might just be a fun little trip to Paris for he and Dubois. It was a big famous city, and tourists loved it. But one glance at Dubois in her bodysuit, and Troy was thinking maybe they should skip the sights and go back to the hotel room for the rest of the day. She reminded him an electric eel in that thing, and Troy thought it might be fun to run the risk of getting shocked.

Then they ran into Gallo.

The bright white hair, the closely trimmed white beard, the broad shoulders and arms and tree trunk legs that Troy suspected came from a needle. The deep tan that this time of year, almost definitely came out of a spray can.

Gallo was standing on the street outside the museum when they met him. He wore a black leather trench coat over tight black jeans and black ankle-high boots. He wore some sort of mysterious ancient blue medallion around his neck, like a third eye. He had a gold watch loosely draped on one thick wrist. He carried a pointy black umbrella in case of rain, or in case the need arose to jab someone in the face.

He seemed like he was waiting for something, maybe a bus.

"I saw you guys go in," he said. "I figured I should talk to you when you came out. For old time's sake."

Together, three of them walked to a café a few blocks from the museum. Gallo was a guy in late middle-age, late 50s, Troy would guess. His deeply lined face looked every minute of that, his body not so much.

Miquel had brought him on board as a consultant at El Grupo. Gallo was American, ex-CIA to hear him tell it, and he and Miquel knew each other from the days of Basque separatist bombings in Spain. They were friends, maybe. Miquel had seemed to think they were.

Gallo had done a few operations with El Grupo, but had been repeatedly injured on the job. He had been shot several times during the crisis at CERN - light body armor had saved his life. One shot had grazed his face, although the scar wasn't obvious now.

He had been pistol-whipped into dreamland during the train hijacking in the Austrian Alps. He had finally taken a powder after the mission in Albania, and the crazy shootout at the hillside mansion of Mateos Baruti. He had also taken a few bee stings during that one, as Troy recalled.

That was the last they'd seen of him.

"They stole it themselves," Troy said, repeating what Gallo had just said.

The three of them were sitting at an outside table on the patio, watching the foot traffic out on the boulevard. It was a cold day, but the sun was trying to peek out from behind some clouds. It was pleasant to sit here, even with the chill.

Troy and Dubois had ordered coffee.

Gallo had ordered red wine.

He nodded, taking a sip from his glass. "Self-evident," he said. "The Poitier Museum has a reputation for being underhanded. There are all kinds of rumors what you'll find locked away on the third floor of that place, and in their warehouse annex out in the suburbs."

"For example?"

Gallo shrugged. "If you believe what people say, then we're talking about *Poppy Flowers* by Vincent Van Gogh, *The Pigeon with Green Peas* by Picasso, and *The Storm on the Sea of Galilee* by Rembrandt."

"Is it a little convenient that the most important and valuable missing artworks in the world are all hidden inside the Musee Poitier?" Dubois said.

Gallo smiled. "Believe whatever you like. The Poitier ancestors were slave traders. The apple doesn't fall far from the tree."

"What are you doing here?" Troy said.

Gallo shrugged. "Same as you, I guess. Looking into the theft of the Star of Versailles. A client in Amsterdam was interested in buying it, if I could find out who has it, and the price wasn't in deep space."

"Did you find out anything?" Dubois said.

Gallo looked at her. He smiled, but it wasn't clear that his smile reached his eyes.

"Yeah. I found it, more or less. I don't know where it is at this moment, but I know where it's going to be by tonight. When I told my client, it was enough for him to back away. I told him that was probably a wise decision. I made a few bucks and got a little trip to Paris out of it. Not bad."

Troy smiled. "All right. You've got us. Are you going to spill it?"

Gallo shrugged and grinned. Now, he looked almost sheepish.

"Why not? You guys are crazy. Miquel is always trying to get the people who work for him killed. I'll tell you. I hope you won't go there, but knowing you…"

Troy made a gesture with one hand, as though waving Gallo toward him.

"Come on. Give it up."

Troy wasn't sure if he believed a word Gallo said. Troy was never sure, when Gallo was with El Grupo, if Gallo was really with them, or using them to get close to events for his own reasons. Gallo was slippery. But he was also capable and courageous. He took out a bunch of mobsters that night at Baruti's house.

He could have his sources, and they could know things.

"Don't ask me how I found this out," Gallo said.

Both Troy and Dubois stared at him. Neither one said a word.

"The stone will be in Palermo, Sicily, this evening. It was stolen on the orders of La Cosa Nostra. the Sicilian mob. It's going to be delivered tonight. The museum was involved in the theft. Outside thieves were brought in, but the museum staff looked the other way and allowed it to happen."

"A guard at the museum filmed the theft," Dubois said.

"Low-level employee," Gallo said. "He was just doing his job. He wasn't in on it and didn't know anything about it."

There was a pause. Out on the street, a guy went zipping by on a bicycle.

Troy considered the situation. His trouble was with the 'Ndrangheta, the powerful mafia based in Calabria, as well as whatever was left of the Baruti clan in Albania. Even so, as much as they sometimes clashed, the Sicilian and Calabrian mobs were also known to work together.

"You'll notice that they haven't publicized the theft," Gallo said. "The official story is they're closed today because they're recovering from the riot. It's not even clear to me that they've told the French cops about this at all."

"What's the price?" Troy said.

Gallo shook his head. "I don't know the price. I don't even know if there is a price. The thing is supposed to be priceless, right? It's got some kind of magical powers, so they say."

That was the first Troy had heard about magical powers.

"What kind of magical powers?"

Gallo shrugged. "I don't know that, either. Just rumors. Something to do with the ancient world. A prophecy. I don't know. That's why certain people want it."

"Mystical," Troy said. "Mysterious. I thought the thing was like ten years old."

"I don't know what to tell you," Gallo said.

Now, Dubois spoke up. "Why did your client back off?"

Gallo smiled. "Oh, simple enough. He doesn't want to get murdered by the Sicilians. Can't say I blame him."

Troy was looking directly at Gallo now.

"What?" Gallo said.

"You going to tell me?" Troy said. "Where's the drop off? What time?"

Gallo shook his head. "My man, Agent Troy Stark. You'll have to find that out on your own. You know I can't tell you."

"Why not?" Troy said. "We're buddies, remember? We go back. Have you forgotten Mateos Baruti?"

"I don't even want to think about that stuff," Gallo said. "Baruti. Istvan Gajdos. CERN. I thought Miquel was my friend. But it turned out he was trying to make me dead, or maybe just hurt me very badly."

"He does that to everyone," Troy said. "Ask Agent Dubois here."

"We were friends once. Friends don't send friends to their deaths."

Troy looked at Gallo. He was serious. His eyes said he was sincere. There might even be real pain in those eyes. Gallo came on board El Grupo Especial, maybe for the money, maybe for the adventure, maybe for old time's sake. He got a lot more than he bargained for, so he left. Now, he held some resentment against Miquel.

"Why won't you tell me the drop off?" Troy said.

Gallo sighed. "Because when you go there, and inevitably ruin the delivery of the precious gem, and the Sicilians capture you, and then torture you, you'll end up telling them my name before you die."

There was another long pause at the table. Dubois took a sip of her coffee.

"I don't want you to do that," Gallo said.

CHAPTER EIGHT

1:20 pm Central European Time
Hotel Quebecois
Near des Champs-Elysees
Paris, France

"It's not even clear why they invited us," Dubois said.

Troy stood by the only window of this tiny hotel room, staring out at the city. They were on the eighth floor of this boutique hotel, and it afforded lovely views. Most of the nearby buildings were lower than this one. Troy could see all the way to the Arc de Triomphe from here.

And as an extra benefit, he could see the surrounding rooftops, and he was high enough above the street, he didn't need to think about getting shot.

But you ARE thinking about it.

Yes, he was, but he wasn't worrying. There was a big difference.

"The meeting seemed like a formality," Dubois said now. She wasn't talking to Troy. She was talking to the mobile phone sitting on the round wooden table that passed as a sitting area or breakfast nook.

El Grupo had booked them two rooms at the hotel. Both were small. They had chosen to consolidate in this one because the views were better. It was silly. One room was going to sit empty. Troy wondered, not for the first time, how much their employer knew about what was going on here.

As fate would have it, they were on a conference call back to headquarters at the moment, with Miquel and Jan, and whoever else was there.

Also, whoever is eavesdropping.

Troy shook that thought away. He was becoming paranoid. Jan was a master of end-to-end encryption. That had become clearer than ever when Troy was in Hong Kong, became a fugitive from the local cops, stayed in touch with headquarters over the phone, and yet his location was never pinpointed. The Chinese ran a high-tech surveillance state, and Jan managed to beat them at their own game.

"Our guide was not forthcoming with information," Dubois said. "He showed us the fake diamond, but declined to answer questions. The fake is still where the thieves placed it in the exhibit. It doesn't seem as if they've contacted the Paris Police. They haven't sent the fake out to be examined to determine what it's even made of. It almost seems like they plan to…"

Jan Bakker's tinny voice came through the speaker.

"Pass the fake one off as the real one," he said.

Dubois nodded. "Yes."

"Agent Stark, would you agree with that assessment?"

"I hadn't thought of that," Troy said. "But I could see it, maybe. When we talked with Carlo, he claimed the museum was in on the theft."

"But why would they call us in?" Dubois said.

Miquel spoke. Troy knew he must be lurking there somewhere. "Sometimes, the left hand doesn't know what the right hand is doing. If it was an inside job, and of course we don't know that to a certainty, some people there would be unaware of it, even decision makers."

"Carlo thinks the stone went to Sicily," Troy said. "He said the Sicilian mob ordered the theft. I don't where he learned this, or if any of it is real."

"There have been accusations in the past that the museum, and the Poitier family, was affiliated with various mafias," Jan said. "I have just started running network searches on chatter among southern Italian gangs to see if we get anything that seems relevant. There are listening devices planted all over that region by various law enforcement and intelligence agencies. And, of course, there are massive databases that scrape phone calls, tests, and emails. I can pull a lot of data."

"How long will that take?" Troy said.

"I could take a little while," Jan said. "Or five minutes. Or it might never happen. There might be no relevant discussions because Agent Gallo is simply incorrect."

"How does he look?" Miquel said.

"Who?" Troy said.

"Gallo. Who do you think?"

Troy looked at Dubois. She smiled. Miquel and Gallo were supposed to be friends, but Gallo had run off from El Grupo, apparently after taking a few bullets too many.

"I don't know," Troy said. "He looked okay. I noticed when he drank any liquid, it mostly ran out of various holes in his body."

“He was like a fountain,” Dubois said, joining in the fun.

“I should call him,” Miquel said.

“I think I might have something,” Jan said, derailing the Gallo topic.

“That was quick,” Troy said.

"Palermo is a smaller city," Jan said. "And the people who might be involved are a relatively closed and tight-knit group. It's not like trying to pull data from vast criminal networks in a mega-city like Mumbai, let's say."

“Have you done that?” Troy said.

"Sometimes I do," Jan said. "Just for fun."

There was a pause over the line.

“What is it?” Dubois said.

"Uh… I don't know for sure. I'm running it through a translation program."

“I thought you speak Italian.”

"I do," Jan said. "I do. But I'm not perfectly fluent. I like to back up my own knowledge with automated translations, so I don't miss any nuances."

“You have some idea, then?” Troy said.

“One moment, please.”

Troy and Dubois traded looks again. Now there was a tug of war going on inside Troy. One part of him wanted to stay here in Paris with Dubois, maybe for one night, maybe forever. The other part wanted to go to Sicily and get that diamond back.

The Italians wanted him dead, wasn't that true? It seemed that way. And if so, Troy wanted to face down that demon, as well. He couldn't go the rest of his life, being nervous about standing next to windows. It wasn't like him, and it was no way to live.

"There's a meeting tonight," Jan said. "It's in Palermo. Something is going to be delivered. It's not clear what. They are speaking about it in barely concealed code, referring to it as sausage and peppers, as well as dinner, and the meal."

“What if it’s really just supper?” Dubois said.

"I don't think so," Jan said. "It's coming from France."

“Where is the delivery?” Troy said.

“Do you know the city well?”

"No," Troy said. "I don't know it at all. You'll just have to put me in the right place. What time?"

"The meet is 9pm. It's a late dinner, but this is Sicily we're talking about."

Troy checked his watch. "It's 1:30 now. How long is the flight from here?"

“About two and a half hours,” Miquel said.

“I can easily be there in time.”

Dubois raised her eyebrows. She gave Troy a long look. If a problem was going to arise, it was coming right now.

“I can probably be there in time, too.”

Troy instantly shook his head. "No, you can't."

Her voice was flat. "Agent Stark, what are you talking about? We're on an assignment together. If you intend to go to Sicily to continue the assignment, and Miquel agrees you should go, then I’m going, too.”

“Miquel, isn’t Agent Dubois still on injury leave?” Troy said.

Dubois's eyes were on fire. Maybe Troy should back off here. Maybe he should say that he thought Carlo is wrong. Maybe he should tell Miquel that he’s exhausted and doesn’t want to go to Palermo.

But he did want to go.

“Yes,” Miquel said. "Technically, Agent Dubois is still on leave."

“I came back voluntarily,” Dubois said.

"If her injuries aren't healed, then she isn't ready for a field operation," Troy said. "Not physically, not mentally. She's not 100%. She will compromise my freedom of movement. You can't put her in the field. She's a danger to me, and she's a danger to herself."

He was all the way out on a limb now. But these were his feelings. He didn't want Dubois on dangerous missions anymore, not now while she was injured, and probably not ever. Was that a crime? Was it really so bad?

"What are you talking about?" Dubois said. Her voice was rising now. "You have a hole in your arm. I've seen it. I've seen you change the bloody dressings. The whole thing looks like a sausage about to burst."

She was going too far. She was revealing too much. Why would she have seen him changing the dressings? In what context? She hadn't been coming into work. It could only meet that she was seeing him somewhere else.

Troy shook his head. "The injury won't limit me."

That could be a lie. The arm was still stiff and sore. Of course, in the event of an emergency, he would use it however he needed, and simply re-injure it. He would do that without hesitation. He'd done things like that many times before.

He'd more or less knocked out that English drug trafficker yesterday, using both arms, one good one, one bad one.

Miquel weighed in, agreeing with Troy.

"Agent Dubois, unfortunately I think Agent Stark is right about this. You stay in Paris and continue to recuperate. I'm not assigning you to this Palermo operation. Agent Stark, we'll have the plane fueled and ready by the time you arrive at the airfield. Interpol has undercover apartments salted through the city. The location of your apartment will be on your phone when you land in Sicily. From there, we'll work out the details of the meeting and how we can stop it."

“Any chance of local backup?” Troy said, already knowing the likely answer.

“From Sicilian law enforcement?” Jan said.

Troy nearly laughed. "Yes."

"That would be much like calling the gangsters directly and informing them that you are on your way," Miquel said.

Troy nodded. "Ah."

“We'll talk soon,” Miquel said.

“Thanks Miquel. Thanks Jan."

The line went dead.

Dubois was furious. Her entire body seemed to be thrumming with electricity. If someone's head could explode, it would happen to Dubois now.

"This is the most male chauvinist thing you've done! I can't believe what is happening here. You're a pig, Troy. Is that what you are?"

“You're beautiful when you're angry,” Troy said.

He did not try to approach her.

"Don't try to make a joke of this." She pointed at the mobile phone lying flat on the table. "Were you trying to humiliate me in front of them? I'm an agent, the same as you. You can't treat me like this."

Troy felt his own anger rising, just a little bit.

“Dubois, you're off your feed.”

She stared at him. It was an Americanism, and it didn't translate at all.

"I've had to rescue you again and again. You nearly died in Belgrade just a week ago. You would be dead now if I hadn't risked my life, killed ten men, and destroyed an entire city block of warehouse buildings, to get you back. If Alex hadn't suddenly showed up when he did, I don't know how I would have done it. There was no way to get in there except from the sky, and I can't fly a helicopter."

Dubois's jaw had dropped. She seemed frozen, her mouth open.

"You need to rest up and repair," Troy said. "I don't have those same needs. I was a special operator before I came to this job."

“You were a black operator,” Dubois said.

"Call it whatever you want," Troy said. "You need to let me operate. The state you're in right now, you're going to get us both killed."

They stared at each other. He had never seen her so angry. He had never seen her look so pained. The truth was out, and the truth hurt. She was an exceptionally good cop. She was a great investigator. She was good at arrests and takedowns. In regular police work, she brought many good things.

She was not on Troy’s level.

“I love you,” he nearly said, but didn’t.

"I care about you a great deal," he said instead. "After Belgrade, I am terrified about you getting hurt. That's me being honest."

She sighed. There might be no coming back from this conversation. All the same, these things had to be said. Her dark eyes were blank. The anger seemed to have gone away. But she wasn't going to show him a drop of vulnerability.

Her voice was cold, like the frozen north.

"You have nothing to worry about, Agent Stark. I'm not going to get you killed. You had me taken off the assignment instead. I guess I'll just stay here, rest and recuperate. Maybe I'll go visit with my mom. Thanks for the free time."

Now Troy sighed, too. He shook his head.

There was nothing he could say to fix this. If he said anything more, it would only make matters worse.

He began to stuff the few items he had unpacked back into his bags.

CHAPTER NINE

4:15 pm Central European Time
A Walkway
The left bank of the River Seine
Near Place de la Concorde
Paris, France

Dubois's phone was ringing.

The chilly afternoon was already ending. The sun never had appeared, and now the gunmetal gray sky was turning a shade darker. The brown water of the river flowed by, as above her on the street level, the evening lights of Paris began to come on.

In an earlier part of her life, she had often walked here. This submerged walking path along the Seine might be her favorite part of the city. To a great degree, Paris was a city for tourists, and that was fine. These paths were for locals.

As she walked, two men on bicycles, outfitted in form-fitting clothing as though they were preparing for the Tour de France, zipped by, going in the other direction. They were moving fast. Perhaps they really were competitive cyclists.

Others walked nearby, moving at varying paces. A woman in shorts and a green fleece jacket jogged slowly ahead of her.

The telephone buzzed and vibrated in her coat pocket, insistent, relentless.

"Go away, Miquel," she said.

She was on injury leave, as Miquel and Stark had so kindly indicated. She did not have to answer the phone. She could just walk here, resting and recuperating, and clearing her head. After a moment, the buzzing stopped.

Stark had treated her as a liability.

It hurt so much to think that. He felt he was better and safer, going to Palermo on his own. And Miquel, tacitly if not explicitly, had agreed with him. She would worry about Stark's safety right now, but she was too angry with him. Her entire body was overcome with the feeling, almost rage. The things Stark had said felt like a betrayal, possibly the ultimate betrayal.

"We're partners," she said. "Or we aren't."

There could be no halfway, as far as she was concerned. She wasn't Stark's research assistant. She wasn't his data analyst. She wasn't his language interpreter.

She wasn’t his European tour guide.

She was his girlfriend.

She nearly screamed out loud at the thought of it.

Stark was a killer. She understood that. He had trained as a Navy SEAL, one of America's elite groups of soldiers. He was a veteran of numerous wars and clandestine missions. He might have worked for the CIA and for a mysterious entity known as Metal Shop, although he downplayed these things. He might be an asset for American intelligence even now, although he denied it.

He had skills that were hard to categorize. He seemed to know the details of nearly every weapon system. On past missions, she had seen him commandeer guns from enemies, glance at them, and immediately begin to use them.

He was an experienced skydiver to an astonishing degree. She thought him more athletic than any man she had ever met. He was immensely strong, and his reflexes seemed closer to the invisible speed of a cat than an actual human. He could overwhelm and defeat nearly any opponent in seconds. And he had honed and developed these abilities in actual life-or-death combat.

Dubois, she was forced to admit, was a police officer. She considered that she was very good at investigations. She could think about, make sense of, and find patterns in large amounts of information, though Jan Bakker was better than her at this. Jan's algorithms were vastly better than either of them.

She was a decent shot with her service firearm, but that came from many hours on training ranges, and anyway she abhorred violence. It made her sick the first time she killed a man while on assignment with Troy Stark, as a matter of fact.

She had good, not great, martial arts skills, again after years of training and dedication. Those skills were becoming rusty now anyway, because much to her dismay, they weren't super useful in real world situations. She had tried to use them on the men in the alleyway in Belgrade.

It didn't work, to put it mildly. She got one good kick in before the men subdued her and carried her (carried her!) away.

She was a good pilot of small airplanes, a very useful skill, which she had learned from her father. She was pretty good at jumping out of airplanes, another skill he had taught her. If you added it all up…

She was a drag on Stark. She was his junior partner.

Abruptly, absurdly, she began to cry. She would be dead now. She would be dead, or worse, except Stark caused a mini-apocalypse and rescued her.

She walked on, thankful that the daylight was fading. At least no one could see the tears streaming down her face.

She hadn't even told her mom that she was here. At first, she hadn't mentioned it because she thought she and Stark might have a romantic getaway for a day or two. This stolen diamond case seemed like a lark, or even a dead end. Diamonds, paintings, and other incredibly valuable items were often stolen, and then found decades later.

But Stark had decided to take it seriously. Worse, he had decided to leave her behind. Even worse, Miquel, her mentor of nearly ten years, had decided Stark was right. Now, Stark was gone and she was alone, and she wasn't sure she even wanted to see her mother in her current state of mind.

The phone started buzzing again.

She took it out her pocket, looked at the number. She sighed and rolled her eyes. She pressed the green TALK button, and held the phone to her ear.

“Yes Miquel. What can I do for you?"

She heard the icy tone in her voice. If she could make it even colder, she would.

"Dubois," he said. "I've been trying to reach you."

She didn't respond to that. She hadn't been in the shower. She wasn't on another call. She didn't answer because she didn't want to speak to him.

"Jan picked up some chatter through network surveillance that he does. He's running algorithms that catch references to certain search terms in mobile telephone calls, texts, emails, transmissions of all kinds. Star of Versailles, Musee Poitier, tanzanite, some others. A woman, apparently an American, though no one is quite sure, crashed a car off the cliffs near a small village in the Cote d'Azur late last night. The car was an old convertible with the top down, and she wasn't wearing a seat belt. She was thrown clear of the car, fell a long way, landed in the sea at high tide, and somehow survived. She has very serious injuries. A man found her washed up on the beach early this morning. She was brought to a hospital in Nice by helicopter, straight from the beach. She has been under sedation most of the day as they worked to save her life."

"Good thing she wasn't wearing a seat belt," Dubois said.

She could not imagine where this conversation was going. Jan is sifting through thousands of possible mentions of the word "tanzanite." A tourist crashed a car in the South of France.

Okay...

"They had to cut open her skull to relieve swelling in her brain."

Dubois shook her head. Then she shrugged.

"All right. I'm sorry that happened."

"At one point, she awakened," Miquel said. "She was in a panic, as you might imagine. She said she was run off the road and that her two friends were murdered. She said they stole the Star of Versailles in Paris yesterday, then traveled to the coast to hand it over. The people who hired them killed the other two and then tried to kill her."

"A crazy person," Dubois said. "She must have seen the theft in the…"

"It hasn't been publicized," Miquel reminded her.

Dubois stopped walking. She froze, as if she had suddenly turned to stone.

"Almost no one knows about this," Miquel said. "Staff at the museum. Trustees of the Poitier Family Trust. You, me, Jan, Agent Stark. Carlo, it seems. Maybe a few others. The hospital staff do not know. They think the woman is mentally ill or traumatized by the crash. They think she just *believes* she stole the Star of Versailles."

Dubois ran scenarios in her head. The most direct route between the South of France and Palermo, with the least amount of scrutiny, was probably by boat. There was a ton of pleasure boat traffic in those waters, and the coast guards probably wouldn't give a small motor yacht a second look.

Stark might really be going to the place where the diamond drop-off would take place. And if this story was true, the people bringing it, and the people receiving it, were all cold-blooded killers.

"Should I go to Sicily?" she said.

"No. We've told Agent Stark to watch, get pictures if possible, but not interfere."

Dubois was silent. Again, that feeling, these men didn't want her put in danger. They didn't think she could handle it.

"We need you to go to Nice. You'll have to fly commercial air because Stark has the plane. But there are two dozen direct flights between Paris and Nice each day. We'll get you on one. Go to the hospital, see if you can gain access to this person, and interview her. If we can get some details, we may be able to build a working hypothesis about how the theft took place and who else was involved."

Dubois nodded. Okay. That was a reasonable request.

“Also, if any of this is real, then the woman is probably in danger.”

Voila! Agent Dubois was back in business. The woman was in danger, and Dubois would have to protect her. This was a real assignment. It demonstrated that Miquel did trust her, and value her contributions. No, she was not leaping into the open jaws of danger with Stark, but so be it.

“They tried to kill her once, they might do it again,” Miquel said. "We need you to assess the security situation in the hospital there. We want to keep the woman alive. We don't have the resources to do that by ourselves, at least not for long. We need to determine whether we should reveal this theft to a wider audience."

“And if I can’t, for some reason, get in to see her…”

“Find a way,” Miquel said.

CHAPTER TEN

8:50 pm Central European Time
A narrow street
La Kalsa (the old Arab Quarter)
Palermo, Sicily

"This is definitely the place," Troy said.

Troy's soft boots whispered against the cobblestones, as he navigated the serpentine alleys of La Kalsa, the old Arab Quarter of Palermo.

His shadow stretched and contracted under the weak, sporadic street lights. The neighborhood was a labyrinth by night, with its narrow pathways bordered by buildings that leaned into each other like tired old men.

He had noticed the city's beauty as the plane descended through the early evening skies - Palermo was a twinkling gem nestled between the mountains and the sea. Yet on the ground, that same beauty was weathered, a patina of decay overlaying everything. Structures stood cracked and peeling, their facades pockmarked with the passing of time.

He emerged into an open plaza. On a crumbling brick building just ahead, a crude red cross was daubed onto the flaking white paint of the third floor. Was it a church or a medical clinic? Either way, it was in sad shape.

Below the building, festering mounds of garbage lay unattended, plastic bags ripped open. A pack of stray dogs, mangy and skinny, scavenged through rotting food and household junk.

Troy pressed the phone to his ear.

"The plaza is quiet," he said, speaking in a low murmur. "There's a red cross painted on a building - it matches the description you gave me."

"That's the location," Jan said, a faint hiss of static coming over the line. "Look for the pale blue house, two stories, just off the plaza. That's where the delivery should take place. But the meet-up will happen in the plaza."

"Got it," Troy said. He ended the call and slipped the phone back into his jacket.

He went to a far corner near a closed restaurant and backed into the shadows. He sat on a stone bench and watched the action, such as it was, out on the plaza. A solitary violinist played a somber melody, his notes rising into the night air. The sound was lovely, but it went underappreciated by the sparse crowd. No coins clinked in his open instrument case; no applause greeted the end of his songs; no one cared. Across the way, some children kicked a soccer ball around, laughing and shouting.

Troy felt the familiar weight of the small .25 caliber pistol in his pocket. It was compact, chosen for stealth and ease of transport, which he'd kept stashed away inside the cabin of El Grupo's airplane. It wasn't much of a gun by his standards - he had it as a last resort.

Don't use it. There was no reason to bring it.

Despite everything that had happened since he joined El Grupo, he was beginning to think like an Interpol agent, possibly even like a European. Gunplay was an American thing, a Middle Eastern thing, maybe a Russian thing. Brazil, Mexico, Colombia.

A lot of cops on this continent didn't even carry guns.

And this was about a diamond theft, not the kind of violent crime or terrorist act that could justify pulling the trigger. The stone at the heart of this op was priceless, sure, but life was more valuable.

Three men entered the plaza. They seemed unhurried, casual, as if they were just locals enjoying the quiet night. One of them took a bite from a sandwich, the bread falling apart at the edges, crumbs falling to the ground. They were talking, but their conversation was low, a private dialogue that Troy couldn't crack.

As if on cue, the violinist stopped playing. He laid his instrument in its case, closed the cover and slipped away, disappearing into a narrow side street. The musician knew from long experience when something was about to go down.

Despite the small size of the plaza, the trio paid Troy no more attention than they did the trash pile and the dogs. To them, he might as well have been a ghost. Maybe they didn't even notice him here.

From his vantage point, Troy noticed two more figures emerging at the far end of the square. Both were men, their shoulders hunched, hands buried in the pockets of their windbreakers. The dim glow from a nearby window did little to illuminate their features. They were shadows among shadows.

These new arrivals carved a cautious path opposite the first three, keeping a deliberate distance as they skirted the edge of the open space. The two, who had just come in, led the way out through an alley to Troy's left, the other three falling into step behind. Troy waited just enough for their forms to blur into the darkness before he got up and followed a ghost trailing phantoms.

The narrow street ahead wound gradually to the right, the voices of the men echoing off the ancient walls, distorted and fragmented. They were out of sight already, so he was going to need to pick up the pace.

Without warning, two men came out of dark, open doorways to the left. Their movements were sharp and sudden.

Behind him, another man came out of a doorway to the right. Troy barely saw that man, a blur moving in the corner of his eye.

Guns were out, pointing at Troy from three directions. Troy caught how the men triangulated quickly and carefully, each staying out of the other's line of fire. If a trigger got pulled, Troy was the only one who would get hit.

"Don't you move a muscle, you punk."

There was barely a single light on the street. The man was practically invisible. His accent was a slice of Brooklyn here in Sicily.

Troy stood as still as stone.

The man who had spoken stepped closer, his face obscured by darkness as he reached into Troy's jacket. He pulled the gun out and held it up with two fingers, as if he didn't want whatever it had rubbing off on him.

"This? Stark. You came here with this?"

"You know my name."

"Of course we know your name. Why do you think we're out here for our health?"

Italy. Baruti. This was a setup.

"I'm sorry to hear that," Troy said.

He felt calm, even blank. If he survived the night, there would be time enough to figure out how this happened. But right now, he needed to find a way to escape.

Three men. Three guns. He probably should have fought them right away.

His body tensed. He took a breath.

The cold steel muzzle of a gun pressed into the nape of his neck, right where his spine met his skull.

"Don't even think about it."

His shoulders slumped. He let all the air go out of him.

"Walk."

They guided him along down the darkened street. Two more men appeared, little more than broad silhouettes. Five men now, gangsters, all likely armed, all here for Troy. The group of six turned left and entered an unassuming building whose door hung open.

Inside, the atmosphere immediately shifted. A quaint courtyard bathed in the soft glow of scattered lanterns lay before them, the scent of some subtle perfume in the air.

They crossed the courtyard to a green wooden door, which was closed. One of the men knocked on it. A voice on the other side said something Troy didn't catch.

They opened the door, and they all went in.

Against the far cinderblock wall, a fat man sat a small round table. A white and red checked tablecloth covered it. A plume of blue smoke swirled around the man, coming from the cigar between his first two stubby fingers. There was a lit candle on the table, an open bottle of red wine, and two empty glasses. The seat opposite the fat man was vacant, silently waiting for its next occupant.

"Troy Stark, meet Bernardo Vizzini," said the American who had disarmed Troy minutes ago.

Vizzini gestured at the chair, but didn't speak.

Troy took his offer, the metal chair scraping softly against the tile. Vizzini filled one of the glasses with a practiced tilt of the bottle, then he filled the other.

"Drink."

Troy looked at the glass like it might bite him.

"Don't worry about the wine. If we wanted to kill you, we would have just shot you in the street like a dog."

Vizzini's voice was thick and gravelly, each word deliberate, carrying the weight of a man accustomed to giving orders.

Troy shrugged. That made sense, as far as it went. He and Vizzini clinked glasses.

Vizzini spoke a word. It sounded like "sah-loo-teh."

"It means to your good health," he said.

Troy smiled and said the word back to him. They could kill him any second, and it was frustrating that he'd let himself get into this situation. Maybe Dubois wasn't the only one off her feed these days. On the other hand, something about this was kind of fun.

He allowed himself a sip of the wine, which had a deep rich flavor, bold, not even a little bit dry.

"Good?" Vizzini said. He took a sip of it himself.

Troy nodded. "Very good."

"We make it ourselves," Vizzini said with more than a hint of pride.

He leaned back, his eyes narrowing with a semblance of respect as he broached the subject at hand. "I suppose you wonder why you're here."

"I came here about a diamond," Troy said. "There was going to be a delivery."

"There was a delivery," Vizzini said. He knocked back another gulp of the wine, and Troy did the same. "But it wasn't a diamond. It was you."

The men around them laughed just a little bit.

"The diamond is why you thought you came here," Vizzini said. "You came here to see me. Anyway, that Paris thing? I wouldn't worry about it. It's none of our business. The rock was stolen by Al Qaeda. They're the ones that mined it twenty or thirty years ago. They wanted it back because they can sell it again and use the money to fund these games they play." He raised his hands. "You and I don't want to get involved in that."

On the contrary, it was exactly the kind of thing Troy wanted to get involved in. But he didn't think this was the opportune time to mention that.

"You mine a rock," Vizzini said. "Sell it, make a bunch of money. Later, you steal it back and sell it again. That much I understand. But those people are crazy. Money doesn't interest them, as a thing in itself. They want to die now, killing their enemies, because they're sure that will get them to Paradise. Best to leave that sort of thing alone. Don't involve yourself with people you don't understand."

"So why are you and I meeting?" Troy said.

Gallo. Gallo sent him here. Carlo Gallo was working for the mob.

"I wanted to thank you personally," Vizzini said. "You did us a favor by getting rid of Baruti, so I feel a sense of obligation to you. Baruti's friends want revenge."

"The 'Ndrangheta," Troy said.

Vizzini raised a hand and waved that idea away. He sighed. "Let's not throw names around. Friends of ours. Friends of Baruti's. We're all friends, technically speaking. But you aren't. They would kill you, but I hear it's too hard."

He looked up at the gunmen standing around them. Now, they all laughed heartily, including Vizzini. They could have killed Troy at any time.

"They're going to kill one of your brothers instead. In New York. They think it'll be easier. Your brothers are cops, no? We don't like cops in Italy. We don't like them in New York either."

Troy's heart seemed to stop beating in his chest. He froze. For a long second, he thought he might not be able to say another word.

"Which brother?" he managed.

Vizzini shrugged. "I don't know. The eldest? I guess. Yeah, the eldest. Donald, is that a brother of yours? A Mick name for sure. They thought that would be fitting. But if they miss him, they'll get whichever one they can get, probably."

"What can I do to stop it?" Troy said.

Vizzini shrugged. "Send them into hiding, your whole family. That's what I would do. Or maybe you can talk to our friends, and surrender yourself. They want you, not your family. We could even sell you to them. Or, as a gesture of goodwill, just kill you and give them the body."

Vizzini shook his head. "I don't want to do that. I never liked Baruti. This thing with the swords. What the hell was that? He was arrogant. I'm glad he's dead, that's the awkward truth. And a lot of his business fell into the hands of people loyal to us, which has been very nice."

"Why did I have to come here to learn all this?" Troy said.

Vizzini looked into his eyes. He had hard, cold eyes.

"Would you have believed me if I called you?"

Good point.

"Anyway, I want to run something by you. There's an opportunity here. You could work for us. Consider this a personal invitation. The money is very good. You can keep the job you have now."

Troy was starting to breathe again. In fact, he was going to hyperventilate. He still had his phone. They hadn't bothered to take it from him. He had to get out of here. He had to start calling his family - *everyone in his family* - right now.

"Well, that's flattering," he said. He raised his hands. "You know, all of a sudden, I got a lot to do."

Vizzini raised a thick hand. "One minute. Listen to it. You owe me that."

It was true. He owed this man a minute of listening.

"We have enemies all over the world," Vizzini said. "People who need to go. You're good at making people go, Stark. We know that. I'll say the word. Murder. You're good at it. And usually, maybe not tonight, you're good at not getting murdered yourself."

Troy shook his head. This was it? Vizzini wanted to make him into a hitman?

"I have to pass."

"You already killed a lot of people. What's the difference?"

"I kill people who do bad things, usually to innocent people."

Vizzini smiled. "Everyone I have you kill will be bad. They all hurt innocent people. I can promise you that."

Troy tried to imagine it. Working for Interpol as an investigator and special operator. Working for Missing Persons and American intelligence as a double agent. And working for Sicilian La Cosa Nostra as an international hitman.

No. It was a bridge too far.

Vizzini saw the answer in his eyes. He shrugged his shoulders and sighed.

"That's fine. I tried to help you. If you change your mind, just show up here in Palermo again and hang around. We'll find you. You're like a walking signpost."

Vizzini paused, and now his eyes said he was deadly serious again.

"Either way, I wish you good luck. You're going to need it. I understand the shooters are already in New York."

CHAPTER ELEVEN

10:05 pm Central European Time
Hospital Magdalene
Nice
Cote d'Azur (the French Riviera)
France

"You're a ninja," Dubois said.

She took a deep breath to steady her nerves.

Infiltrating a hospital. No one will kill you for this.

That might be true, but her body wasn't experiencing it that way. She was trembling, her entire body, from her head to her feet. Her hands might be the worst. She could understand why Miquel sent her on this assignment rather than to Palermo to watch the Mafia take possession of a precious stone.

You could get killed doing that. Her body probably would have rebelled and shut down. Miquel knew a lot about trauma, and he seemed able to anticipate how his people might handle it.

"Good for him," Dubois said. "He's smart. That's why he's in charge."

Dubois lurked in the darkness on the grounds of the small hospital. It was perched on a rolling green hillside, above a suburb of stacked together, multi-colored four and five-story buildings, marching downward to the beaches.

The grounds were not well-lit, and were ringed with dense copses of trees. The main hospital building was old white stone, possibly built before World War II. It was long and low, only two stories high. The rooms on the second floor had small balconies with ornate iron railings. The rooms on the ground floor had sliding glass doors and tiny outdoor patios with shrubs planted on either side.

The building must come from a time when the medical profession was less pharmaceutical in nature, when it was good for patients to "take the air." That would be especially right here, where the air had the scent of the Mediterranean in it.

Dubois stood back in the trees near the edge of a wide lawn. She wore a black jumpsuit. Her hair was tied with a black sash. Everything she had on tonight was black. She was dressed for maximum invisibility.

Jan Bakker had determined that the woman, who as yet had no name, was in room 119, which was on the floor above the ground floor. There were no maps of the building layout available online, perhaps because the hospital was run by an ancient order of nuns, or perhaps because it was small enough that no one thought a map was necessary.

"Now I need to take a guess here," Dubois said quietly, speaking to herself. "I don't want to go into the building because I don't want anyone to see me. I want to go straight in through the balcony to the woman's room."

She paused, staring at the building.

"If I was Room 119, which one would I be?"

Easy enough to narrow down. It would be a room close to the end of the building, away from the main entrance.

Dubois gazed at that end of the building. There was a room all the way at the end, mostly dark inside, except for a flickering TV set. She wasn't sure if that fit her idea of how the woman would be. She survived a car crash down a mountainside and into the sea. Would she really be awake and watching TV?

The staff think she is American.

An American, if she had the ability to do so, might turn on the TV set just to have it playing in the background. It might give her comfort, even keep her company, whether she was awake, asleep, or in a coma.

It would serve as a guess to work from, anyway. She'd go for that room. All that was left was figuring some way to get up there.

All the way to the far left was some kind of wide dinner patio on the ground floor. There were numerous round white tables and chairs. It almost looked like a wedding might take place there. Maybe it was a place where nurses could wheel patients outside and they could sit with visitors.

There was a decorative trellis over there, which climbed up the side of the building. It looked flimsy from here, but if it was sturdy, she could go up the trellis like it was a ladder. At the top, the roof above the ground floor ran the entire length of the hospital. The roof sloped downward at a mild angle, and it stopped every ten meters or so at another room balcony.

It would be very easy to move across that roof.

But was the trellis sturdy enough? And was the roof sturdy enough?

Don't worry. Verify first, then figure it out. Move forward.

Dubois walked over to the wide patio. She stood at the bottom of the trellis and stared up at how it went straight to the roof. The horizontal beams were very much like the rungs of a ladder.

She raised her hands above her head, grabbed a rung there, and stepped up onto the bottom rung. She stood for a moment, then bounced a tiny amount on the rung. It was strong enough to hold her weight.

Well, well, well.

Dubois started climbing.

The crossbeams creaked dangerously each time she stepped on a new one. She was very light, between 50 and 55 kilograms (she rarely weighed herself, to be honest, but that was a pretty good guess). Someone heavy like Stark would probably snap every one of these beams, one right after the other.

She was on the roof in a minute or two. She crept to the patio of the room with the TV set on. A woman lay there in dim light, the TV flashing images of some adventure show. Whoever the hosts were, they appeared to be in a hot air balloon over the African savannah, a million wildebeests running below them in the annual migration.

It was hard to say much about the woman. Her mouth seemed to be hanging open. Her hair was tied up or maybe shaved off. One of her arms was in a long white cast. Her legs were hidden under the blanket. There were machines around her, monitoring her vital signs.

Dubois slipped over the railing and crossed the tiny patio to the sliding door. It was open. Only the screen was closed. Dubois could just hear the TV set, on low. She could hear a faint beep from a machine.

She took a breath, slid the screen door open, and went inside.

The door to the hallway was open, but the lights were dim out there as well. If she was lucky, the nurses' station was at the other end of the hall, and the night shift only came to the rooms if they were called.

The woman in the bed opened her eyes and turned her head toward Dubois. Her mouth snapped shut and her eyes opened WIDE. Her head was covered in a thick white bandage. Her face was bruised, swollen, and battered, bringing back uncomfortable feelings for Dubois.

The woman's right arm, although also swollen and dark purple with bruising, was not in a cast. She had some sort of device with a large black button in her hand.

Dubois raised her hands.

"Don't press the call button," she said in English. "I'm here to help you. Good guys. I'm one of the good guys."

The woman held up the device, moving with what seemed like infinite care.

"It gives me more morphine when I press it." Her voice was slow, running like syrup. "It doesn't call anybody."

She gestured with her head in slow motion at an IV drip on a pole next to the bed.

"Holly?" Dubois said. She was almost certain she had the right room, but she might as well confirm it.

"Holly Danger," the woman croaked, nodding slightly. "That's me." A rueful smile slowly spread across her face.

Dubois moved to the chair by the bedside. She felt that would be less threatening if she sat, instead of looming over the woman's broken body.

"You're very beautiful," Holly said. "Like an angel."

Dubois smiled. "Thank you. You're very beautiful, too."

Holly gestured down the length of the bed.

"Maybe once."

Dubois took her phone out, set the audio recorder, and placed it on the table. She didn't mention this to Holly one way or the other, and she didn't seem to notice.

"I understand you stole the Star of Versailles."

Holly nodded, a tiny bit. "I was the getaway driver. We used a car made to look like a police car. I was wearing a fake police uniform. That was funny. We used to do funny stuff. That was always part of our deal."

She gazed wistfully into the space in front of her, as though she was gazing at a place in the past.

"Go on," Dubois said.

"We ditched the cop car for an old Citroen sedan. Later, we ditched that for an old Mercedes convertible. I set the pick-ups ahead of time. It went off without any problem. Smooth as glass." She breathed heavily. "Smooth as silk."

"The Mercedes was the car that went into the sea," Dubois said.

"Yes."

"Someone tried to kill you?"

Holly nodded again. "Yes."

She gestured at a Styrofoam cup on the table. Dubois reached, picked it up, and handed it to her. Holly dropped the morphine controller. It slid off the bed and onto the floor. That was fine. It was better, for now, that the woman didn't take any more painkillers. She took a sip from the cup, then took a deep slug of it.

"Water," she said. "I'm so thirsty."

Dubois nodded. "I understand."

"They killed my friends," Holly said, unprompted. She was ready to talk - more than ready. "My friends were the ones who actually went in the museum and stole the diamond. They were murdered. I heard the gunshots, and one of them told me to run. I drove away, but got run off the road. They launched a sort of flaming wagon at me."

She shook her head. "It was the strangest thing. I thought I made it, escaped from them, but then this fiery… What was it?"

She drifted off into silence.

"Do you know where this happened?"

Holly nodded, and then looked at Dubois. She stared at her as if she was noticing her for the first time. "Are you the police?"

There was no sense lying. Holly had already admitted she was one of the thieves. It was among the first things she told the hospital staff as soon as she woke.

"Yes. I'm an investigator with Interpol."

"Cops aren't usually as pretty as you."

Dubois didn't answer.

"I don't care if I go to prison," Holly said. "I just want to live. I don't want them to kill me."

Tears began to stream down her face.

"They murdered my friends. We had the diamond. A million euros cash for each of us. It was supposed to be the biggest score of our lives. We were so stupid. We should have just run with it."

Dubois said nothing about that. If they had run with it, the client probably would have found them eventually.

"Where did it happen?"

Given the location where the car went into the sea, and now this flaming wagon description, they were probably already at a point where Jan could narrow it down to a few places. But it would be better to know the exact location.

Holly said an address. "It's in a village called Eze. Off the Moyenne Corniche road, up on the cliffs. It's a nice spot, an old estate house with a large barn. There are a few rolling fields. It looks like they might have grown grapes up there at one time. They have those wooden things in the fields that the vines grow on. The house looked empty, but there were chickens running around, so I don't know. The meeting was supposed to take place in the barn. That was where they shot my partners. It didn't even seem like anyone was there. Then all hell broke loose."

Holly had just shot the arrow into the heart of the target. A house. An address. An old farm. All of this meant there was an owner on a real estate deed.

"Do you know who the client was?" Dubois said, trying to win the jackpot, everything all at once.

Holly slowly shook her head. "Dick said they were the Diamond Dogs. I don't even know what that is."

"Dick?"

"Richard," Holly said. "Richard Tickler. That's who our leader was."

Dubois let the name slide. It was an obvious alias. They could worry about who the thieves were later. Right now, she had a possible murder site. She also had a possible gang name, or criminal network. She turned off the audio recorder and stood.

"Thank you, Holly. This is very helpful."

She reached onto the floor, picked up the morphine controller, and put it back in Holly's hand. She took the Styrofoam cup off the blanket, where Holly had left it. It was empty in any case.

"Will you take me with you?" Holly said.

Dubois shook her head. "I can't. You're injured. You have to stay here. These people are keeping you alive. You have a long road of recovery ahead of you."

"You have to get me out of here," Holly said. "I can't stay here. If you got in, how hard will it be for *them*?"

"They don't know where you are," Dubois said.

"You found out."

"We're going to protect you," Dubois said, although she wasn't sure if they were capable of that or not. El Grupo, with its limited resources, certainly wasn't capable of it. Interpol proper wasn't involved. The local police didn't know the theft had taken place and could probably be compromised.

"I promise."

Okay. Now, she had promised. She would have to make it real somehow.

"I don't believe you," Holly said, the tears streaming down her face again. "All cops are liars."

CHAPTER TWELVE

10:45 pm Central European Time
Hotel Gran Sicilia
Politeama / Liberta
Palermo, Sicily

"Donnie, listen to me!"

Troy was back in his hotel room. It was a clean, somewhat nondescript room in a large hotel meant for tourists. The walls in the room were light blue. There was a stylized map of Sicily on one wall. There were various pictures of Palermo street scenes, and ancient mountain villages on the other walls.

Everyone downstairs in the lobby had been wearing a mask when he walked in.

This was a good place, generic, anonymous. He felt safe here. Troy's entire body was shaking in a delayed adrenaline rush. He was probably going to spend some sleepless nights thinking about how easily those gangsters had gotten the drop on him.

"I'm at mom's house," Donnie said, his voice faraway. "This isn't the best place to talk about this."

Troy looked at the cell phone in his hand. His brother was stubborn and overconfident. You might even call him arrogant. His head was made of cement.

"I just told you that people are trying to kill you. It's kind of important."

"I get it," Donnie said. "But this isn't a good time."

"Where are you now?" Troy said.

"I'm in my old bedroom upstairs. I came up here so mom wouldn't hear. She's downstairs cooking."

"Do me a favor," Troy said. "Look out the window and see if there's a car down the street. It should be a nothing sort of car, something you wouldn't look at twice. Should be a couple of guys in it. They're federal agents. They're there to protect mom. They can protect you, too."

He didn't mention that Donnie supposedly had his own agents trailing him.

"I can't see anything out the window, Troy. It's almost dark, and we're having a snowstorm."

Something about Donnie's voice was off.

"Are you drinking, Donnie?"

"I've had a couple."

Troy shook his head and rolled his eyes. "How many is that, four?"

Donnie didn't answer.

"Look, I'm going to start over," Troy said. "I just met with a guy who runs a crew in the Sicilian mob, La Cosa Nostra, okay? He told me the Calabrian mob has gotten frustrated trying to kill me, so they're going to kill you instead. My eldest brother, that's what he said."

"And this is because you…"

"I killed a guy, that's right." Troy winced as he spoke. He hated revealing this part of his life to his family, even his brothers. They must know some part of it. After all, he was a former Navy SEAL with multiple combat deployments. They knew he had been used on clandestine missions by Joint Special Operations Command. They had watched the testimony he gave to the US Senate about the existence or non-existence of Metal Shop. Donnie knew something, but there was no way he knew the extent of it.

"A guy in the Albanian mob," Troy said. "A guy the Calabrians did business with. They liked this guy. He made them a lot of money. They're not happy that he's dead."

"And you killed this guy because why?"

Troy sighed. "Because he was trying to kill me."

"I guess I'm not too worried about it," Donnie said. "I'm a big boy."

Troy nearly screamed into the phone. Nothing intelligible, just a long scream of anguish and frustration.

"Donnie…"

"Come on, Troy. I'm a copper. A New York City cop. An Inspector. If they kill me, the NYPD and the feds will rain a shitstorm on them, the likes of which they've never seen. Every made man in the five boroughs will be up on RICO charges inside the first week. Every elderly boss with Alzheimer's and a weak bladder will do a perp walk for the TV cameras. Every money laundering front and every so-called legit business will be up on tax evasion charges. Guys who are out will go back inside for 20 years on minor parole violations."

"How will any of that help you if you're dead?" Troy nearly said, but didn't.

"The mob doesn't kill cops in New York City," Donnie said. "They would never allow the Italians to come over here and do it."

"That assumes the Italians are going to ask for permission."

"That's how these people operate," Donnie said. "If you want to do something that's going to cause everybody problems, you ask for permission first."

Troy nodded. This is how his brother was. This was how it was going to be.

"All right, Donnie. I just came out of that meeting. I need to make another call."

Meeting. It was like a sick joke.

"Do me a favor and keep an eye on Mom, will you?"

"You know I will."

"Give my love to Kelly and the kids."

Troy hung up and stared at the phone for another little while. Invisible fingers seemed to tighten around his throat.

He rang another number, and waited as the call bounced from cell tower, to undersea cable, to cell tower again.

"Agent Stark," a deep, gravelly voice said. "To what do I owe this pleasure?"

Troy picture the one-eyed wonder the voice belonged to. Salt and pepper goatee combined with a military-issue crew cut. Square jaw, thick neck leading to broad shoulders. One blue eye. One black eyepatch with a black strap keeping it in place. A pair of thin, steel-rimmed glasses over the whole mess.

Colonel Persons, Troy's commanding officer once upon a time, now his spymaster. Missing Persons was what his soldiers used to call him, though never to his face.

"Colonel Persons. I have a problem."

"Tell me," Persons said. "I live to help Troy Stark solve his problems."

"It's a problem we've talked about before."

"Then it shouldn't be a problem," Persons said. "The problem we talked about is under control."

"I just met with a Sicilian mafia boss."

"Everybody's a mob boss in Sicily," Persons said.

"He told me they're going to hit my brother Donnie."

"Who, the Sicilians?"

Troy shook his head and sighed. He felt like he was carrying a giant stone on his shoulders. It weighed about a hundred thousand pounds at the moment.

"No. The Calabrians. The Sicilians don't care about Baruti. In fact, they're glad he's dead."

"Why would they tell you these things? It's practically a death sentence for them, if that ever got around. It would be open war at the very least."

"They wanted to thank me personally for getting rid of him."

Persons made a sound like a tire being punctured. That was him laughing. It didn't last long. "Agent Stark, you're becoming quite credulous in your old age."

Troy didn't bother to ask what credulous meant. Persons threw out vocabulary words sometimes. It was a bad habit. Missing Persons had any number of bad habits. In many ways, he was an easy person to dislike.

"I'll be 33 this year," Troy said.

"I've heard it said that cognitive ability peaks in your mid-20s. Now I'm starting to believe it."

"I went to talk to them about something else."

"Something you're working on?" Persons said. "Something that went missing, perhaps?"

"I guess everyone knows about that by now," Troy said.

"Not everyone. Not even close."

"Listen," Troy said. "I'm very worried about my brother. I'm worried about my whole family. It's impossible for me to be effective when this is hanging over my head. I feel like I need to go back to New York and protect them myself."

"Troy, you have nothing to worry about. I gave you my promise. Your people are safe, all of them."

"Give me something that makes it believable," Troy said.

Okay, I will. One minute, please."

There was a pause over the line. After a few moments, Persons came back on.

"Here's what I have. Donnie works from 7am to 3pm. He got off work today and went to your mother's house in the Bronx. He's there now. We've got agents doubled up, one car on your mom's street, one around the corner so as not to attract notice. Your brother Patrick is at work."

"Pat," Troy said.

“Fine,” Persons said. “He drives around the city in an ambulance, so it’s a little hard to stick with him at all times. What we do is follow his rig via GPS. We put a satellite tracker on his rig. He takes the same one out every day.”

“Mikey,” Troy said.

"Since he stopped doing undercover work, he's been riding a desk downstairs from me. I suspect they were annoyed when he came in from the cold, and this is how they punish him. They're going to bore him to death. Remember my office? One Police Plaza. There are hundreds of cops in this building. Our guys follow him down here in the morning and then follow him home again at night. He looks miserable."

“What about their families?” Troy said.

“The Italians don’t hurt wives and children,” Persons said. “It’s beneath them. I hope I don’t need to explain that to you. They also don’t hurt mothers. The agents watching over your mother 24 hours a day are a waste of taxpayer dollars.”

“Did you ever fly inside of a C5 Galaxy?” Troy said. He tried to shrug off the suggestion that keeping his mom alive was a waste of money. It was getting harder to shrug things off these days. “*That’s* a waste of taxpayer dollars.”

The C5 was an enormous cargo plane, basically a flying warehouse. It consumed so much fuel, Navy pilots had nicknamed it FRED. The acronym stood for Freaking Ridiculous Economic Disaster, or Freaking Ridiculous Environmental Disaster, whichever you preferred. Only Navy pilots didn’t say “freaking.”

“Touche,” Persons said. “I was only joking before. It was a joke in poor taste. Your people are safe, and it’s worth every penny.”

Troy nodded. It sounded… all right. It wasn’t perfect by any means, but nothing ever was.

“Okay,” he said. “I guess that’s good enough.”

"Good," Persons said. "I'm glad we could put that to rest again. Now, do you want to talk to me about that missing item? It's important."

The Star of Versailles? It was a stolen diamond, or whatever kind of stone. Expensive, yes. Important? A little over a week ago, they were dealing with a massive bio-weapon attack.

“It’s fluff,” Troy said. “Maybe some bad guys took it.”

“That much seems clear,” Persons said. “Bad guys took it.”

"I don't know much," Troy said. "I probably don't know anything you don't already know. I'll have to talk to you when I get more information."

"Please do," Persons said. "I'll be waiting for your call."

Troy hung up. Persons could wait for a month, or forever, for all Troy cared. It had been an awful day. He and Dubois's romantic getaway to Paris was ruined by running into Carlo Gallo. Now Dubois was furious with him, the Sicilians had captured him and then benignly let him go (punching a giant hole in his confidence in the process), and Donnie's life was at risk. At least Donnie, and maybe all of his brothers.

Troy sat in one of the chairs by the little round table. Basic hotel furniture. What he would like to do was go to sleep. Then again, how could he sleep with all of these things piling up on top of him?

The cell phone rang, and he nearly howled in agony. He glanced at the number. Headquarters. He answered it.

"Stark," he said.

"Agent Stark," Miquel said. "How did the surveillance go?"

"Strange," Troy said. "Unexpected."

"What does that mean, please?" The voice now was Jan Bakker's. Jan was uncomfortable with ambiguous speech.

"I talked to them," Troy said. "It wasn't a drop-off at all. It was a ruse to get me here to meet with them. Turns out our friend Carlo Gallo will take anyone on as a client. He tricked me into coming here. They were waiting for me."

"Why would they want to talk to you?" Miquel said.

He didn't touch the idea of his old friend working for the mafia.

"It's a long story, Miquel," Troy said. "And probably off topic. It's enough to say that in terms of the other thing we're looking at, this was a dead end."

"We have a break in the case," Miquel said. "A woman on the southern French coast was run off the road. She went down the cliffs and into the sea, but survived the crash. There was a possible double murder. Close to Nice, in the surrounding area. Jan is already piling up data about it. I'd prefer not to say more over the phone."

"All right," Troy said.

The words seemed to wash over him. They didn't really make a lot of sense. There was a double murder in Nice, which had something to do with a stolen gem. Troy couldn't make sense of it, and he didn't really want to try. A hot shower suddenly seemed appealing. A hot shower, scalding hot, might help him sleep.

He spoke mechanically, like a robot. "The Italians told me that Al Qaeda originally mined and sold the diamond, and they're the ones who stole it back."

Jan came on the line. "That would make a certain amount of sense. There is a long history of conflict or so-called 'blood' diamonds. There isn't much regulation in that industry, and the regulation that exists is mostly for cosmetic purposes."

"It keeps up the appearance of legitimacy," Troy said. "So young ladies in the West can show off their engagement rings without feeling guilty."

"More or less," Jan said. "For at least a decade and probably more, Al Qaeda was deeply involved in diamond mining and smuggling from the failed states of Central Africa. They were using the raw diamonds to fund their own activities. They set up illegal mining operations, often using slave labor, as well as criminal networks to move the diamonds around the world."

"What would you like me to do?" Troy said.

"If Palermo is a dead end, perhaps you should go to Nice in the morning," Miquel said, without much commitment. "Dubois is already there."

"Investigating a double murder?" Troy said.

"Yes."

"Is the plane still here with me?"

"Yes."

Troy shook his head. Crazy Dubois was in Nice, suddenly on a double murder case. She did it to deliberately put herself in danger, and demonstrate to Troy that was she was a big girl and didn't need his protection. This was a day that refused to end.

"In that case, I'm going right now," he said.

CHAPTER THIRTEEN

February 15
1:05 am Central European Time
In the hills near the village of Eze
Cote d'Azur (the French Riviera)
France

"Scary, like a horror movie."

Agent Dubois guided the nondescript sedan along the winding road, its headlights slicing through the darkness. The vehicle, a blubber boat chosen for its anonymity, complained as it climbed to the isolated farmhouse perched on the cliffs near Eze.

Gravel crunched underneath the tires, announcing her arrival to anyone who might be listening for an approaching car.

She parked the car at the end of the rutted driveway and killed the engine. The world around her fell into a deep silence. She sat motionless for a moment, surveying her surroundings. Outside, the sky was painted with a billion stars.

This was Miquel's newest gesture of confidence in her. Jan was convinced that he had found the farmhouse, so Miquel sent her here. This time, Dubois wasn't completely sure she was ready.

She stepped out of the car, the cool night air wrapping around her. With practiced ease, she checked the magazine in her gun. Loaded. The weight of it was comforting.

Flashlight in her other hand, Dubois moved away from the car. Each step took her downhill, closer to the dark silhouette of the old homestead. It stood as a testament to forgotten times. It would make a decent hideout for a criminal gang.

The large barn loomed ahead, its doorway gaping open like a dark mouth. She approached it with caution, every sense alert. Her breathing was even, her movements precise - nothing betrayed the adrenaline coursing through her veins.

Suddenly, a massive shape unfurled from the darkness, wings casting a momentary eclipse over the stars. An owl, colossal in size, took flight mere meters away from where Dubois stood. Its silent departure was almost surreal, the only evidence of its existence the rush of air that brushed against her face and the slight rustle of feathers.

Dubois staggered back, heart hammering in her chest.

"See? A jump scare, just like in the movies."

Stark had abandoned her, left her behind because he thought she was a liability. And now here she was, shaken by an owl's sudden flight. She cursed under her breath. Stark was right. The fear was palpable, a weight upon her shoulders, and on top of that, now there was the creeping doubt that she might indeed be what Stark believed her to be.

With each shaky exhale, Dubois pushed the terror down, forcing it into the recesses of her mind. There was no place for it here, not in this line of work. Her resolve hardened and she advanced toward the barn, the darkness ahead beckoning her to confront the very thing she feared most.

The gnawing pit of her stomach brought back the memory of Belgrade's darkness, as she huddled in a cage that bit into her flesh, a prison meant for an animal. Her captors' hollow laughter still echoed in her mind, a constant reminder of her vulnerability.

She had to overcome it. She had to FIGHT to regain herself.

The night air carried the rustle of feathers and the clucking of chickens in the dooryard. A silhouette strutted with instinctive authority; the rooster, guardian of this moonlit domain, eyed the area with a confidence that came with being so heavily armed - claws, beak, spurs. In her youth, she had once seen a rooster murder a hawk that had tried to carry off a chicken. The rooster attacked the hawk with a speed and a mindless ferocity that was both astonishing and disturbing.

She stood near a wire fence, her eyes tracing the movements of the poultry flock. The chickens remained blissfully unaware of the owl that had taken flight moments before, a predator deterred by the rooster's unyielding presence.

In that small interaction of the cutthroat natural world, Dubois saw a parallel to her own world - a world where threats loomed large and protectors often stood alone.

No. This was silly. She was scared, and her mind was playing tricks.

"Get it together, Dubois," she said.

The rooster paused, tilting its head, and seemed to watch her for a moment. Then it continued its patrol, not caring a bit about the fragile psyche of an agent trying to claw back her confidence one step at a time.

The farmhouse was just to her left, a shadow against the backdrop of the night sky. She tested the front door. The knob wouldn't turn; locked. She tried to peer through the windows, but drapes were pulled across them. It seemed like no one lived here or had been here for a long time.

The chickens must have wandered over from a nearby property.

The barn was maybe twenty meters distant. Its gaping doorway yawned wide, blacker than the dark night.

"Back on your horse, Dubois," she whispered.

Her fingers curled around the grip of her gun even as her hand trembled the slightest amount. She took a step towards the barn, then another, until the darkness swallowed her whole. Panic fluttered in her chest. She forced a slow, deliberate breath in through her nostrils. In… hold… out through the mouth.

Her flashlight pierced the blackness as she crossed the threshold. Dust motes danced in the beam of light, twirling madly. The emptiness of the barn loomed large around her, dark shadows high above her at the edge of her flashlight's reach.

Her heart hammered a frenzied tempo, a reminder of her recent captivity.

But this was not Belgrade. This was Eze, and she was no longer caged. With each sweep of her flashlight, Dubois reclaimed a small piece of herself, her determination growing stronger than the fear that wanted to cripple her.

Her beam settled on two stains on the dirt floor. They were wide, maybe a meter apart, consistent with where two men might stand while being shot. More, there were indentations in the dirt floor, and two tracks where bodies might have been dragged away.

Dubois exhaled sharply. She crouched and extended a quivering finger towards the first stain. The moist earth clung to her skin immediately, its dampness cold and almost sickening. She lifted her finger to her nose. The metallic smell confirmed her fears before the word formed on her lips.

"Blood," she whispered into the silence. "There's a lot of blood here."

At that moment, a sound shattered the stillness - a voice so unexpected it sent an electric jolt through her spine.

"Hey."

It was deep, a man's voice, and far too close behind her.

Dubois leapt to her feet. She turned, practically a pirouette.

The flashlight's beam swung wildly before fixing on the figure in the doorway. Her gun hand whipped forward, pointing the pistol.

"Don't move!" she shouted in sharp French.

A large man raised his hands slowly, deliberately. A smile played across his face, a touch of amusement despite the danger. Stark's eyes met hers, and he shook his head.

"You have to be more alert than that, Agent Dubois."

"Agent Stark! Are you stupid? I could have killed you."

He shrugged, a casual lift of his shoulders.

"Yeah, but I could have killed you first."

CHAPTER FOURTEEN

8:45 pm Eastern Standard Time (2:45 am Central European Time)
A quiet neighborhood near the Hudson River
Piermont, New York

"Excuse me, while I kiss this guy!" Donnie Stark shouted, singing along to the song playing on his favorite satellite radio station.

He had a lousy singing voice, and alone in his car, he really didn't care.

He liked to sing. And he liked to sing the lyrics incorrectly, in funny ways. It was a quirk of his, which very few people knew about. It didn't really fit his tough guy image. It had started when he was a kid. In grammar school, they used to make all the little kids sing a song called, "My Country 'Tis of Thee."

The opening lines of the song went, "My country 'tis of thee, sweet land of liberty, of thee I sing."

For the longest time, young Donnie thought the line was "of the icing."

Which kind of made sense. Snow-capped mountains, all of that.

What didn't make a lot of sense was he used to think the first words were "My country tis-o-vee." No one ever explained what tis-o-vee was.

He sighed. Memories.

His riverfront suburb was quiet, its upscale homes casting warm glows onto the snow that blanketed their lawns. On the passenger seat, a Glock 19 lay loaded next to his police badge.

Beside the gun and shield, there were a dozen roses. A bottle of chilled champagne, hopefully kept that way by the winter air seeping through the window cracks, lay next to Valentine cards for his two little girls.

Snowflakes swirled in the beam of his headlights. His mind was just a bit clouded by the whiskey he'd had at his mom's house back in the Bronx. The familiar guilt tugged at him; he knew better than to mix drinking with driving, especially on a night where every turn could hide a patch of ice.

He glanced down at his wide belly nearly pressing against the steering wheel, the seatbelt straining against his girth. He patted it.

His height often fooled others, but not the bathroom mirror, nor the way his knees ached climbing the stairs. At forty-one, Donnie felt the weight of years more than he cared to admit.

"Time to hit the gym, fatso," he said, his voice now a whisper.

His mind churned darkly as the Lexus rolled quietly up into the driveway. The pale glow of the dashboard illuminated the frown on his face. Troy seemed half a world away in Europe, but suddenly the shadows of his life loomed over Donnie' own.

It was ludicrous, wasn't it? Yet there it was, gnawing at his insides, a feeling that he couldn't shake off. More than anything, he was annoyed as he considered the enigma that was his youngest brother - always abroad, always unreachable, and now, his secrecy apparently had some kind of price attached.

He eased the car to a stop, headlights casting long shadows across the snow-dusted driveway. Kelly's BMW sat on the other side of his passenger seat.

With a sigh, he glanced forward at the garage, where his 1969 Mustang slumbered under a film of dust. The clutter that filled the other half mocked him now - an old lawnmower, broken gym equipment, his old bicycle - symbols of procrastination that suddenly felt foolish, even dangerous.

There was a doorway at the back of the garage that led into the laundry room and then into the kitchen. A man who kept his garage clean could park in there, close the electric bay door behind him, and then enter the house.

"If your life is in danger," he said. "It's probably better to park inside the garage."

He reached over to grab the roses and champagne when a flicker of movement to his left caught his eye. His hand froze midway to the passenger seat.

Through the snow-dusted side window, he saw a figure walking briskly across the neighbor's front yard, heading straight for him. A long trench coat flapped around the man's legs, shrouded by the darkness and the thickening snowfall.

It was impossible to make out the man's face.

A sudden thump from behind jolted him. He looked into the rearview mirror. There, framed in the reflected glow of the streetlights, stood another man directly behind his Lexus. The man wore a dark ski mask - all that showed were his eyes. In a swift motion, the man raised a shotgun, its barrel aimed at the back window.

"Oh no."

The words barely left his mouth before Donnie threw himself sideways, heart pounding against his ribcage.

The rear windshield exploded inward, showering him with glass. He lay on top of the champagne bottle, practically squashing it, while the roses scattered across the leather seat, petals crushed under his weight.

I didn't hear the shot. He's got a silencer.

Donnie's hand dug underneath him on the passenger seat, fingers finding the grip of his Glock. He wrenched it out from under his body and shoved the barrel into the gap between the front seats. He tilted it up and out toward the missing windshield.

He pulled the trigger several times in rapid succession.

BANG! BANG! BANG! BANG! BANG!

Each shot made the weapon buck wildly against his grasp, but Donnie held on, firing blindly through what remained of the back window.

"Eat that, you prick!" he shouted.

Donnie's gunfire was deafening, making his ears ring. He hoped the noise of the gunshots, and his scream, would be enough to alert the neighborhood.

"FIRE!" he shrieked. "FIRE!"

With the gun still in his hand, Donnie swiveled to look out his driver's side window. The trench-coated figure had closed the distance with terrifying speed, materializing at the glass like a specter of death. And there it was - another shotgun in his hands, the sound suppressor grotesquely oversized.

The adrenaline surged through him, sobering him up in a split second.

He acted on pure survival instinct now, aiming through the window.

BANG! BANG! BANG! BANG!

The window shattered and sprayed outward.

The man staggered back, arms flailing from the impact as bullets hit home. Then he was gone, out of sight. An instant later, he popped up again and started running.

Body armor. Bulletproof vest. Some damn thing.

Donnie's breath came in harsh gasps, the gun still ringing in his ears.

He kept firing out the window, the muzzle flashes blinding, after-images dancing across his vision, the shots deafening. He screamed, a long wall of sound without syllables or meaning that he could barely hear.

There was glass all over him.

Am I hit?

The thought ricocheted through Donnie's mind as he lay sprawled across the seats, the gun's weight suddenly immense in his shaking hand. He couldn't seem to move. His body was like lead.

Somewhere behind him, car doors slammed. An engine revved furiously, tires squealing on snow and asphalt as a vehicle tore away into the night.

People were screaming now, people were running, their shadows cast long by the neighborhood porch lights suddenly coming on.

His wife Kelly appeared, framed in the doorway of their home, her silhouette stark against the warm glow behind her.

A face materialized in the remains of the driver's side window. It was a man's face, weathered with age and experience.

Mitch. It was his neighbor Mitch. Retired firefighter.

"Get Kelly inside," Donnie managed to croak at him, forcing the words out. "I don't want her to see this."

"See what?" Mitch said. "What the hell is going on?"

Donnie tried to piece together a response. A numbness was spreading through him, and there was a sharp pain that seemed to stab at his chest. He struggled for breath.

"Am I shot? Am I bleeding?"

The questions tumbled out, but he already knew the answer. There was no wet warmth, no searing agony of a bullet wound. This was something else.

Mitch leaned in, the beam of a flashlight probing the interior of the car.

"I don't see any blood."

In the distance, there was the approaching wail of sirens.

"Cops are coming now, Donnie. What happened here?"

"Somebody tried to kill me," Donnie said, his voice barely above a whisper.

He locked eyes with Mitch. "I think I'm having a heart attack."

His gaze shifted past Mitch, back to Kelly and beyond, to the house that held his entire world. "Bring my girls into your house, all right? Keep them safe for me."

The sirens grew louder. The first ones were almost here.

"Will do," Mitch said, and was gone.

Donnie Stark lay across the front seat of his car, the snow gently falling through his shattered window, wondering if he was going to die.

CHAPTER FIFTEEN

3:25 am Central European Time
Boutique Hotel Jacobins
Nice
Cote d'Azur (the French Riviera)
France

"Stark," a female voice, thick with sleep said. "Telephone is ringing."

Troy's eyes opened a crack. He had been asleep, dreaming about a beach somewhere. It was a different kind of beach, open, a long stretch of deserted white sands, not like this one.

Which one?

He grunted. He felt Dubois's warmth next to him, under the covers.

It came back to him. They were in a small beachfront hotel in Nice. The beach here was the opposite of deserted. There were dozens of hotels and thousands of people here. He had been dreaming of the South Pacific, maybe.

"Agent Stark," Dubois said again.

He nearly laughed. Even in her sleep, she called him Agent Stark.

His phone was ringing. Its lights were flashing. It was late for someone to call him. He looked at the name and number.

Mikey.

It was his brother. He answered it.

"Mikey."

"Troy?"

"The one and only."

"You awake?" Mikey sounded dead serious. He was a pretty serious, no-nonsense type in general. This sounded even more serious than that.

Troy's heart seemed to skip a few beats.

"I am now. Everything okay?"

"No. Donnie almost got killed. Two guys tried to take out in his driveway with shotguns."

Troy sat up all the way, his back against the headboard.

"What?"

"Yeah. It's snowing pretty hard here tonight. A couple of guys tried to kill him. He had just pulled in. They came out of nowhere. They were clearly waiting for him."

Troy's throat was suddenly tight. The invisible hands were there again, trying to choke the life out of him.

"Is he all right?" he said.

"They've got him in the hospital for observation."

Now Troy slipped out from under the covers and was standing in the small room. Rooms in France. Rooms in Europe in general. They were small. He didn't know what to make of that.

He was in bare feet, boxer briefs, no shirt. It was cool in the room. There was a window open, and the moon was glowing out over the sea.

"Was he shot?"

"No," Mikey said. "He didn't get shot. He didn't get injured at all, except a few cuts from flying glass. After it was over, he thought he was having a heart attack."

"Was he?"

"Seems like no," Mikey said. "He just got a little excited, that's all. Guy's been riding a desk too long. He hasn't been in the real shit for a while."

In spite of himself, in spite of everything, Troy nearly laughed.

"Where are Kelly and the kids?" he said instead.

"They went to my house. A neighbor brought them there. A retired fireman."

"Where are you?"

"I'm at the hospital."

Troy felt something rising in him, a sense of helpless terror. His breath caught in his throat. His lungs didn't seem to work. He had never had a panic attack, but he thought maybe this was what one felt like when it was starting.

He had to impart a lot of information to Mikey, and quickly.

"Mikey. Listen to me. Are the cops there?"

"I'm the cops."

"More cops. Other cops."

"Yes."

"Then you have to go home and…"

"Save it," Mikey said. "We've got coppers everywhere. Guys I work with are watching the house. Guys Donnie knows who retired and still do security are doing the same. Local town cops are in the lobby downstairs here and posted at the door to Donnie's room. The door is open, so they can see what's happening in there."

"Where's Pat?" Troy said. Pat was the fourth brother. He was not a cop. He was a paramedic for the New York Fire Department.

"Pat went with his family, and picked up mom, and they're all converging on my house. The place is like Fort Knox right now."

"It won't last," Troy said. "Eventually, people lose interest and go home."

He wasn't sure if he was telling Mikey this, or himself.

Mikey ignored the comment anyway. "What's this Donnie said about you called him earlier, and told him someone was going to try to kill him. The whole reason he survived was he had a Glock on the seat next to him. So I guess he has you to thank for that. He said he put two or three rounds into a guy's chest."

"Good man," Troy said.

"The guy got up and ran away."

Troy sighed. "Body armor."

"Duh-uh," Mikey said. Again, Troy nearly laughed. Mikey was a full-grown, dead serious adult, who had worked Vice and Homicide, and who sometimes acted like a fifth grader. "So what's this all about? How did you know that?"

Troy took a breath. He knew it because he'd been lying to his family all along about what he was doing over here. And now he had to come clean about it.

"I don't work for a government food charity."

"I'm pretty sure we all know that," Mikey said. "Maybe not Mom."

"I work for a small sub-agency of Interpol. We do deep cover stuff. Special ops. Rapid investigations. A little while back, I killed an Albanian mobster who was trafficking kidnapped girls to North Africa."

There was quiet over the line. Troy had just admitted to murdering someone. This sort of thing set him apart from his brothers. They were cops. As far he knew, neither of them had ever killed anyone in the line of duty. And of course Pat hadn't.

Then there was Troy. He'd lost count.

"I'm not supposed to talk about this stuff."

"Are you an assassin?" Mikey said

"No. It just happened. It was him or me. Girls were getting taken from London. We were trying to get them back."

"Mateos Baruti," Mikey said.

"Yeah. You read about it."

"What other Albanian crime lord has been murdered recently?" Mikey said. "He was stabbed or killed with a sword. Something like that. They said it created a power vacuum where his old rackets are up for grabs. The papers seemed to indicate it was a mob hit."

"It was a duel," Troy said. "Him and me. He was the sporting type. Given the circumstances, I didn't really have the option to decline."

"He deserved it," Mikey said.

"Yes. But he had powerful friends. Namely the southern Italian mob. Calabrians. They've been trying to kill me. They're the ones who blew up my car."

"I remember you telling us," Mikey said. His voice was beginning to sound flat and dead. He was connecting the dots on his own. They just hadn't created a fully formed picture yet. He didn't know if it was an elephant, a hippo, or what.

"Nothing has worked so far," Troy said. "They keep missing me. So now they've decided to kill my family."

His voice was starting to shake. He didn't like that feeling. It wasn't the killer trying to choke him to death. It was the sense that he was going to cry.

"I just found that out tonight," he said, to be clear. It sounded like he was trying to get himself off the hook.

There was another long pause.

"Ah, Troy," Mikey said finally. "Ah, kid."

"I know," Troy said. "It's too horrible. I am so very sorry."

"I have to think about this," Mikey said. "I need some time."

"Okay."

Just like that, the line went dead. Troy smacked himself in the head with the phone. Hard. If he did it again, he might smash it into pieces against his skull.

"Stark!" Dubois said. "Don't do that."

She was fully awake now.

"What is going on?"

Troy raised a hand to her as if to signal STOP.

He had another number on speed dial. Normally, he wouldn't make this call in front of her. But he didn't care anymore. If they were going to be together, she was going to have to find out sooner or later.

The phone range a few times, then deep gravel voice answered.

"Hello, Troy. I was wondering when you'd call."

Missing Persons. Troy couldn't remember the last time Persons called him anything besides Stark. Troy could barely control his anger.

"Colonel, my brother almost got killed tonight."

Over on the bed, Dubois gasped. Her mouth hung open, and she covered it with a hand. She looked like someone on a TV show, overselling a surprise.

"I know," Persons said mildly. "He acquitted himself very nicely. You'll be happy to know that. And we're on top of it."

Troy's voice was rising.

"On top of it? In what way are you on top of it? What are you on top of? I just talked to you a few hours ago. You told me you were on top of it then. Then my brother almost got murdered in his own driveway."

"It was snowing. Our guys…"

"Oh, God!" Troy shouted. "It was snowing? That's why?"

"They screwed up," Persons said calmly. "I admit that. It was hard to see who was who in all the snow. They reacted too late. But they fixed it. They were there when it happened, saw it, and they chased down the hitters. Two professional guys from Italy. We identified them. I can give you the dossiers, if you want."

"Where are they now?" Troy said.

This conversation was getting off track. There were a million other hitmen out there. Troy's family was in immediate danger. Even so, if Troy got his hands on those guys…

"The hitters?"

"Yes." Troy had a feeling of unreality wash over him. Maybe none of this was real. He was in a lunatic asylum somewhere, hallucinating all of it.

"They've been retired," Persons said. "Neutralized, you might say. Since it's a snowstorm, we left them on the back porch of the Black Raven Social Club in Howard Beach, and they're being covered up nicely. Their Italian-American friends hang out there and should stumble on them in the morning. It sends a message. The right parties will receive it."

For a moment, Troy was rendered speechless. Of course, this is how it went. They send hitters. We kill them and send them back.

Missing Persons was that kind of man. If he could call in a Vietnam-style napalm strike on the Calabrian mob, he would probably do it. It would send a message.

"Jesus," Troy said.

"I'm not sure Jesus had anything to do with it," Persons said. "But I'm very sorry it got to this point."

"What am I supposed to do now?" Troy said.

"I've got agents staked out. Cops, active and retired, have come out of the woodwork to gather around your family. Friends, I suppose. Between our guys and theirs, there must be 20 or more people guarding your family at the moment."

"I know that," Troy said. "But that's tonight."

"Right," Persons said. "They're safe tonight. As I indicated, the two hitters are gone. If your people are willing to do it, tomorrow I can take the whole group of them into protective custody. We can hold them until it seems safe to come out again."

"It's thirteen people," Troy said. "Without getting into cousins, aunts, extended family."

"I know. We can handle thirteen. The kids can go to school under aliases, or they can home-school for the time being. The adults can hang out by the pool. I don't think your cousins need to worry."

How could he be sure of that? Disappear Troy's close family, and then the cousins become the only ones the bad guys can still reach.

"When will it be safe?" Troy said.

"We can talk about that later," Persons said. "We need to get these people off your back. I understand that. I was shying away from the nuclear option because I thought there wasn't a good enough reason to go there. But they've made it clear, through their actions, that it might be necessary."

"What is the nuclear option?" Troy said.

Persons didn't respond.

Was he going to decapitate the 'Ndrangheta? Was he even capable of that?

"Troy, I want you to be comfortable in your role," he said. "I'm willing to do what it takes to achieve that. It probably won't take more than making an example out of a few people. If it takes more, it takes more."

Why haven't we done that already?

Simple. It was against the law to assassinate people.

Troy sighed. He had made a mess here. His entire family was going to have to go into hiding. Would they even do it? Donnie, maybe, after what had happened.

But headstrong Mikey?

“Ah, God,” Troy said. It was so bad. It was the worst thing he had ever done.

“I need to talk to you about this other thing you’re pursuing,” Persons said, changing the subject abruptly.

Troy's head seemed to be floating. He looked down at his feet to make sure they were still touching the ground. "What thing am I pursuing?"

“Come off it, Stark. I know you’re after a stolen gemstone.”

Of course he did. His phantoms nearly let Donnie get killed, but he kept tabs on Troy at all times.

“What about it?” Troy said.

“Chatter says there’s more there than meets the eye.”

“There is,” Troy said. “Is it safe to talk on this thing?”

“You called me,” Persons said. “I’m not worried about it.”

"Al Qaeda took the stone. That's what I heard. They stole it to use the money to fund future activities. So it's got a link to terrorism. I have no idea how accurate that is. There's a lot of other stuff about the museum and the people who own it. Who they know, what they're up to. It's a lot of loose ends."

Now that he was saying it out loud, it all seemed silly. *Al Qaeda took the stone?* The man who gave him the idea was a Sicilian mobster who might think it was funny to send cops down blind alleys. The Sicilians could have easily stolen it, and claimed otherwise. Anyone could have been behind this.

“I don’t know who was involved,” Troy said now. “But it seems like it might have passed hands down here. That’s why we came.”

“Where is here?” Persons said.

“You don’t know?”

“No.”

"French Riviera," Troy said. "We have a lead on an old cliffside estate where a couple of murders might have taken place. The ownership is dark, but our guy will track it down."

Troy turned. Dubois was staring at him from the bed, watching him.

He had blown his cover completely. He realized that he no longer cared. If he got cut from El Grupo, and from Interpol, then maybe he wouldn’t put his family in danger anymore. He was burning alive right now, burning from the inside. He had nearly gotten Donnie murdered in his own driveway, right in front of his family.

Troy ached, positively ached, for revenge. The nuclear option sounded pretty good at the moment.

"Could be Al Qaeda," Persons said. "But that's not what we're hearing. We're hearing Al Qaeda originally mined the stone in a slave labor camp they controlled near the border of Tanzania and Burundi. We're hearing someone else, possibly someone quite a bit more unhinged, may have stolen it."

"Like who?"

"I couldn't say," Persons said. "But if it was them, they might not be planning to sell it for money."

"What are they going to do with it?" Troy said.

"Possibly something bad."

Troy rolled his eyes and shook his head. It was a diamond, a gemstone… whatever it was. Were they going to hit someone in the head with it? Drop it off a tall building in a busy downtown area.

"What possible bad thing could they do with it?"

There was no answer. It was like a sudden howling emptiness had suddenly opened on the line between them.

If Troy could reach through this phone and grab his old commanding officer by the throat, he would do it now.

A moment ago, Persons wasn't worried about the phone line. Now he had clammed up. Either he was concerned about who might be listening, or he simply didn't want to tell Troy what he knew. That's who he was.

Troy had nearly thrown his brother's life away for people like this.

"Colonel, I have to run."

"Keep in touch," Persons said.

Troy hung up.

Dubois was still watching him from under the covers, about a million questions in her dark eyes.

"My brother nearly got murdered."

"I know. I heard you. I'm sorry. That's terrible."

"Yeah. He's okay."

Dubois grabbed her phone from the bedside table. Her eyes met Troy's as she pressed the buttons. The fear in her big eyes was all too obvious.

"Who are you calling?" he said.

"I have to check on my mother."

Troy could tell her that it was nearly four in the morning. He could explain to her that the Italian mafias had a soft spot for mothers, and didn't generally kill them, or hurt them in any way. Mothers were off limits. None of this would reduce her fear, and it might only make it worse. So he didn't bother.

Anyway, it might be wrong.

"I hate this," he said instead.

CHAPTER SIXTEEN

6:40 am Central European Time
Plage Des Ponchettes (Ponchettes Beach)
Nice
Cote d'Azur (the French Riviera)
France

"Thanks for getting me killed, kid."

Troy walked the stone beach, his soft boots on, in the pre-dawn darkness. There might be the faint beginning of daylight in the sky, or it might be the glow from the lights of the city. He couldn't tell.

It was chilly out, not cold. The air was heavy with mist. The dark sea was calm, lapping gently at the rocks. The water retreating after each tiny wave made a strange sound. To Troy, it was like dead skeletal fingers rubbing across the naked bones of someone's rib cage - like a xylophone that didn't play musical notes, but just made the sound of bone on bone instead.

Troy had been up for hours. He had been wide awake ever since the call that came about his brother Donnie. Agent Dubois, to her credit, had almost instantly fallen asleep after waking her mother in the middle of the night, and frightening the wits out of her. Minutes after hanging up, she was gently snoring again.

Troy felt nothing about the stolen diamond, the case they were supposedly here pursuing. He thought nothing about it. He was aware that there were things he could think and feel about it, but none of them were occurring to him right now.

Every time he blinked against the dark canvas of this early morning beach, it seemed he watched Donnie nearly get murdered in his own driveway.

He wasn't there, he didn't really know how it played out, but he watched the scene nevertheless. He knew what Donnie's driveway and house looked like, he knew what a snowstorm looked like, and that was enough.

"I didn't kill you, Donnie. You're not dead."

Troy wasn't in the mood for Donnie's hard-nosed sarcasm at the moment. Donnie was alive, he was fine, and that filled Troy with a sense of relief so overwhelming, there were flashes here and there when he thought he might pass out.

"I'm just joking with you, kid."

Kid.

Donnie had been calling Troy "kid" since Troy was probably nine years old, and Donnie was 18.

"I'm glad you're alive," Troy said. "I love you very much."

"Maudlin," Donnie said. "Sappy."

It was late at night in the hospital where Donnie was. Troy had lost track of time, so he wasn't sure how late. But Donnie was awake, energetic, and something like cheerful. All of these were good signs. He was probably proud of himself, the way he fought his would-be assassins to a stalemate. Troy wasn't going to ruin his mood by telling him where those assassins ended up.

"So be it," Troy said.

Donnie had called him. Troy figured it was to let him know there were no hard feelings. But it was impossible to say if that was true, because Donnie refused to be serious about it. Then suddenly, as if someone threw a switch, Donnie's attitude shifted.

"You probably saved my life," he said.

Troy shrugged. "I warned you, that much is true. I never meant for any of this to happen, I feel terrible about it, but I did warn you. Not that you listened."

"Oh, I listened," Donnie said. "I didn't want it to be real. But I had my Glock loaded and on the seat next to me, inches from my gun hand. I did that because of what you told me. It's the only reason I'm still alive. When it all went down, I had the gun and was firing in two seconds. Emptied the clip."

"Mag dump," Troy said. Some guys did it to be thorough. Some guys did it because they were panicking.

"The first half was to defend myself," Donnie said. "The second half was because the gun was loud, and I figured it would bring help."

"Good man," Troy said. "Smart."

"I want to tell you something," Donnie said. "One, it was the most excitement I've had in a long time. Looking back, it was kind of fun. Don't tell Kelly or Mom that, but it's true. There's something about fighting for your life. You don't get a rush like that any other way."

Troy understood the feeling. It was not a thing he normally talked about. He very much didn't want to talk about it now.

"Okay," he said.

"Two, a couple of G-men came to see me a little while ago. They laid it all out, the situation, and what they can do for us."

"What can they do?" Troy said.

Missing Persons promised they would offer his family protection, but Troy wanted to hear confirmation of it from another mouth.

"They can put us all in protective custody, kind of like witness protection. Two weeks to a month, for starters. Then they said we could see what the intelligence networks are picking up. We'd live under new identities for the time being, and the kids would be home-schooled. We'd all be required to lay low. Obviously, we'd have to take time off from our jobs. The feds are talking about Colorado, in the mountains, maybe Denver. Or maybe on the West Coast somewhere. Both ideas sound okay."

Troy forced a deep breath into his lungs. On the off chance that someone somewhere was listening, Troy hoped the feds announced a last minute change of plans, and sent his entire family to Kansas.

"What do you think?" he said.

"I'll be honest," Donnie said. "I don't love it. But given what happened, I'm going to try to push everybody into doing it. Wives, kids, everybody. Mom will go along. I think Mikey will be the hardest one to convince. He would enjoy it if somebody tried to kill him."

"Maybe he can stay behind and everyone else can go," Troy said.

"I'll get him," Donnie said. "His kids. They need him. That's all I'll have to say."

"Okay, Donnie. That sounds good."

"You don't have to worry," Donnie said. "That's what I'm telling you. You don't have to feel bad. We'll all get paid leave from our jobs, and we'll disappear for a little while. When we come back, I'm guessing it will have all blown over."

Was he hinting something here?

Troy wasn't sure. Donnie was usually about as subtle as a brick thrown through a plate glass window.

"I am very glad to hear that," Troy said. "It is a huge relief."

It would be an upheaval for the moms and the kids. Maybe they could tell the kids they were all on vacation together.

It was mortifying to Troy that his actions had brought this on. Mateos Baruti was a bad man. He was the poster child for bad men.

He had trafficked abducted women and girls. He kept some of them as his own personal slaves. He would force men he had captured to have sword fights to the death against him, something he trained in and no one else was ready for. He was a man who deserved his fate.

And yet killing him had caused all this. It was a dark world.

Troy thought back to Missing Persons' mentioning the "nuclear option." Troy didn't care if the 'Ndrangheta were angry about Baruti and wanted to kill Troy. It wasn't very nice, but it had a certain crude logic to it. But this was taking it too far.

Troy would nuke a lot of gangsters to make it stop.

"I love you too, by the way," Donnie said. "We all do."

CHAPTER SEVENTEEN

9:05 am Central European Time
Boutique Hotel Jacobins
Nice
Cote d'Azur (the French Riviera)
France

"Without a corpse, it's unlikely we'll find a match from blood alone."

"I understand," Dubois said. "But it was almost certainly blood, and there was a lot of it, in two different spots perhaps two meters apart. It's consistent with the woman's account of two men being shot in that barn."

They were on an encrypted call with headquarters. Troy sat in an accent chair by the window, sipping his third cup of coffee. There was coffee here in the room, and it was very good. You had to go the long way around to make it.

There was a stainless steel electric pot which you used to heat the water. There was a real tin of gourmet ground coffee. And there was a tiny glass French press, where you actually made your coffee, one cup at a time.

It was worth every extra minute, and then some.

Except Troy was tired, and the coffee wasn't waking him up. He needed something stronger. He had inspected the coffee tin again and again for evidence of the word "decaffeinated." He hadn't found any.

He was not focused on this meeting. He gazed out the window at the beach and the blue sea beyond. He and Dubois kept ending up in these lovely places, just in time to move on to somewhere else.

Miquel's voice came from the tinny speaker in Dubois's mobile phone.

"Are you with us, Agent Stark?"

"Yes, I am. I'm hanging on every word."

"Would you say the stains on the dirt floor were blood?"

Troy looked at Dubois. This was not a video call, and she had only gotten out of bed 20 minutes ago. She was wearing a long, thin t-shirt that came down to her thighs and hugged the curves of her body. Her Afro was huge, up, out, and all over the place, unkempt and wild like the jungle itself. She looked yummy.

"It was kind of dark, but yes. I would say Agent Dubois's assessment is accurate. It looked to me like a couple of people got shot full of holes."

"Jan has found the owner of the estate," Miquel said. "He may be implicated in the murders, if that's what they are. We know where he is. We probably don't have enough evidence to charge him with a crime, but we may be able to pressure him to divulge information."

"The woman Holly," Dubois said. "How can we protect her?"

"Difficult," Miquel said. "Jan has also looked at her digital chart. She has multiple fractures, multiple internal injuries, and damage to organ systems. She was very lucky to survive, but moving her to a more secure facility at the present time would be problematic to say the least. Her treatment plan indicates stabilizing her over the next few weeks, then airlifting her to Paris for a long recovery. It will likely be a month before she attempts to walk again."

"I slipped into her room easily," Dubois said. "The night nurses were not around. It wouldn't surprise me if they were asleep somewhere."

"No one knows who she is," Miquel said.

Jan spoke for the first time. "While I was inside her record, I took the liberty of deleting any reference to what she said when she first awakened."

Dubois was shaking her head. "It's not good enough. She is basically helpless in there. I could have killed her silently with a pillow."

"Our resources are limited," Miquel said. "Without revealing this matter to our superiors…"

"Then that's what we need to do," Dubois said. "Call Interpol headquarters in Lyon, tell them what we're working on, and what has happened."

"It will compromise the case," Miquel said.

Dubois was silent. Her silence was a statement in itself. Troy felt the weight of it. The bad guys would kill, without remorse and for entirely selfish reasons - for revenge, or to cover their tracks, or to take an expensive item without paying for it. The woman in that hospital bed was a thief, but probably not a killer. She got mixed up with the wrong people. Dubois did not want her to die for that.

Also, Miquel was doing it yet again. He was being secretive. He was being paranoid. It was possible he was being selfish. He was keeping information from the organization that employed him, that employed all of them.

Would Interpol knowing what was going on compromise the case? Sure, it might. They would contact the Paris police. They would contact the Nice police. The theft would quickly become public knowledge. Whoever was behind all this would know that it was time to go dark, disappear, evaporate.

Troy shrugged. He had bigger problems on his plate than a couple of jewel thieves getting murdered by their employer.

"Of course," Miquel said now. "I was remiss. I understand and accept your argument. I will send two agents today to watch over the woman. They can announce themselves to the hospital staff, and stand guard at the door to the woman's room. They can work in tandem with hospital security. None of this should require contacting Lyon, and maybe not even the local police. They will be there this afternoon."

There was another long pause.

"Does that alleviate your concerns, Agent Dubois?"

Dubois shrugged, then nodded. Her giant head of hair bounced.

"Yes, thank you. That should work."

"Then we'll move on to the next point," Miquel said. "If everyone is ready."

"Ready," Troy said.

"Hermann Ranker," Jan said, as if he'd waiting this whole time, with decreasing patience, to utter those two words.

"I tracked the ownership of the estate in Eze to him through a series of shell companies. One of the companies was named in the infamous Panama Papers leak, which revealed the tax evasion and anonymous offshoring of money by the global elites."

Troy, despite himself, began to perk up. Maybe the coffee was working after all.

"So Hermann Ranker is among the global elite?" he said.

It would make perfect sense. A wealthy guy hires a team to steal a priceless gem, and then has them killed so no one knows he was behind it. Maybe they could wrap this case up by lunch.

Sure, there were nuances. Was it an inside job? What did the people at the Poitier Family Trust know, if anything? Where did the diamond even come from? But those were details that could be tracked down later, or just as likely, not at all.

"He's not exactly a member of the global elite," Jan said. "He might aspire to reach that level, though. He's an Austrian hacker, 46 years old. He's run numerous underground companies, including one called Massive Upload. It was a hosting service where people would store pirated content, including music and movies. Tens of millions of people used this service, especially in Asia. It was thought to contain nearly every Bollywood film that was ever made, and maybe 30 or 40 percent of the Hollywood and Hong Kong movies. It was one of the largest copyright violations in history, at least at that time. There have been larger ones since then."

Troy sighed quietly.

Copyright violator. Probably not a murderer.

“When was that time?” Dubois said.

“He was continually harassed by the FBI and India’s Intelligence Bureau, beginning about 15 years ago. His sites were shut down in multiple countries, would appear on new hosts, then get shut down again. He moved from country to country, trying to stay a step or two ahead of the law. For a period, he lived in Venezuela, because they have no extradition treaty with the US. But he has expensive tastes, and there is very little luxury available in Venezuela anymore, so he moved back to Europe.”

“Funny,” Troy said.

“Eventually, about ten years ago, his sites were completely shut down and the data seized. That’s when the enforcement agencies discovered he was hosting illicit materials on encrypted servers. We are talking about enormous-scale identity thefts, including credit card and banking information, government and financial records that could be used for blackmail purposes, and troves of child pornography. Many of the files were never successfully decrypted, so we don’t know what’s in them.”

“He sounds lovely,” Dubois said.

“He’s not a good person,” Jan said. “He issued a statement to the FBI, through a law firm in New York, that he was a mere hosting provider, had no idea what was in the files that clients uploaded to his servers, so he was not accountable for any of it.”

“Was that an acceptable argument?” Troy said.

“No.”

“Was he arrested?”

"Also, no," Jan said. "He is very much at large. My theory is that once the copyright violations ceased, the film studios and other large copyright holders stopped demanding action from the intelligence agencies. There were more pressing matters for everyone, so Ranker became an afterthought."

"Is he still wanted?"

"Yes," Jan said. "In the United States, Canada, India, England, and the EU."

"Where is he right now?" Troy said.

"He lives in Berlin, in a penthouse flat."

"If everyone knows where he is, why doesn't anyone just pick him up?"

"As I indicated, once Massive Upload was shut down, no one was that interested anymore."

"Tax evasion?" Dubois said. "I assume he made money from this business."

"Millions, in all likelihood. But his sites were hosted all over the world, popping up and dropping down like prairie dogs. He's officially an Austrian citizen and resident, but he hasn't lived there in years. Collecting a tax debt would be their problem. He's never officially been a resident or done business in any other country."

"All right," Troy said. "He's free to go. Would you say he's retired?"

He tried to picture why someone who had walked away with millions, and who no one was seriously trying to capture, would risk his freedom for this. If they could hang him with accessory to a double murder, he would lose everything.

"I would say he is not retired," Jan said. "He's still very much active. For example, he is someone who, for a fee, is thought to be able to generate flash mobs in major cities across Europe, usually flash mobs of young migrants."

"Like the one at the Musee Poitier," Dubois said.

"Of course," Jan said. "Criminals often use flash mobs as cover for thefts and other activity. It's a misdirection. Look what's happening here, and while your eye is on that, something bigger and more important is happening over here, which you don't see. And governments sometimes use riots and unrest to let people blow off steam after unpopular decisions or economic setbacks. It channels anger and resentment into silos where the energy can then burn away."

"This is how he makes his living these days?"

"Some part of it," Jan said. "He also runs a new company called *Fights from Underground.* The fights most often take place at a small venue in Berlin, though satellite locations are beginning to crop up. He is often at the fights in Berlin. They are illicit, unsanctioned fights, which are filmed and broadcast on hundreds of internet sites and social media channels worldwide. Often the fights are bare-knuckle boxing matches, and sometimes they are martial arts or mixed-style fights in a fenced cage. Usually the fighters are migrants, or sometimes they are local people who are poor and may be homeless. They may be drug addicts. When they are migrants, he tries to match fighters with reason to be hostile to each other, for example, a fight between a Hutu and a Tutsi from Central Africa. He's had Shiite Muslims from Syria fight Sunnis from Iraq. I believe online advertising revenue from the fighting is how he makes the bulk of his income."

Troy took a deep breath. He was in a bad place. He recognized that about himself. The thought of this Ranker character exploiting vulnerable people to this degree…

Troy's anger felt like a gathering storm - magnetic, with rolling booms of thunder and sharp, ear-splitting whip cracks of lightning. Driving rain. Tornados hurling cars and cows and single-wide trailers into the distance. This guy had better not give him trouble or resist him in any way.

Tolerant was not a word that would describe Troy Stark at this moment.

"What about this other thing the woman mentioned to me?" Dubois said. "The Diamond Dogs?"

"I haven't found much," Jan said. "It appears to be a criminal network based in Istanbul. Very shadowy. I haven't found any specific crime we know they've committed, or the names of anyone we know for a fact is a member. It is believed by Turkish intelligence that ten years ago, they might have been involved in trafficking individuals from Europe through Turkey, and into Syria."

"What sort of individuals?"

"Young men and women who wanted to join ISIS."

"You think Ranker was involved in that?" Troy said.

"I think it likely he was NOT involved. That's a dangerous business. But he clearly has contacts among human traffickers and migrants coming from the direction. It would be good to speak with him and find out more."

"I'd like to speak with him," Troy said, his voice calm, masking the turmoil inside of him. He didn't like to think of himself as someone who would look for a convenient scapegoat to unleash his frustrations upon. But then again he had all these frustrations, and here came a bad man named Hermann Ranker, wandering into the picture.

"You can do that," Jan said. "There is a fight card at his venue in Berlin tonight. It is very likely that he will be there."

"What is the place?"

"The place is called the Viper Room, and it's an old stage theater from the 1920s or 1930s. It's in the neighborhood near what was once the Berlin Wall crossing called Checkpoint Charlie. He calls it the Viper Room because he often goes by the nickname The Viper."

"How can we get close enough to talk to him?" Dubois said.

"He has one weakness."

Troy doubted there was only one. "What's that?" he said.

"He has a fondness for beautiful black women. One might call it an obsession."

Troy shook his head. "No."

Dubois smiled. It was a wicked smile.

"Speak for yourself."

Troy almost couldn't believe what she was saying. He wanted to scream at her, but he raised his hands, almost in a gesture of supplication, instead. "After everything that's happened? You want to put yourself in that position?"

Miquel's voice came on the line. "The man is a hacker, as Jan indicated. I suspect this won't be anywhere near as dangerous as recent missions you've both been on."

Troy thought back to a Russian hacker he'd had to interview in Brooklyn once. It was at the time of the slaughter bot drone attacks. The man had a bodyguard who took his job way too seriously and had tried to fight Troy to the death.

A hacker? Yes, probably easy. Bodyguards? You never could tell.

"It's merely an interview," Jan said. "Agent Dubois lures him away from whatever crowd is there, Agent Stark follows, and you both question him in a secluded location."

"You people are crazy," Troy said. "Listen to what you're saying."

He was mindful that little more than a week ago, he and Dubois had entered a hot zone after a cholera attack that killed thousands of people, where the barely functioning medical system had collapsed in the face of it, and he had hardly batted an eye beforehand. In other words, his behavior was inconsistent, and these guys must be painfully aware of that. But things had changed since a week ago.

Dubois looked at Troy and shook her head.

“I think it will go fine,” she said.

CHAPTER EIGHTEEN

6:55 pm Central European Time
Bar L'Etranger
11th Arrondissement
Paris, France

"Yes, one more, why not?" Jacques Trudeau said.

There were six empty pint glasses on the small round table in front of him. Jacques was a Frenchman with an Englishman's taste for strong beer, in particular, India Pale Ale. The tall, skinny waiter went away to fetch Jacques another.

In earlier days, now would be a normal time for Jacques to light up a cigarette, but of course they had murdered that little tradition, the same way they were killing every freedom a man in this country ever had.

Jacques sat in a dark corner, in a round booth made for maybe three people at most. He came to this little pub often. At one time, it was a gathering place for poets writers, and other members of the counter culture and avant garde.

Now, the last vestige of that scene was the pot-bellied, bespectacled, white-haired antique holding court among six or seven sycophants at a long table along the far wall. He was Philippe Pontif, the aging radical cartoonist.

In the distant past, he had made a name for himself, lampooning the super-rich, the complacent bourgeoisie, the corrupt and venal politicians, and the French military. Some years ago, alarmed that he was fading into obscurity, he had decided the way to stay relevant was to punch down, and begin drawing unflattering caricatures of the Prophet Muhammad.

It was one thing to draw Muhammad at all, which Jacques knew was forbidden in Islam and was practically a death sentence in itself. But what Pontif did was beyond the pale! He deliberately made Muhammad ugly, and portrayed him in the most outrageous ways - picking his nose, sitting on the toilet with his robes up and his shorts around his knees, and gleefully eating pork, among even more unsavory images.

The man was daring them to kill him.

Pontif was here almost every night, apparently hoping to drink himself to death before the irate Muslims got to him.

Truth be told, Jacques was here almost every night as well. It was quiet, except for the bursts of laughter from Pontiff and his obsequious gang of bootlickers. Often, Jacques could get this table, which was his favorite. It was a good vantage point to watch the entire bar, which was something he enjoyed.

People left him alone here. He was a big man, and he could be surly. Generally speaking, that was enough.

The skinny waiter floated by and slid the pint glass onto Jacques's table with hardly a glance. See? That was what Jacques wanted. If there was no good reason to interact, then don't. This waiter had mastered the art.

This was a good place for Jacques to think, as well. A few drinks, a background hum of conversation, and his mind was at ease. He was a deep thinker and often pondered the world and his place in it.

Tonight, he had a new wonderment to ponder. It was more of a problem, you might say. His six years of employment as a guard at the Musee Poitier had abruptly come to an end. The manager claimed it was because they believed he was drinking on the job. The man had documented half a dozen instances when co-workers claimed Jacques was visibly drunk or smelled like alcohol while at his post.

Jacques knew it had nothing to do with his drinking. They decided to get rid of him because he knew their little secret. The Star of Versailles was gone, and they were acting like it was still there.

When Jacques first discovered the theft, he insisted on speaking alone with the Director of the Museum, and no one else. This was a HUGE event, and not one to be shared with the gossip columnists who worked the front desk. He showed his video to the Director. The Director asked Jacques to forward it to him and then delete it from his own phone.

Jacques forwarded it, as requested, but he did not delete it. At least, not until he transferred it to the laptop computer he maintained at his flat.

Jacques Trudeau was not born yesterday.

The Star of Versailles, arguably the most important, most valuable exhibit in the entire museum, had been stolen. The museum had not announced this to anyone. Aside from a small handful of people who might be private detectives, no police or law enforcement of any kind had been alerted. There was nothing in the newspapers.

They're going to cover it up.

What could this possibly mean?

He noticed that the lights inside of the bar were beginning to have auras around them. The people did, too. It was like there was a soft filter around everything. Okay, Jacques was drunk now. He might as well admit that. The beer that had come recently was completely drained. Anyway, he did his best thinking when he was drunk.

He made a vague hand gesture at the waiter, which indicated something like "one more," and the waiter, experienced professional that he was, made a barely perceptible nod, which indicated that the message had been received and would be acted upon.

They're in on it.

The Director, maybe members of the Poitier family, or staff at the Poitier Family Trust, had participated in the theft. Perhaps they had stolen it themselves. It was an item worth millions of euros. They had stolen it, replaced it with a forgery, and would now go blithely on as if nothing had happened.

The full weight of decades as a wage slave suddenly landed on Jacques's shoulders. He had to work for his money, in thankless dead-end jobs that he could lose at a moment's notice, while the insiders simply robbed their way to impossible wealth.

A new pint appeared in front of him, as if by magic.

"Merci," he said, but no one was there.

He stared across at the garish laughing face of Philippe Pontif. The man was a grotesque. He and his little coterie of yes-men and concubines aging like milk (and long past their expiration dates), were all convulsed in a sort of uncontrolled cackling madness. Red-faced Pontif, his mouth wide open as though he was howling in agony, appeared to be in the throes of a life-threatening cardiac incident.

Jacques breathed out. "When they finally get you," he said, his voice low, his mouth barely moving, "I for one will not be bothered by it."

***

The young man opened the door and entered the bar.

It was dark inside, a wall of sound, and a feeling of heat from the two dozen bodies in the tiny space. The man felt nothing about these people. He wasn't here to feel something about them.

It was raining and a bit cold outside. The young man was wearing a long dark coat and carrying a heavy backpack. He carried the backpack lightly, as if it wasn't heavy at all. One might think he was a university student with his textbooks in there.

He didn't wear a mask, and that was the right thing to do. No one in this bar, not the waiter, not the bartender, not the patrons, was wearing a mask. These people didn't care if weaponized cholera made it to Paris. They didn't care if they came down with cholera. They didn't care if they lived or died.

All of this was good.

Immediately, the man spotted the table where Jacques Trudeau would normally be sitting. It was a small round table in a semi-circular booth in the corner. This had all been mapped out for him beforehand. In fact, he had studied a floor plan of the bar, so he would know exactly where to go without hesitation.

Jacques Trudeau was indeed at the table. He was a large, broad, pale man. His neck was thick, and his face was stern. He had big workman's hands. In his youth, he must have been no one to mess with. The young man walked directly to him, smiled and nodded as if they were good friends.

He slid into the booth next to Jacques, slipped the heavy bag off his own shoulders, and placed it under the table, very close to the soft fake leather seat of the booth. He quickly counted eight empty glasses in front of Jacques. There was a ninth glass, which the young man moved in front of himself.

Amazing that a man could ingest this much alcohol, and remain seated upright.

"I can order one for you," Jacques said, practically shouting to be heard over the loud buzz of the bar patrons. "That one is mine."

Even more amazing - the man had ingested this much alcohol, yet he could still speak clearly and in full sentences. He must be as bad an alcoholic as they said.

Somewhere, music was playing. The young man couldn't tell what song it was, or even what kind of music. It was more that he felt the bass line than heard the song.

"No, thank you," he said. "It's just for show. I don't drink."

"Arab?" Jacques said.

The young man shrugged. "I like to think I can pass for Italian, or Greek."

Jacques laughed. "Good one. You pass for camel jockey."

The young man smiled. It was entertaining to play along, at least for now. "You saw through me right away. You're very observant."

Jacques gestured across the bar at a boisterous group at a long table. "That's who you're after, over there. Not me."

The young man followed Jacques's gesture. "Who is it?"

"The fat man, with glasses. He's the one who draws Muhammad sitting on the toilet bowl."

"Is he?"

Of course, the young man knew that, too. He knew a lot about what went on inside this establishment.

Jacques nodded solemnly. "Yes. He is."

"Well, that's terrible. He shouldn't do that."

Jacques watched the young interloper closely. "No, he shouldn't."

"It's *haram*," the young man said, using the Arabic word that meant forbidden. "But I don't care about that man."

Jacques was still staring at him.

"I came to talk to you."

"Oh?" Jacques raised his eyebrows. He reached and pulled the full pint glass in front of him again. He had incredible control of his motor functions this far into a drinking session. On the one hand, you might say he was a pathetic drunk. On the other hand, he must have almost superhuman tolerance to alcohol. These Westerners and their drinking - it was something to behold.

"Yes," the young man said. "There are rumors going around town. People are saying the Star of Versailles was stolen and replaced by a clever fake. This supposedly took place the day there was a riot inside the Musee Poitier. People are hinting there is a cover-up going on. Someone told me you might know something about this."

"Are you the police?" Jacques said. "A detective?"

The young man shrugged and smiled. "I'm not free to discuss that."

"In that case, why would I tell you?"

"Because you know what they did was wrong."

Jacques seemed to stare at the empty space in front of him for a moment. Then he nodded. "It's true. During the riot, or the invasion if you prefer, two men came and stole the Star of Versailles."

"Did you witness this?" the young man said.

Jacques shook his head. "I was away from my post, dealing with the mob downstairs. I left the camera in my mobile phone on. It filmed the whole thing."

"Do you still have the film?"

"I gave it to my Director. There's also a copy on the computer in my flat."

The young man's heart skipped a beat.

"Who else has it?"

"No one," Jacques said. "As far as I know."

"Did you upload it, store it somewhere on the internet?"

Jacques shrugged. "I'm not computer savvy in that way. I wouldn't know how to do that, even if I wanted."

The young man nodded. He reached a hand across the table. Jacques's big hand swallowed his, but didn't crush it. The two men shook.

"We'll be in touch soon," the young man said. "Until then, please keep all of this to yourself."

"I will."

The young man stood and without another word, he walked to the door. He left the backpack under the table, nestled up against the long seat of the booth.

A second later, he was out in the cold and in the rain. He walked quickly down the street. A few people were out under umbrellas. It was dark, but of course there were cameras everywhere. He knew that. The plan - the promise - was that he would be out of the country this very night.

He pulled gloves on, then took the phone out of the pocket of his long coat. It was a throwaway phone, which was going into the sewers as soon as he made this call. Still, you couldn't be careful enough.

He pressed the buttons, dialing a number from memory, the only number this phone would ever call.

"Yes," a voice said.

"He knows everything," the young man said. "There's a film of it on the computer in his flat. The film is stored locally on his hard drive. That's the only location."

"You know this?" the voice said.

"It's what he told me."

"In that case, proceed as planned."

"And the computer?"

"We'll deal with that ourselves," the voice said.

The young man hung up. He was two blocks from the bar now, still moving fast. The rain began to come down a little harder. He took the detonator from his other pocket. The thing's range was not far, a few blocks at most. It was a simple device, with a clear plastic casing over it, and just two buttons on the small black body.

Press the red button, and while holding that one down, also press the green one. Two buttons eliminated the chance of making a detonation by mistake. The buttons were a little stiff and hard to press. You really needed two hands to do it.

The young man didn't hesitate. He stepped into an alcove, opened the casing, and pressed both buttons. A second or two passed, during which a fleeting thought occurred.

Maybe it's a dud.

BOOOM!

Somewhere to his left, there was a giant explosion. The sound of it was almost impossible to believe. He plugged his fingers in his ears and squeezed his eyes closed. The ground shook so much that he lost his feet and fell to the concrete, forcing him to open his eyes again. A bright orange and red light rose into the sky. All along the street, glass windows shattered, like a line of mini-bombs. Car alarms began to screech.

The young man pulled himself to his feet. He breathed heavily, as if he had just run several kilometers. His body was shaking. He began to walk again.

"Mashallah," he said.

In English, it meant, "God has willed it."

CHAPTER NINETEEN

9:30 pm Istanbul Time (8:30 pm Central European Time)
Zephyr Raki Bar
Nisantasi District
Istanbul, Turkey

"Is all this necessary, Hassan?"

The group of men stood in the back alley behind one of Hassan Celik's bars. Hassan did many things for a living, and had done many others. More than forty years old now, he had lived a life full of risk. His favorite way of making a living, without a doubt, was serving the national alcoholic drink of Turkey, raki, to the masses.

The conservatives saw it as a crime against Allah's word. If so, then it was a victimless crime.

"We've been on the road 36 hours, and this is how you greet us?"

Hassan stared at the two young jihadis down the alleyway from him. They looked exhausted, with black circles under their eyes. But they were both smiling, as if something humorous were going on here.

A tall delivery truck was sandwiched into the tight space, and men were loading it from the back exit of the bar. They were filling the truck with canned food, bottled water, blankets, clothes, flashlights, batteries, and medicines of various kinds.

It was not at all strange or out of character for Hassan to send aid trucks to brothers and sisters in need across the Middle East. He had done it many times, sending needed supplies into war zones and disaster areas.

This time, he was sending an aid truck with these two on board.

Can they even drive a truck?

"We aren't here to hurt you," one of them said. "We are just passing through, and you are helping us. We are doing the work of God."

They were both dressed in jeans and football jerseys. They could be anyone. They could be Turks. They might even pass as Westerners.

Hassan had four bodyguards with him while dealing with these two. He didn't see any other choice. The mujahideen were dangerous people. He had learned that firsthand. He regretted the path he had taken in life that brought him to this place.

Hassan's bodyguards were big men. Three were Turkish combat veterans. One was a convicted murderer from Russia. All of them had no qualms about killing. All were holding rifles out in the open. It was dark in this alleyway, but one thing was clear enough: two of Hassan's men were aiming their rifles directly at the jihadis.

"You kidnapped my daughter," Hassan said, trying to keep his voice even.

Now, the faces of the two young men became flat and deadly.

"We didn't take her. It wasn't our task."

"Your people," Hassan said.

"She was returned to you, safe, well and unharmed, was she not?"

An image flitted through Hassan's mind. His five-year-old daughter Aysegul. She was a beautiful young thing, as beautiful as a flower. The thought of her almost made him scream right now in terror and rage. They had held her for two and a half weeks, forcing his participation and compliance. She had been released less than two days ago.

Hassan immediately put the little girl and her mother, his estranged young wife Afet, on a plane for New York City. From there, they had caught a connecting flight to Cleveland, where his cousins had picked them up.

They were safely in Akron, northeast Ohio, USA. They were only supposed to be visiting, but maybe his cousin Ahmed could find a way to keep them there.

Afet hated Hassan, and he didn't blame her.

"You brought this horror on us," she said, when he dropped them at the airport. "I will never forgive you. Your daughter will grow to womanhood, and she will not know you. You will be a stranger to her, if God will allow it."

"I wish you a good and happy life in America," he said in return.

If he was truly a man, he would have his guards simply kill these two monsters right here in the alley. Just murder them in cold blood, and dump their bodies in the sewers, where they belonged. Only monsters would believe they were doing the work of Allah.

"Everyone is dying," Hassan said. "This makes it a low-trust situation."

"We know nothing about that," said the jihadi that Hassan was beginning to think of as the leader.

"The thieves I hired were murdered," Hassan said. "I assume you did it."

"Oh, that," the young man said, and they both laughed.

"A bar blew up in Paris a little while ago."

Now the lead man shrugged.

"Allah is full of mystery. When you walk his path, you accept that you will not always understand his methods."

Hassan nodded.

Like all true believers, these two were good at regurgitating standard phrases and statements. They were also good at plotting murder, and at slipping through checkpoints and roadblocks. They were single-minded in their pursuit of death.

They were not really human.

"You would kill me with the same mocking smile on your faces, and the same blank look in your eyes."

The young man shook his head. "Our orders are not to bring harm to you in any way. We are to avoid bringing even the hint of suspicion upon you. He likes you, you know. He respects you. You have behaved honorably."

They were talking about the man people called al-Shabah, or "the Ghost." He was somewhere in the combat zones of Syria, living on the run, still fighting the forces of Assad, still fighting the Americans and the Russians and the Iranians, still fighting everyone. The Ghost had set all of this in motion.

These young men were carrying the jewel stolen in Paris to the Ghost. Not because the Ghost craved wealth, but because the Ghost craved death. If Allah was truly loving, they would not reach him.

"That's wonderful to hear," Hassan said.

"It's true. He did not want harm to come to your daughter, and as a result, she was returned to you unscathed. He also does not want any harm to come to your family. He would harm them if you forced his hand, as I think you understand by now."

Hassan said nothing. Much more talk from this man, and he would order them both killed after all, and then he would suffer the consequences.

He would also drop the Star of Versailles to the bottom of the sea. The wretched thing was cursed.

But of course, he would never do it. It would be one thing if the Ghost killed Hassan, which he could easily do. For someone trapped inside a war, the man had incredible reach. And after everything that had happened, perhaps Hassan would welcome death.

But he could not allow it to happen to his family.

"He kills them so they cannot identify you," the young man said. "When all connections to you are eliminated, that means we are not in an awkward situation regarding you. If they are dead, you can remain alive. He wants you to live on and keep your freedom. You are not Allah's perfect servant by any means, but you are his faithful servant nonetheless. You have done many good deeds."

Hassan still could not find his voice.

"If I encountered you, my orders were to tell you that."

Hassan took a long, deep breath. His lungs felt the many years of smoking. His body felt the many years of drinking raki and eating rich foods. What to say when someone like this told you that despite everything, you were a good servant of Allah?

"Hassan," a voice said from behind him.

He turned. One of his young bar workers was standing near the rear exit of the bar, holding a stand-up dolly. Next to him, another was yanking down the sliding door of the delivery truck.

"The truck is ready."

CHAPTER TWENTY

10:35 pm Central European Time
The Viper Room
Friedrichstadt
Berlin, Germany

"This was a bad neighborhood at one time."

Troy walked down the city street next to Dubois, barely hearing her. It seemed like he was a foot taller than her. In fact, that was about right. He was aware of how uncomfortable his left foot was - there were brass knuckles inside his boot. He had a sick feeling in the pit of his stomach.

Jan had sent VIP passes to tonight's event at the Viper Room to their phones just a few moments ago. Obtaining them had required convoluted navigating on the dark web, and payment in crypto. For a while, it had seemed like maybe Jan wouldn't be able to get them. But now the path was cleared - they were going in.

Dubois was prattling on, maybe to soothe her own nerves.

"There was a red light district here in the aftermath of World War II and during the partition. Lots of poverty in this neighborhood. Plenty of murders. The East Germans and the Russians inserted their spies, and the spies played cloak and dagger with the American and English spies, and West German secret police. Bodies would turn up in the alleyways in the mornings."

Things were tense between Troy and Dubois.

He replayed the scene in their Berlin hotel room again and again. He had been watching TV news coverage of the bombing in Paris when she came out of the bathroom wearing a neon yellow bodysuit he had never seen before.

The bombing targeted a newspaper cartoonist who drew insulting pictures of Muhammad. It had killed the cartoonist, his entire entourage, and perhaps a dozen other people. Troy remembered thinking vaguely that it couldn't be a coincidence - the theft, then the bombing.

But then Dubois's attire drove any productive thoughts from his mind.

The bodysuit was made of some soft fabric, like terrycloth, that clung tight to her insane female curves like body paint. The fabric seemed to glow. The contrast between the yellow and her dark skin was surreal, like she was a lava lamp come to life. Her facial bruises were fading, and she had rendered them invisible with makeup.

She completed the fashion statement with black combat boots and a black belt at her waist. She wore a neon yellow sash in her hair, to match the cat suit. The whole look was unbearably sexy. It should be illegal to dress like this in public.

Troy felt the fingers on his throat again. "Jesus, Dubois."

She smiled. Was Dubois evil? Was she doing this to torture him with worry? Troy was beginning to wonder.

"How do I look?" she said.

His voice was flat and dead. "You look like a bumblebee."

"I'll take that as a compliment," she said.

He shook his head. "Don't."

They stared at each other for a long moment.

"To catch the fly," Dubois said, "you need a little honey."

Troy gestured at the outfit. "For the record, I'm against this."

Dubois shrugged. "I hear the morality police in Iran are hiring."

Now, on the streets of Berlin, Dubois was still talking. Mercifully, at least for the moment, she was wearing a long leather jacket that covered her up.

"Many immigrants have lived here, and many still do," she said. "Turks and Lebanese looking for better economic conditions, Libyans, Iraqis and Syrians displaced by the wars in their countries."

Troy glanced at his phone. "The place is right up ahead."

There was no sign or anything. The street was mostly dark. The club was on the ground floor of an old five-story building. If it had been a theater at one time, there was no longer a grand entrance. The only windows were on the top floor, and there were no lights in them.

There was a small cluster of people around a double doorway. A large man was scanning phones with an electronic reader. Two others were patting down the ticket holders for weapons, or maybe other contraband, before allowing them to enter.

Dubois stopped. So did Troy.

"Be careful in there," he said.

Dubois didn't even look at him. "We're partners. If I'm the bait, you're supposed to protect me."

"You volunteered for this."

She sighed. "I hear the Taliban…"

He waved a hand in the air to dismiss what she was saying. "I know. They're hiring for the modesty enforcement team. That's not the point here, and you know it."

She raised a hand, palm upward.

"After you."

Troy moved ahead without a backward glance. The plan was he would enter the venue first, to make sure he could gain entry. Then he would stake out a spot near Ranker's roped-off area, but not so close as to arouse suspicion.

Moments later, Dubois would arrive. She would try to deposit herself into the mouth of the lion, like a slice of fresh meat, and from there they would see what developed.

That was it. That was the whole plan.

Troy reached the doorway. There were only one or two people ahead of him. The first man scanned his digital ticket, and there was no problem.

"VIP," the man said.

Troy stepped to his right, and one of the big men frisked him. The man ran both hands up the insides of Troy's legs, checking carefully around the ankles and behind the waist. He felt inside Troy's jacket on both sides. Then he gestured with his head.

"VIP is upstairs," the man said in English.

It was a cursory pat down, to put it mildly. Maybe VIP got you the friends and family treatment. Troy glanced around. A few more people had arrived. People were appearing in ones, twos and threes.

"Upstairs," the man said again.

Troy went inside. There was a short hallway with a staircase to the right. At the far end of the hall, dim lights were on, gleaming white, and he could hear shouts and laughter. A crowd of people were standing around down there.

He climbed the stairs, and came to a small threadbare lobby. The lights were low, maybe so people couldn't tell how dilapidated the place was. There was a bar with two bartenders along one wall. At least a dozen people were waiting for drinks. Another big man stood in front of Troy, behind a red velvet rope. He was also holding a digital scanner. Troy held the phone out to him, and he scanned the document again.

The man unclipped the velvet rope and stepped aside for Troy to pass.

There was a wide double doorway across the lobby from him. Troy skipped the line at the bar and went to the doorway. He stepped into the main hall.

The place was crowded. He could see right away how the place was an old theater. On the ground floor, the original seating had been removed. There was a boxing ring installed in the center. To the left, the stage was still there, perhaps five or six feet high, with rows of folding chairs. All of the chairs appeared to be taken.

On the floor level, people simply stood. There were no chairs, and if there were, they wouldn't have a view of anything.

Up here, the VIP level, was the old theater balcony. The balcony was sloped upward, and most of the original seating had been retained. The view wasn't bad. Cameras were trained downward towards the ring.

There was standing room to the left. Troy moved over there. To his right, there was a special VIP area within the regular VIP area, roped off with bright blue velvet. Troy, who had studied the target's photos for an hour earlier today, spotted Hermann Ranker immediately.

He sat at a table along the balcony railing with three or four other men. Ranker was perfectly bald, wearing a blue dress shirt and a dark dinner jacket. He had earrings in both ears. He was reasonably well-kept for a man in his mid-40s, maybe carrying a few extra pounds. He probably wore the jacket to hide it.

Below them, in the ring, a fight was going on. Two skinny sub-Saharan Africans circled each other warily, both trying to jab, neither committing to anything. The fight was slow, as though they were heavyweights past their primes. Troy could tell right away they weren't trained fighters. Their hands were taped, but they weren't wearing gloves. For both of them, the primary motive was not to get hurt.

The crowd hooted and jeered at them.

Here in the Viper Room, and out there on the internet, the spectators wanted blood.

Troy glanced at Hermann Ranker. Ranker was leaning in, speaking closely with one of his men.

Then Dubois appeared. She was close to the blue velvet rope. She took her long jacket off and draped it over the back of one of the balcony seats. Suddenly, the yellow bodysuit was there, with the body inside of it, like a bomb had gone off here.

Eyes were on her from everywhere, like lasers.

Almost instantly, Ranker noticed her, as he was intended to do. If sexy black women were his weakness, then Dubois had just dropped a chunk of kryptonite in his lap. He said something to her and smiled.

Troy looked down at the fight. Nothing had changed, except the jeers were louder than before. This must be the undercard. These guys looked like they hadn't thrown a real punch in their lives. He felt sympathy for them, and pity. The journey here couldn't have been easy. Whatever they left behind was probably worse.

Now this.

They were inside a ring, likely making pocket change, trying to fight and trying not to fight at the same time, while a crowd of drunks surrounded them on all sides, screaming and laughing at them.

Troy thought of the Roman Coliseum, and how many of the fights weren't skilled gladiators fighting to the death. It was hapless losers being fed to wild animals as a form of entertainment for savage mobs. Not much had changed in all this time.

Jan Bakker had said the VIP tickets were the crypto equivalent of 300 euros a piece. Whatever Ranker was making on the internet off the backs of these guys, he was doing pretty well here in the real world as well.

Troy allowed himself to feel his visceral dislike of Hermann Ranker, the people who worked for him, and everyone here at this event.

He glanced around the theater. The emergency exits, if there were any, were not clear. The place was a fire trap. On the ground floor, there was another bar along a back wall. It was doing a booming business. From here, Troy could see at least three dozen people smoking cigarettes, cigars, or something else.

There were code violations everywhere you looked.

Troy glanced at Ranker again. Dubois was already inside the blue velvet rope and sitting at Ranker's table. Her back was to the action down in the ring, probably because she didn't want to witness it.

Troy watched as Ranker reached across and took her hand.

This is going to happen fast.

That sick feeling was back. Never mind the fight, the people involved, or the venue. All of the bad things were closing in on him. Dubois getting kidnapped, twice! And yet, here she was, putting herself in harm's way again. Donnie nearly getting murdered. The Sicilians taking Troy into custody with almost no effort.

The villages in rural Romania, eerie, empty, men covered head to toe in white biohazard suits, piling bodies onto bonfires.

The hired killer, straddling Troy, trying to choke him to death, and then Troy getting the knife out, stabbing the man and stabbing him.

Suddenly, a roar came from everywhere. Troy looked at the fight again. One of the combatants had closed on the other and was beating him with a flurry of punches. He backed him toward the ropes, the victim with his hands up, trying to protect his face.

Troy sat down in the old theater seat behind him. The fight had gotten interesting, and no one was looking at him. He reached down to his left foot, unzipped the boot, and pulled his foot out. He took the brass knuckles out of there and slipped them into his jacket pocket. Then he put the boot back on and zipped it closed again.

He looked over at Ranker's section. Ranker and Dubois were standing. They were holding hands. Troy watched as Ranker led Dubois out of the section and toward a back hallway. In a few seconds, they were simply gone.

He moves fast.

Troy took a deep breath. He fought the urge to follow them down the hall immediately. He had to give it a moment, let it unfold.

Dubois did this. She brought this on herself.

All right. Enough of that.

He counted down from ten to one, as slowly as he could.

Then he stood and moved toward that back hall. He already had some luck with him. The hall was not inside Ranker's little sitting area. Troy went to the opening and looked inside. The hall was long, narrow and poorly lit, with brick walls on both sides.

There were two men at the far end, standing in front of a door. There were no other doors in the hallway. That was it. Dubois and Ranker must have gone in there.

Troy moved down the hallway. He put his hands in the pockets of his jacket. His right hand found the brass knuckles and slipped them on. He tottered, sort of lumbering from left to right, as though he was drunk. He skimmed one wall, and moved along it.

One of the men shouted something to him.

It sounded like “Verboten!”

Troy kept coming. The men were about his height, but thicker. They were big guys, as goons normally were.

Troy felt a surge of something, something he didn’t normally feel. Adrenaline was one thing. This was anger, hate, and terror, all wrapped into one storm of emotion.

He was nearly there. He narrowed his eyes, as though he was drunk and could barely keep them open.

“Bathroom,” he said.

One of the men pointed back the way Troy had just come.

“Other way.”

Troy turned slightly, as if to follow where the man was pointing. His right hand came out of his jacket. He twisted and drove his body into the punch. He caught the guy’s jaw perfectly. The CRUNCH was solid, amplified by the metal of the knucks.

The impact went straight up Troy’s arm. He was going to feel that tomorrow.

A couple of teeth went flying, along with spit and blood. The big man’s head spun to his right. His body followed, spinning around, showing Troy his wide back, doing a sort of graceless pirouette.

The next man up stared at Troy, his mouth open in an O of surprise. He reached into his jacket pocket and came out with a small pistol. It was a dumb move. The space was too tight for a gun.

Troy grabbed the gun hand at the wrist. He stepped forward and delivered a punch straight to the guy's face. The brass knuckles ripped a cut above the guy's nose. Instantly, blood was flowing down. Troy punched him again in the same spot. The cut became a deep gash.

The guy was still in the fight. He was trying to free the gun hand. He brought his other hand up and clubbed Troy on the side of the head. Troy stepped close, body to body, and drove his right knee up into the man’s groin.

That hurt. The pain was all over the man’s face. The gash was one thing. The knee was on another level.

The man had a full head of blonde hair. Troy grabbed him by it and slammed his head into the red brick wall. The bricks dented in. They weren’t bricks at all. They were some kind of decorative wallpaper plastered over drywall.

It’s an old building. There has to be bricks, right?

Troy spun the guy around, exchanging places with him. Now, he rammed the guy's head into the opposite wall. Here were the actual bricks.

He slammed the head again, then again.

The light in the guy's eyes went out. His arms went slack. Troy took the gun from the guy's hand.

The man slid down the wall, his knees buckling. He sat for a second, then keeled over sideways.

Troy looked at the first man. He was still on his feet, his arms pressed against the fake brick wall, his head hanging down. Troy approached him.

"Hey."

The man turned and looked up. Troy wound his shoulder and clocked him under the jaw with a peek-a-boo uppercut, brass knuckles and everything.

Now, two guys were down. Two wankers down. Quickly, Troy took the plastic zip ties from inside his sleeves and bound the men's wrists behind their backs.

He glanced at the door. It was probably locked, and these guys probably had a key to it. But Troy didn't feel like he had the time, or the inclination, to search them for it. The door was a basic wooden door, with your typical heavy lock.

He stood and raised his right foot, ready to blast the door as hard as he could.

***

"You're a very beautiful woman," Ranker said. "Sexy. You look like a sex machine. The best I've seen all week."

Dubois didn't know whether to laugh, or what.

A sex machine? How flattering.

"You're like an animal. Raw, like a jungle cat."

They were sitting on a soft blue couch with a small round table in front of them. Ranker had brought out a bottle of red wine from a cabinet on the wall. The bottle was already open, the cork sticking out of the top. He had made a show of pouring a glass for each of them.

Dubois noticed that Ranker made no move to take a sip from his.

She did the same.

"Don't you like wine?" he said.

Dubois nodded. "I love it."

"Then why don't you drink?"

She gestured with her chin. "You first."

Ranker smiled. The canine tooth on the top right side of his mouth had turned dark. It was still there, a discolored tooth surrounded by teeth that were mostly white-ish. Dubois was no dentist, but she felt that wasn't a good sign.

"You're very clever," Ranker said. He raised his glass, but didn't drink from it.

There was some kind of commotion going on outside the door. Dubois turned to the door, but Ranker waved at it.

"Always something. Don't worry."

A second later, a brutal sound came and the door cracked in the middle. Dubois and Ranker stared at it.

BOOM!

The door broke apart, the bottom half splintering from the lock, and falling backwards into the room. The top half hung in place on its hinge for a moment, then leaned sideways and dropped down into the doorway. It leaned against the door frame. The man looming behind it, Troy Stark, kicked it over and stepped into the room.

For a second, Dubois saw Agent Stark as Ranker must be seeing him. Big, strong, square-jawed and rugged. His eyes looked like they were on fire, like he was a demon, a vision of hell. His right hand dripped blood, and there was a gun in his left hand.

Ranker didn't seem concerned. He placed his wine glass back on the table. He had never brought it anywhere near his mouth.

"Have I had the pleasure?" he said to Stark.

"Uh… this is my friend," Dubois said.

Ranker turned to Dubois. He looked her up and down as if assessing her value on the open market, and then he nodded. "Yes. Of course he is."

Stark came closer. He gestured at the wine.

"What's in the glass?"

Ranker shrugged. "Wine. What does it look like?"

"Roofies."

"How very year 2000," Ranker said. He turned to Dubois again. "More than just a friend, I gather?"

Dubois rolled her eyes, but said nothing. A hint of something was starting to creep into Ranker's voice. He was beginning to sound a bit petulant, like a child. Maybe he had noticed, as Dubois had, the two big guards in a pile out in the hallway. Neither one of them seemed to be moving.

"How did you get in here?" Ranker said.

Stark shrugged, slowly coming closer. "How does it look like I got in? I destroyed two of your bodyguards and kicked down the door."

As they watched, Stark pulled a pair of bloody brass knuckles from the fingers of his right hand. There were a handful of white paper napkins on the table near the wine bottle and glasses. Stark reached over, picked a couple of them up, and wiped the blood away.

He slipped the brass knuckles into his jacket pocket and tossed the used napkins onto the table. They were saturated.

"You've caught me at a bad time," Stark said. "I'm not in a good mood."

Ranker shook his head. "Nothing happened here. You and your girlfriend are free to leave. We were just chatting."

"We're free to leave, are we?" Stark said. His voice was rising.

Dubois watched him. There was something very threatening, almost malevolent about him now.

"Yes," Ranker said.

Stark shook his head. He loomed above them. "I'm not ready to leave just yet. I'm going through some things right now, difficult things, which make me frustrated. Also, I don't like people like you. Do you see how those two problems might dovetail nicely?"

Ranker's hands began to snake backward along the table.

Stark pointed the gun at him.

"Keep your hands where I can see them."

Ranker stopped, still as a statue.

Stark gestured with his head back out the door. "I don't like what you're doing here. Do you understand?"

He was very close now. Even Dubois began to feel afraid. The muzzle of the small gun was centimeters from Ranker's face.

Ranker nodded.

Without warning, Stark brought his right fist around and clobbered Ranker on the side of the head. Ranker flinched and raised both hands on either side of his head, as if this might protect him. Dubois knew that Stark's fists would overwhelm any feeble attempt at defense Ranker might make.

She watched as though this incident was taking place on a TV screen. She felt strangely frozen, helpless to intervene. Or maybe she didn't want to intervene. Ranker was clearly a bad man, and the whole point of this exercise was to bring all three of them together in exactly this way.

"Speak!" Stark shouted

"I understand!"

Stark sat down on the couch next to Ranker. He slipped the pistol into his jacket pocket. Now, both hands were free. They formed an oddly intimate group - Dubois and Stark as bookends, with Ranker in the middle.

"I'm going to ask you some questions," Stark said. "And you're going to answer them. If you hesitate to answer them, or lie to me in any way, omit information, try to obfuscate, I'm going to hurt you. To put that in context, I punched you a minute ago, but I haven't started hurting you yet. There's a big difference. Do you understand?"

"Yes," Ranker said.

"How much I hurt you is mostly up to you," Stark said. "But not entirely. The lovely lady here is free to leave, as I understand it. But she's going to stay and listen because I might get too excited to pay attention to what you say. Does all of this sound okay to you?"

Ranker seemed unable to speak.

Stark poked him hard in the side of the head with two fingers.

"Does it sound okay?"

Ranker flinched.

"Yes." His voice was automatic, almost robotic.

Stark nodded. "Good. Here we go. We'll start with an easy one. You own an old house with a barn on the cliffs in the village of Eze, on the French Riviera."

Ranker opened his mouth in a sort of half smile. He looked at Stark, then back at Dubois. His eyes showed not fear, but surprise. He looked like he might even laugh.

"What? That sounds lovely, but I own no such…"

BAM! Stark punched him the side of the head, much harder than before.

Ranker's entire body spasmed, like a jolt had gone through it. He turned to Dubois again. His eyes were red and watering. He seemed like he was not entirely there.

"How can you allow him to do this?"

"I couldn't stop him, even if I wanted to."

"This could be a long night," Stark said. "You enjoy fights, don't you? It hurts the morning after a fight. It hurts a lot. You're about to find that out."

“You can’t do this.”

“I’ll start again,” Agent Stark said. “You own…”

Ranker nodded.

“I own the house, yes.”

Stark nodded. “Very good. See? It’s not so hard to be honest. You might get used to it. Next one. You organized a flash mob at the Musee Poitier two days ago.”

Ranker eyed stark warily.

“Yes.”

“Who hired you to do that?”

Ranker shook his head. “What makes you think…”

BAM! Stark punched him in the side of the head again.

Ranker closed his eyes. His body began to tremble.

“Wrong answer. Here’s a little ground rule I forgot to mention. You don’t answer a question with a question. That irritates me. I’m already irritated. You don’t want to make it worse.”

“Are you the police?”

BAM! Stark hit him again.

Tears were streaming down Ranker’s face now. He was openly crying. Dubois stood up and positioned herself on the other side of the table. Ranker’s face was contorted into a grimace. There was something unseemly about this man crying. Not too long ago, he was calling her an animal and trying to get her to swallow a spiked drink.

Ranker looked despondently at the shattered door, as if hoping someone would appear there. The sounds of cheering and shouting came down the hallway. He had probably told his men that he didn’t want to be disturbed.

“What did I just say about asking questions?”

Ranker was breathing hard, almost gasping for air.

“Hermann, I will beat you to death right here.”

“I was hired by an outfit that calls itself the Diamond Dogs,” Ranker said.

Stark nodded. "Very good. Diamond Dogs. It's a quaint name. It's what I wanted to hear. Those were test questions, and I already knew the answers."

“Okay,” Ranker said. He took a deep breath. He didn’t seem to know what was next, but he looked like he was trying to steel himself for it.

“They hired you to create a diversion so they could steal the Star of Versailles.”

Ranker shook his head. “I don’t know why they hired me. Is that what happened?”

Stark looked at Dubois. Their eyes met. Dubois looked at Ranker. Was he lying? She couldn’t tell.

"There was a murder at your house in France," Stark said. "In fact, it was a double murder."

Now Ranker’s eyes went wide. His head was shaking, very slowly.

“No.”

“You don’t know about that? It’s your house.”

“I haven’t been there in nine months. No one contacted me about a murder.”

“Nine months?”

“Yes. I have wished I could get back there more than I do. The place is starting to fall apart.”

“Does anyone use it in your absence?”

“Yes. Sometimes I let people stay there.”

“Like who?” Stark said.

“People in my circles. No one who would commit a murder.”

Stark’s fist slowly rose, but he didn’t launch it.

“The Diamond Dogs?”

Ranker shook his head. “No. Definitely not.”

“Do they know the house is empty?”

“I don’t know,” Ranker said. “They might know about it. They might not. I hope they don’t.”

“Who are they?” Stark said.

“I don’t know that, either.”

“Look at me, Hermann.”

Ranker shook his head. He was staring straight ahead at Dubois standing on the other side of the table. He was staring at the middle of her torso as though he couldn't raise his eyes. "I don't want to."

“Look at me.”

Ranker turned to Stark.

Stark slapped him across the face, an open-handed slap. The sound of it was loud. SMACK! Then Stark raised his fist again.

Ranker had stopped crying for a few moments. Now, he started again.

“You don’t know much, do you?” Stark said.

Ranker raised his hands to his face and began to cry into them. He cried for a little while, then seemed to compose himself again. He lowered his hands. His eyes were red and puffy. The side of his face was bright red where Stark kept hitting him.

"I don't know anything about them," Ranker said. "I don't. They're thieves. They steal jewels, art works, antiquities. Rare cars, in a few cases. They're not even *the* thieves. They hire thieves. They're the middlemen. They put these deals together. They've hired me a few times. I don't ask questions. I get paid, and that's enough. People work with me because I'm not curious. I don't ask, I don't tell. If you knew anything about me, about the things I've done, you would know that."

"I know all about the things you've done," Stark said.

Ranker said nothing.

"How do they get in touch with you?"

Ranker seemed to be broken now. He wasn't trying to resist the questioning at all. He answered flatly, and matter-of-factly. "Burner phones. Shifting portals on the dark web. It's anonymous."

"How do they pay you?" Stark said.

"Crypto, sometimes. Blind transfers to offshore accounts. It depends on the job. I trust them as far as it goes, but I stay at a remove from them, and they do the same."

"The real thieves, the people who actually took the Star of Versailles, were murdered at your house," Stark said. "In the barn. That's what led us to you. If we know who you are, the murderers do, too. They didn't pick your place by accident."

Stark and Ranker stared at each other, eyes full of meaning. Ranker squinted. His mouth hung halfway open.

"We should take you in," Stark said.

"You *are* the police."

Stark shrugged. "Police of some kind, I guess you'd say. Secret police."

Ranker shook his head. "What have I done, that you can prove? My testimony has been compromised by police brutality."

Stark gestured out into the man's little arena. There was a distant roar of the crowd again. "Unsanctioned fights. Unlicensed liquor sales. Smoking in an entertainment venue. Too many occupants to meet fire code. No emergency exits."

Ranker shook his head. He was returning to secure footing. "Berlin Polizei has jurisdiction here. They are well-paid to stay out of my business. It would be embarrassing for the spooks and the cops to step on each other like that."

"Yes, but it might keep you alive," Stark said.

Ranker breathed deeply. Dubois could see the wheels spinning in the man's head. He was looking for a way out. He was going to ground after this, possibly five minutes from now. He was going to be a rabbit hiding inside a hole.

"This is probably the last time we'll see each other," Dubois said. It was the first thing she had said in what seemed like a long time.

Ranker nodded. "Yes, I think so."

"We can help you," Dubois said.

"No, I don't think you can."

"If you tell us who the Diamond Dogs are, we can protect you from them."

"I told you already," Ranker said. "I don't know who they are."

Stark stood up. Without a word or a sign between them, he and Dubois headed for the door. Dubois stepped over the men on the floor. She noticed that one of the men was moving just a little bit. There was blood on the floor all around the two men.

"Good luck," Stark said. "You're going to need it."

Emboldened because Stark had stopped hitting him, and was in fact leaving, Ranker suddenly shouted. "I don't need luck, policeman! I was born lucky." His voice was almost a shriek.

Stark shook his head. "Tell that to the bad guys."

CHAPTER TWENTY ONE

February 16
1:05 am Central European Time
Hotel Berlin Wall
Kreuzberg
Berlin, Germany

"It would be cool to go out."

Troy sat in the wide window sill, looking three stories down at the ground level of the hotel. He had his right hand in a small white bucket of ice. That hand was going to be sore tomorrow. It was already sore now.

Below him, a length of the old Berlin Wall, painted in bright graffiti, ran along the street outside. There was an outdoor beer garden down there, which was part of the hotel, and the Berlin Wall served as its exterior wall.

Something about that appealed to Troy immensely. An outdoor bar, nestled right up against the infamous Wall. He tried to picture if this building would have been east of the wall or west of it. It seemed to him that this was East Berlin once upon a time.

"Radical," he said out loud.

The beer garden was strung with colorful overhead lights and crowded with revelers, even at this hour. There were tall metal fireplaces deployed at strategic places on the patio, meant to keep the place warm.

Dubois was changing into her jammies. The yellow bodysuit, a potential fire hazard itself, was in a pile on the carpet. The pajamas were light blue, with a series of cartoon characters on them that Troy couldn't quite place.

"We did go out," she said. "We just came in."

He shook his head. "That didn't count."

The room was small with a double bed. It was a little bit tight in here.

"We should probably just tell them to never mind booking two rooms."

Now, Dubois shook *her* head. “You take up the whole bed. I reserve the right to move down the hall if necessary.”

At least she was smiling. She was back on her horse, Troy supposed, and enjoying the work again. Okay. That was okay, as long as the worst they ran into were lightweights and wastes of skin like Hermann Ranker.

If things got any heavier…

They were going to get heavier. There were murderers on the loose. The Star of Versailles *might* be in the hands of Islamic terrorists.

“And I reserve the right to keep you prisoner here,” he said.

Dubois’s phone began to ring. Troy fought the impulse to pick it up and throw it against the wall. Then he shrugged and smiled, too.

They were making progress. They had set up Ranker, and knocked him down like a large bowling pin. He owned the house in France. He had organized the flash mob. The Diamond Dogs, whoever they might be, were real.

Now, he and Dubois would find out exactly how badly Ranker had been shaken.

Dubois pressed the green button on her screen. She pressed the speaker phone button. She turned the volume down just enough so they could both hear.

“Dubois?” Miquel said. “Stark?”

“Did it work?” Troy said.

“It worked exceptionally well,” Jan Bakker said. “Almost perfectly, you might say.

“Tell us.”

“As you know, I pinpointed the location of four mobile phones owned by Hermann Ranker,” Jan said. “None are registered to him, but I was able to pierce the veil of ownership. Two of the phones are encrypted. Two are normal, open lines. I broke the encryptions before you even entered the Viper Room. They were easy, commercially available encryption packages. Ranker must think he is immune to surveillance.”

“Amazing that he ran an illicit hosting service so long,” Dubois said.

“Not really,” Jan said. “Those were different times. Massive Upload was always vulnerable to data breaches, but hacking techniques were not as good in those days. The reason the FBI was able to take down all of his servers was his security systems were never particularly advanced. He benefited from being early, not from being good.”

"Ah," Dubois said.

"Anyway…" Troy said.

Jan instantly went on.

"Ranker, in the moments after you left the club, made a call to two mobile phones registered in Turkey, without answer. Then, I suppose because he was desperate, he called a landline in Istanbul. He spoke briefly with someone. They both spoke English. I'll play that call for you now."

A female robot voice said, "The following is a conversation between an unknown male and Hermann Ranker."

"What?" a male voice said. The voice was deep and harsh.

Ranker: "We have trouble."

"Never call this number unless it's an emergency. I told you that."

"You didn't answer the other lines," Ranker said. "It's an emergency."

"Call me back on the safe line. I will answer."

There was a pause, and then Jan came back on.

"That was the entirety of the first call. In Turkey, landlines are still common. We're fortunate that Ranker called it. The phone number is registered to a raki bar in Istanbul. The owner is a man named Hassan Celik. There is a lot of data about him readily available. Interpol ourselves have an extensive dossier. He is 39 years old, was considered a teenage prodigy in math and engineering, and graduated high school at the age of 15."

"Another genius, eh?" Troy said. "That's always a good thing."

"Well, he came from a poor family and didn't pursue any studies after that. He owns at least six hookah lounges and a couple of other raki bars. He has been suspected of opium trafficking, though never charged. Nearly two decades ago, he spent four years in prison, at hard labor, for operating a stable of prostitutes. He is a known associate of human traffickers bringing refugees out of Syria and Iraq, and possibly, bringing Western ISIS volunteers into Syria during the Syrian Civil War and the rise of the Islamic State."

"These guys," Troy said. "He could probably be rich just from running the bars and lounges. But it's never enough. They have to poke the bear. It's a sickness."

Maybe he was describing the same sickness that plagued him.

"Celik is quite well off," Jan said. "He owns several small buildings. The hookah lounges are usually on the ground floor, with rooms and apartments upstairs. He is thought to temporarily houses refugees in those apartments, before they move on to Europe. He may have used the apartments to house ISIS volunteers. The pipeline of ISIS volunteers has obviously dried up in recent years."

"If all of this is known about him," Dubois said, "why doesn't anyone stop him?"

"His Interpol file suggests he may be an asset of Turkish intelligence. Turkey is an enemy of the Assad regime. They are also opponents of Kurdish independence. It's well understood that during the height of the Syrian Civil War, the Turks often did not stop Westerners crossing through their territory to fight in Syria. Celik likely couldn't have trafficked ISIS fighters without Turkish intelligence knowing."

Troy didn't like where this was going. His career as a Navy SEAL ended in Syria. He was leading an American platoon embedded among fighters from the Kurdish People's Defense Units, or YPG. But the Kurds were a mixed group, combining several units that had been decimated in the fighting. Some of the fighters were women, from the YPJ, or Women's Protection Units. Some of the fighters were from the Kurdistan Workers' Party of Turkey, or PKK. Troy didn't really know the difference between the various types of Kurds, and didn't much care.

They were escorting a long caravan of civilians displaced by the fighting, moving across open desert. The night before, Troy and his men, along with the Kurds, had annihilated a group of ISIS fighters pushing up from the south. Some were still out there, and since they didn't care if they lived or died, were likely to try again.

A large force of the Turkish Army crossed south into Syria from Turkey. They demanded that the Americans leave the area.

Troy remembered sitting in the dark that evening, eating tinned meat with his men and some of the Kurdish fighters. It was too dangerous to light any fires.

"If you leave, the Turks will kill us all," a man said.

This was Troy's introduction to the strange and confusing world of American foreign policy. There were maybe 30 million Kurds spread out across the rugged borderlands of Turkey, Syria, Iraq and Iran, in an area they liked to think of as "Kurdistan." Kurdistan didn't exist on any map. It was just a hope the Kurds had for the future. One day, they would have their own country.

The United States considered Kurds from Syria, Iraq and Iran as allies. This was because Syria and Iran were enemies of the United

States, and the United States liked the idea of a free Kurdistan in northern Iraq. But the United States was NATO allies with Turkey, and Turkey had labeled the Kurds terrorists. Therefore, as far as the US was concerned, Turkish Kurds were terrorists. All other Kurds were good.

Except the Kurds saw themselves as one people. And Troy was with a group of Kurds from Syria, Turkey and Iraq. There were at least 200 Kurdish civilians under his protection.

His own commanders ordered him to stand down.

He radioed them back. "Uh… negative on stand down. Please inform the Turks there is a platoon of heavily-armed, extremely well-trained special operators from the United States Navy SEALs out here. We will not stand down. We will not abandon these people. We will fight to the last man, and we will take a lot of Turks with us. It's possible we'll take every last one of them."

Then he turned his radio off.

Troy didn't like Turkey. He didn't like Syria. He preferred not to think of these things at all anymore.

Jan was speaking.

"Ranker called back to an encrypted mobile phone. It took me several moments to decrypt the Turkish side of the next call. So the beginning of the conversation is one-sided, but it is fairly straightforward to understand the context. After a moment, once I broke the encryption, both sides become audible. A line or two of dialogue appears to confirm that the unknown party is Hassan Celik."

The soothing female robot introduced the call again. A few seconds passed.

"The police came here," Ranker said.

A long pause followed.

Ranker: "Tonight. Not five minutes ago."

Another pause.

"I don't know," Ranker said. "It was a woman and a man. The man was an enforcer. He broke down my office door. He beat two of my guards unconscious. He took a pistol away from one of them. He waved the gun in my face. When he walked out of here, he kept the gun."

There was blank air for just a few seconds.

"I know he's the police because otherwise I'd be dead now." Ranker sighed. "I wish you'd never got me involved in this."

“You contacted me,” the harsh, deep voice from the first call said. This was where Jan had broken the encryption. He had made pretty fast work of it.

Probably, the man was Celik. That made sense to Troy.

“You asked me if I had a job for you,” Celik said. “You’ve been asking me for months. This was a job, a well-paid job.”

“I know,” Ranker said. “I know that.”

“Let me remind you. You said, Hassan, I’m going under. I’m up to my eyes in debt. I’m going to lose everything. I need a score.”

“I said *I KNOW*. Hassan…”

“I asked you about the boxing,” Celik said. “And you told me it doesn’t make any money. It’s a tiny fraction of Massive Upload. The Americans killed you. The FBI killed you. Your dreams are dead because of them. Do you remember this?”

“Obviously I do.”

“I wish I had recorded it,” Celik said, “so you would never forget.”

There was another long pause. For a second, Troy thought the encryption had re-established itself.

“This is a terrible, terrible thing,” Ranker said, his voice low. “We’ve done a terrible thing.”

“You said, give me the biggest score you have. I said, I have one, but it will be the worst thing you have ever done. What did you say to that?”

Now Ranker spoke slowly. His voice was barely above a whisper. “I said I don’t care. I don’t care if we kill women and babies. But I didn’t mean it. My drinking was out of control.”

“That was just a month ago,” Celik said. “If it was out of control then…”

Ranker, apparently crying now, cut him off. “That asshole beat me in front of his woman. He beat me like a dog.”

“Who, the cop?”

“Yes.”

“I don’t get it. If they were cops, why is she his woman?”

“I don’t know,” Ranker said. “I don’t know who she was.”

“Why did you let him beat you?”

"Are you listening at all? He knocked out two of my guards and then handcuffed them. They were helpless. One is in hospital. He was a martial artist. The other is Chechen. He refused medical care, but he did not look good when he left."

Celik seemed unconcerned. “Get better guards, I guess.”

"The cop told me there was a double murder at my place in France."

Celik didn't answer.

"He told me they killed the thieves. Hassan. They are killing everyone involved in this. They did it at MY HOUSE! Why did they do that? How did they even know it was there? Did you tell them where I live?"

"I didn't hear about anything like that," Celik said. "I didn't tell anyone anything. Could be the cops are just fishing, and no such thing happened."

"They're going kill me next," Ranker said. "Then they're going to kill you. Don't you know that? You're not safe, either. God, I wish I had never done this."

"What did you tell the police?" Celik said.

"Nothing. Of course, I told them nothing."

"Hermann…"

"Nothing," Ranker said. "I don't care if you don't believe me. To be honest, I wish I never met you."

"It's too late for wishes," Celik said. "Listen to me now. Do you still have the island house in Greece? The one near Thessaloniki?"

"It's near Possidi, but yeah. I have it. I haven't paid any property taxes on it in three years. I don't know why they haven't seized it by now."

"Go there and hide out for a while," Celik said. "Don't tell anyone where you're going, or why. Don't bring anyone. Just keep your mouth shut and leave. Get on the next plane and go. It's not easy to reach. No one can get you there. Call me in a week. I'll keep my ears open. Maybe this will all blow over."

"This was a deal with the Devil," Ranker said.

"There's nothing we can do about that now. What's done is done. We can't stop it. There is too much force behind it. It's out of our hands."

"ISIS is the Devil."

"Don't say that word," Celik said. "You don't know what you're talking about. Don't ever say that word again. Not on the phone, not in person. I will kill you myself."

"Okay," Ranker said. "Okay. I'm sorry."

"Calm down, go to the house. Call me in a week. I'll know more by then."

"What if you're dead?" Ranker said.

Celik laughed. It was the gravelly laugh of a long-time smoker. It sounded like he had pebbles in his throat. "In that case, run. Assume they tortured me."

"You have a wonderful sense of humor. All right. I'll go."

"Good," Celik said. "The cops won't find you there, either."

"Thank you," Ranker said. "I didn't mean what I said about you."

"Be well," Celik said.

The call ended. There was a moment of silence in the room.

"That's all we have," Jan said. "Ranker didn't make another call after that, and if Celik did, he used a phone I'm not aware of."

"Ranker's in trouble," Troy said.

"It seems that way, yes."

"Vizzini told me Al Qaeda took the diamond," Troy said. "They mined it, they sold it, and then they stole it back. Now Ranker says ISIS."

"Some of the people who were in ISIS were previously in Al Qaeda," Dubois said. "They were closely affiliated. ISIS called itself Al Qaeda in Iraq before Abu Musab al-Zarqawi died, and the two groups fell out. Maybe someone from ISIS knew about the stone from their time in Al Qaeda."

"Yeah, but why would they even want it?"

"The Star of Versailles is invaluable," Jan said. "The most obvious answer is what the Sicilian told you. They took it to fund operations. ISIS has fallen on hard times. They've lost everything, including access to oil revenue from lands they once held in Syria and Iraq. They control tiny remnants of the land they once ruled, in units isolated from each other. Most of their fighters are dead. At least ten thousand are held in prisons across Syria, in inhuman conditions. Their international funding from wealthy Sunnis in the Gulf states has dried up. No one likes to back a loser."

Troy had trouble accepting this.

"Why would Ranker think this crime was the worst thing ever? It's got to be more than just ISIS or Al Qaeda getting money. What's a thing like that worth?"

"No one has ever publicly put a price on it," Jan said. "That seems to be by design. The Musee Poitier never divulged the price they paid."

"It doesn't matter," Troy said. "Ten million euros. A hundred million. Even if they could sell it, that kind of money isn't going to rebuild the Islamic State. And that's if they can find another buyer right away. It's not exactly a liquid asset."

"They might already have a buyer," Jan said. "Likely someone with enormous wealth, like a Saudi or emirate prince. The market for stolen gems is more liquid than you might think. There are illicit sales going on all the time."

"Do tell," Troy said.

"There's an auction tomorrow night in Prague," Jan said. "It was only announced on underground channels earlier today. The item for sale was not announced. The price was not announced. They only said that it's more than rare, a one of a kind item you will not want to miss, which has just come on the market. It's likely to become the centerpiece of any collection."

Troy sighed deeply. Madrid, Paris, Palermo, Nice, Berlin, and now Prague, all in the space of a few days. He'd been through worse, he supposed. But he was tired, even exhausted. He could admit that to himself.

His brother had nearly died. That was the hardest part.

"Let me guess," he said. "You have some way of getting us in there."

"Yes, I do."

CHAPTER TWENTY TWO

4:05 am Syria Time (3:05 am Central European Time)
A ruined building
Idlib, Syria

"Out! Out! Out of the cell now!"

A flare went up somewhere very close.

The Ghost's eyes were open, and he could see the room in the arc of light and shadow, two of the walls blasted out, the two others pockmarked with bullet holes, but he was staring into the past.

Nureddine. I am Nureddine.

He was naked, standing on a cold stone floor. The men had hosed him down with a powerful hose, ice-cold water. He tried to cover himself with his hands, but when he did, they aimed the hose at his face. The water was so powerful, it felt like it would strip the skin off of him.

"Out of the cell!" someone screamed.

Blinding lights flashed, there was some loud western music playing, ear shattering. The cell gate was open. He had almost fallen asleep from exhaustion on his steel mesh cot, but of course there was no sleep here.

He stumbled out of the cell. A woman stood there among a line of soldiers. She laughed and pointed at his nudity. She was holding a giant German shepherd on a short leash, a dog she could barely control. The dog snapped and growled at him.

Men with rifles pointed them at him as though they were about to fire.

He ran the gauntlet again, barefoot on the cold wet cement.

A hose blasted him with water, low in the legs, taking his feet out. He fell onto his side. He scraped the right side of his leg and torso on the ground. His vision cleared, and he saw in front of him more naked men on the ground, writhing.

He saw that the men were collared around their necks and wearing leashes. American soldiers dragged them along the stone floor. At the far end, more soldiers were forcing the men to climb on top of each other in a sort of pyramid. It was a nightmare of naked flesh, a vision of hell. The lights flashed. The music blared.

The water blasted him again.

"Get up!" someone screamed, right next to his head. He turned, and the soldier next to him was using a bullhorn to scream at him.

"Kill me!" he shouted, but he could not hear himself.

He must have gone deaf.

Now someone was dragging him by a chain down the hall between the empty cells, toward the pyramid. His hands went to his throat. To his horror, he realized that he wore the same red collar as the others.

WHUMP!

A rocket hit somewhere nearby, and the building trembled. Small bits of masonry showered down on him. He was on a bed that still had a thin, rough mattress. He had rolled some clothes up to use as a pillow. The bed was not uncomfortable.

He glanced around. His trusty AK-47, the best, most reliable combat rifle ever invented, leaned against the wall behind him. He had half a dozen full magazines for the gun and five incendiary grenades. The night was cool. The wrecked building offered enough shelter. It was pleasant to sleep both indoors and outdoors at the same time.

He'd had a bit of dried meat and some flat noodles in the early evening. He required nothing else.

WHUMP!

Another rocket hit, a bit further away this time. Machine gun fire rattled in the night. The moon rode high. The room, the shattered building, and the sky took on tones of blue and white. Allah could reveal indescribable beauty in the most unexpected places. If the Perfect One willed it, perhaps the Ghost would live long enough to take up painting so he could share with the world a scene like this one.

Ali Talib stood across the way, in the threshold to the next room. He was as still as a sentinel, almost more shadow than substance.

"Shabah?" he said.

"Yes. I'm awake. How goes the battle?"

"They are closer, but we are holding. A trap we set killed an entire squad of Assad's pigs tonight, perhaps fifteen men."

"Mashallah," the Ghost said.

"Yes," Ali said. "And there is more news."

The Ghost sat up in bed. He swung his legs and placed his bare feet on the floor.

"Tell me."

"The brothers are on their way to the Bab al-Hawa crossing with the key. They were in Istanbul last night. We received the message 30 minutes ago by satellite phone."

The satellite phone was kept several blocks away because the Russians tended to target satellite signals for their missile strikes. With the dangerous street fighting, it could easily take 30 minutes for a runner to bring a message here.

The Ghost took a deep breath. This was incredible news. The key was creeping closer. It was practically at their doorstep. "Are the roads open between the crossing and here?" he said.

"As I understand it, the roads in Turkey are damaged but open. The roads here in Syria are bad. There is fighting near the border, and the scene at the crossing is chaos. Refugees cannot leave from Syria. There are hundreds of people pressed up against the border, perhaps thousands, trying to escape. Aid shipments are stuck there. Civilian trucks cannot enter Syria. Goods must be transferred to four-wheel armored vehicles."

"No matter," the Ghost said. "Allah can open the crossing with a wave of his hand."

Ali nodded. "Yes. I believe it."

"Did you ever doubt?" the Ghost said, already knowing the answer.

"Yes. I doubted. I did not think the key would make it this far. I thought the Europeans would seize it. Then I thought the Turks would interfere."

The Ghost tapped his head. "Do not think with your mind. Feel with your heart. Allah is moving through us. He has protected us and kept us safe here, against all odds."

"We've lost many men," Ali said.

"We will lose everyone. But we will carry out what Allah commands, as it is revealed to us. We will see his enemies destroyed, and we will meet him in Paradise."

"Inshallah," Ali said. *If God wills it.*

The Ghost nodded. "Yes. How long is the drive from the crossing to here?"

"Years ago, not long at all. But these are the worst circumstances possible. Our brothers are traveling to the border as aid workers, volunteer drivers in a small truck loaded with water, canned food, blankets and other supplies."

The Ghost smiled. It was beautiful.

"They might abandon the truck and the supplies, and slip across themselves. If they do that, they will be forced to walk here or commandeer a vehicle if they can. It will be difficult to find a functioning vehicle while under bombardment."

"Let them walk," the Ghost said. "They will move like shadows. I know they will make it."

CHAPTER TWENTY THREE

7:15 am Eastern European Time (6:15 am Central European Time)
A small island in the Aegean Sea
Greece

"You sweet girl."

Hermann Ranker steered the small motor boat toward the tall, rocky outcropping of land surrounded by pale blue sea. From here, he could see his whitewashed home at the top of the island. The house was made of stone taken from the island itself. It was just after dawn. The rising sun glinted off the glass windows and sliders.

Every time he came here, he was astonished by the sheer beauty of the place. It could make you believe in the existence of God.

It had been a long night, and he was running on empty. He had flown from Berlin on a private charter to Thessaloniki, then had driven to where he kept his boat moored near Possidi. The entire trip, he felt like a coward, running from the things he had done.

But not now. Seeing the house and the island made things clearer. He came here because this is where he was supposed to be.

He bought this place in the name of shell company during the Massive Upload era. Like everything from that time, he was on the verge of losing it. He didn't like to think about the financial losses he had undergone in recent years. Everything was going under.

The penthouse in Berlin was a rental that he couldn't afford anymore. His various companies were deep in debt. The place in France? It was starting to fall apart from neglect. He didn't want to live there if a murder was committed (two murders, he reminded himself). Perhaps he could sell it, but all that would do is buy some time.

He realized as he approached the island that he should make this place his priority. It was so easy to lose sight of what was important and become distracted by what was right in front of you. This house was important. It was possible, if he retrenched everywhere else, that he could save this place.

He pulled up slowly to the dock. The dock was made of a synthetic material that held up well against the elements. Everything here, everything, was the highest quality. He tied the boat up, reflecting that the boat itself was something he owned outright. No rent, no debt, no taxes in arrears.

"At least I have this," he said out loud.

The boat rose and fell with the gentle swells. Ranker stood at the bottom of a long flight of stairs, looking up. The house was not visible from here, hidden behind the steep, rocky hillside.

All he had with him was an overnight bag slung over his shoulder. There were just a few items of clothing inside it. There were also two bottles of whiskey. He knew there were about two dozen beers in the refrigerator upstairs if it was even still on. He had enough to drink for at least five or six days.

There was some canned food in the pantry, plus rice and pasta. He didn't care as much about food. There were also two guns - a pistol and a rifle.

He shook his head. He'd never shot anyone in his life. He had never even pulled a gun on anyone. That hideous cop, pointing the pistol at Hermann's face? That was far more than Hermann had ever done to anyone else.

The guns were just for show. If the terrorists found him here, they were going to kill him. That much was clear.

As he climbed the steps, he began to wonder about Hassan, and not for the first time. Hassan had treated him as a dupe, a pawn. Hassan had put him in a terrible position, where thuggish cops invaded his place of business, and where he was probably next in line to be eliminated.

"All I did was organize a mob."

Hermann couldn't be blamed for what had happened and what was going to happen. If the thieves had been murdered, that was their fault. When you lived on the edge like this, you had to be careful not to fall off.

If the terrorists caused a disaster, whose fault was that?

Theirs, not his.

He reached the top of the stairs. There was a stone patio here, which led to the sliding glass doors to the house. He took a deep breath and turned around. The views from this house were amazing. There was nothing out there but sun, sky, sea, a few boats, and two or three islands similar to this one. In the distance, he thought he could see the mainland. Sometimes you could, sometimes you couldn't.

It was the most exceptional piece of real estate he had ever owned. Not exactly practical, no, but incredible. And right now, it was showing how useful it really was. This was his escape, his refuge. He could stay safe here.

He could rebuild his life from here.

He glanced around. Everything looked fine. The house was intact. He paid a maintenance service to come out here once every month, inspect the place, and fix anything that was wrong.

He stepped up to the gray metal security panel. He opened the door with a small silver key. The door squeaked on its hinge. He should have someone look at that.

The open door revealed the digital keypad, which lit up. He punched in the code. Everything was operational.

He sighed. Okay. This was his sanctuary. Those people were vicious, they were killers, and they were terrorists. But would they really come all the way out here just to murder him? He had helped them.

"Maybe," he said. "Maybe they would anyway."

If so, he would deal with that when the time came.

He pulled open the sliding glass door, almost ready to cry with relief. He had cried last night in front of that cop, and that was unmanly, unseemly. But here, by himself, it would be all right.

He stepped across the threshold.

He saw the fireball rushing toward him before he heard the explosion. An instant later, he was already dead.

***

The woman's name was Gabrielle, and she was very beautiful.

She knew this about herself and didn't deny it. In fact, she relished it. All her life, it had opened doors for her. All of the best things had come, and while she thought of herself as a good person, she knew that goodness didn't bring you the best things.

She sat on the deck of a small blue motor yacht, moored near a series of small but towering rocky islands. She was nude except for a soft robe, drinking her coffee just after sunrise. Her boyfriend Anders was asleep below deck.

She didn't wake him, not because she was being considerate, but because she liked having this moment to herself. It was her favorite time of day.

Everything was incredibly beautiful. No, it was more than that. It was unspeakably beautiful. The boat rocked gently. In a little while, when Anders woke, she would remove her robe and dive into the water.

In the near distance, the top of a mountain island exploded.

She had been looking right at it, her mind a blank. There might have been a whitewashed house there a second ago. Now, the whole top of the island was just gone. The sound of the explosion came to her, a loud ROAR piercing the morning quiet.

Is it a volcano?

It was all she could think of. The island was a volcano, and now it had erupted. She stared at it. Things were flying in the air. A few seconds later, tiny pebbles began to rain down on her. Some of them were hot, still on fire.

She dropped her coffee and threw herself down the ladder.

Anders was there, already awake. He wore blue striped boxers and nothing else. His eyes were open wide. Something heavy hit the outside of the boat.

"What is it?" Anders said. "What is it?"

She could not speak. He pulled her into the bathroom, which was small and just barely fit the two of them. Outside, the boat was hammered by a hard rain.

CHAPTER TWENTY FOUR

9:55 am Central European Time
Hotel Berlin Wall
Kreuzberg
Berlin, Germany

"The phones are going straight to voice mail. All of them."

Troy lay in bed in the room he was sharing with Dubois. His phone was pressed to his ear. It felt luxurious to remain in bed at this hour.

They were going to Prague later today, but lucky for them, it was just a few hours away. They could drive there, if they chose. Dubois had already acted on the clever idea of getting them late checkout. She had also gone downstairs to see if she could scrounge them up something to eat before the hotel closed the breakfast buffet.

Outside his window, the sun was behind heavy gray clouds, trying to do something. It didn't matter. Troy didn't want a nice, sunny day to waste sightseeing in Berlin. If they had this room for a few more hours, he wanted to spend every minute of it right here in this bed. Everything was great, except he hadn't been able to reach any of his family members. When that happened, he made his next call right away.

"Your family is in protective custody," Missing Persons said into Troy's ear. "That doesn't mean you can just call them when you want. They're out of touch for a reason. Anyway, it's four in the morning here. You realize that, don't you?"

"It's shouldn't matter," Troy said. "My brother Pat works the 11 to 7. He's awake this time of night. If he could, he would answer his phone."

"It would be a breach of security," Persons said. "I remind you that you wanted this for them. We'll work out later how you can talk to them and eventually see them. For now, just know that they're safe."

“Eventually?”

“We don’t know how long this is going to go on.”

"Terrific," Troy said. He nearly said, "What about the nuclear option?" but didn't.

His family was hidden in the bosom of the United States government. For now, the mafia couldn't reach them, and that was enough. More than that, Persons had hit back and sent the two hitmen back to their bosses on slabs.

“What’s the story with the diamond?” Persons said now.

Troy rolled his eyes. This man was as persistent as a pit bull with its teeth embedded in someone's leg and its jaws locked.

"I don't know. Why don't you tell me?"

"That's not why I pay you," Persons said. "I pay you so you'll tell me things, not the other way around."

"I've told you a lot of things," Troy said. "I've done a lot of things."

"You've been an exemplary agent," Persons said. "We couldn't ask for better. You've saved a lot of lives. You've saved a couple of important relationships. I trust you feel you're being compensated fairly?"

Persons had dumped a lot of money on Troy. Some of it had come in cash, and some of it had come in transfers to an anonymous bank account in the Bahamas. Troy had stopped paying attention to the money. By the standards of his previous life in the United States Navy, Troy was rich. But that wasn't why he did what he did, and there was more to compensation than money.

"It's not all it's cracked up to be," Troy said. "Being a double agent."

"You're allowed to quit. Just not until this one is over."

“You’re worried about it?” Troy said.

There was a lot of concern about this missing gemstone. People thought it was going to cause something to terrible to happen, but no one seemed willing to come out and say exactly what that was.

“Have you ever known me to not worry?” Persons said.

"Yes," Troy almost said. "You didn't seem too worried about keeping my family safe until my brother nearly got killed."

But of course, he couldn't say that.

“We’re tracking it down,” he said instead.

"What did the punk in Berlin say? Ranker?"

Troy wasn't surprised that Missing Persons knew about Hermann Ranker. As a result, Troy didn't act surprised, and he didn't act offended. Persons, and whoever he worked for, kept close tabs on Troy.

“He said he didn’t know anything.”

Troy grasped that he was now withholding information from his real boss, if that's what Persons was. Had he done that before? He wasn't sure. He did know that he felt a great deal of resentment about the way things had gone. Troy had taken large risks at Persons’s urging, had made powerful enemies, and in doing so had put his own family in terrible danger.

“Maybe you didn’t hit him hard enough,” Persons said.

Troy almost smiled. "I'll take that under advisement. Next time, I'll hit him harder."

"You won't get that chance," Persons said. "He's dead."

Troy stopped. It felt like his face had frozen in place.

“He’s dead?”

"You hadn't heard?" Persons said. "He died two or three hours ago. After you shook him down, he made a run to an island he owned off the coast of Greece. He got to the house, and it blew up. He's gone. Nothing left at all."

Troy stared straight ahead. He did not say a word. As he watched, the door to the room opened and Dubois came in. She wore jeans and a t-shirt, with her Afro wild and crazy. She was in civilian mode today. She carried a tray of food balanced on one hand, and an entire small coffee urn in the other. She held the urn up with a bright smile.

“They were closing down the breakfast, so I took all the coffee that was left.”

"The clock is ticking on this, Stark," Missing Persons said into his ear. "It would be nice if you can figure out where that thing went, and get it back before something happens with it."

Troy noted that Persons said, “Something happens *with* it.” He didn’t say, “Something happens *to* it.”

"Rest assured, I am doing my best."

"I've seen you do better," Persons said. "Thanks for getting me out of bed."

Then he hung up.

***

Troy and Dubois were entangled in the bed, body to body and face to face, when the phone rang.

Troy opened his eyes and disengaged himself. He glanced around the room. It was later. The silver food tray was across the room on a small table. All of the food - eggs, sausage, bread, butter, cheese - was gone. The coffee urn was also on the table. Troy happened to know it was empty. The two coffee mugs were here on the side table, and there wasn't a drop of coffee left in either of them.

Dubois’s jeans and black t-shirt were draped over a chair.

The phone belonged to Dubois. He glanced at it.

Who else would be calling but headquarters?

He answered. "Stark."

“Agent Stark?” Miquel said.

Dubois's big eyes were open now. She nearly laughed.

“Yes.”

"I called Dubois's phone. Are you with her?"

"You know, we're pretty much inseparable as partners go. We're just here, having some breakfast and going over our case files."

“It’s after twelve noon,” Miquel said.

"Lunch," Troy said. "Did I say breakfast?"

“Hello Agent Dubois,” Miquel said.

Dubois's voice sounded thick and sleepy. "Hi, Miquel.”

The niceties out of the way, Miquel got straight to business without another word of preamble. "Hermann Ranker is dead."

"Really," Troy said, not wanting to reveal that he already knew. He tried to put a note of surprise in his voice. "How did it happen?"

"His island house in Greece exploded. He went there alone. Jan just confirmed that it was indeed Ranker who died. He was able to track Ranker's movement from Berlin down to Greece and out to the island. It seems he kept a motorboat in Possidi. He arrived there early this morning on a private charter flight and took the boat from its mooring. Aerial drone footage shows the boat is still docked below the house, which is completely gone. The entire top of the island was destroyed."

“It was a very large explosion,” Jan said.

Troy figured Jan was lurking around there somewhere. These days, Miquel and Jan seemed nearly as inseparable as Troy and Dubois.

"Do we know anything more about the explosion in Paris?" Troy said. His hunch that the two things were connected still stood, but he didn't see how.

“We know that Philippe Pontif is dead," Jan said. "But only because several of his acquaintances said he planned to be at the bar. We know the identities of some of his entourage who were also there. The waiter, the bartender. We know who they were because the owner of the place could verify who was on duty. The bomb is thought to have been a pressure cooker bomb, possibly carried inside a backpack or a suitcase. It was small, portable, but remarkably powerful."

“Any similarities to the bomb that blew up Ranker?” Agent Dubois said.

"There may be," Jan said. "Both bombs indicate sophisticated understanding of explosives and incendiaries. In the Paris bomb, RDX appears to be the chemical used in the explosion. The presence of thermite within the bomb has been theorized as to why the interior of the pub burned so intensely. It's possible that the same composition was used in the Greece bomb, though I can't say that for sure. We do know the interior of the house in Greece burned in the equivalent of a small-scale firestorm, and both the house and the mountaintop were almost completely atomized by the force of the bomb."

"And the bomb in Paris was that powerful?" Troy said.

"It was smaller," Jan said, "but demonstrated the same type of power. Several buildings in the neighborhood have been compromised and will have to be torn down. By all accounts, the bar was crowded, and most people are unaccounted for. People closest to the bomb are thought to have been vaporized. We may never know who they were unless they come up as missing in the next few days."

"Could be the same bombmakers," Dubois said.

"It's a style of bomb common to Islamic fundamentalists," Jan said. "It's very likely that the Paris bombing was the work of Islamists who wanted to kill Philippe Pontiff in a spectacular way. There is a man who appears on security cameras in the neighborhood. He seems young, possibly of Middle-Eastern descent, but he does a good job of keeping his face in the shadows. Earlier in the night, he was carrying something on his back, under a long coat. It's unclear what, probably a backpack. It causes a hump under his coat. Later, in the moments leading up to the explosion, and in the moments afterward, he is seen without it."

"All of that said, it could still be unrelated," Troy said.

"Philippe Pontiff has been aggravating Muslims for years," Miquel said. "He also took no precautions to protect himself. His violent death has been in the cards for a long time, I'm afraid. I doubt that he and Ranker had much in common. It's a nice try, though. Good thinking outside the box, as they say."

Dubois grinned. "Who says that?"

"Americans," Miquel said.

Troy shook his head and smiled. "All right. We need to get ready to go to Prague. Do you want to tell us about it?"

"That sounds fine," Miquel said. "Jan?"

Jan started in right away. He probably had the whole thing in front of him.

"The sale will take place in a 1700s mansion in a wealthy part of the city. Some of the guests are invited, some heard about the sale and reached out. Agent Stark, you are one of the latter. You're not a known quantity to these dealers. Your name is Trent Elon. You're an American, 40 years old. You made your first pile of money acquiring old Soviet and Chinese weaponry and selling it to whoever would buy it, especially African warlords and South American guerrilla movements."

"Lovely," Troy said.

"You went legitimate within the past decade. Now you're a venture capitalist who's been living in Singapore. You claim that you're from a wealthy family, but in fact you're a former Marine who first started buying and selling weapons while stationed at a secret American base in Niger. You happened to be in Warsaw when you heard about the sale of this gem, or whatever it is. You're a collector."

"Why was I in Warsaw?"

"Of course, you're not really a venture capitalist, or at least that's not how you make the bulk of your income. Venture capitalism is your cover story. You still track down Soviet-era weapons when you can. There are old Soviet weapons in Poland."

"Ah," Troy said. "A cover story embedded within a cover story."

"Who am I?" Dubois said.

"You are Trent Elon's consort," Jan said. "You're a Senegalese named Janet Milola. Trent met you while in Africa on a business trip."

"That's it?" Dubois said. "That's my whole story?"

"You can add embellishments, but I don't think you'll need any more than that. Maybe you were educated in France."

"Brutal," Troy said. "I guess Dubois is my arm candy."

"Something like that," Miquel said.

"Well, I knew she was good for something. Last night she was a honey trap, tonight she's a rich man's trophy."

He looked at Dubois. They were still in bed together, tangled up in the sheets, nearly face to face. Troy kept his face deadpan, not the slightest hint of a smile, not even a smirk. She scowled at him.

They were getting better. They were a team again. A team of rivals maybe, but a team nevertheless.

"Ready to go to Prague?" Troy said.

CHAPTER TWENTY FIVE

9:05 pm Central European Time
Nerudova Street
Mala Strana (Lesser Quarter)
Prague, Czech Republic

It was a dress-up affair.

Troy wore a black tuxedo, black tie, and starched white shirt. Dubois wore a dark red sequined mini-dress, ruby lips, with dark red high heels and a matching red sash in her hair. She looked stunning, as always. More than stunning - astonishing.

The parlor was an open space with a white stone floor and wide double doors. A series of tall windows with blue curtains ringed the room. Each window displayed a night view of a different aspect of the city. It was winter, and Prague was powdered with a crust of snow, though it was hard to see that now.

A man nearby was speaking. "The house was built in 1735, during the European Renaissance. It was built for Vladimir Gallas, a powerful landowner and nobleman whose family dated to the 1300s. The Mala Strana, or Lesser Quarter, despite the name was in fact the wealthiest section of Prague. You'll notice that from this room, you have sweeping views of what was the entire city at that time. Out of these two windows, you can see directly downhill and across the Vltava River to the lights of Old Town Tower on the Charles Bridge."

A handful of people had clustered around the man. He must be the one who called himself Ambroz and the host of this evening's event.

The man had a Caesar-like laurel wreath of white hair on his head. He was short, round, wearing an open black dinner jacket and blue dress shirt underneath. He wore a monocle with a gold chain dangling from it in one eye.

They had come up a grand staircase to reach this room. In the hallway was a sort of atrium or rotunda with a glass ceiling. Here in the main gallery, there was a table of some kind in the center draped with a white cloth. There was a bar along one wall, with a single bartender. The choices available were wine of various kinds and two different brands of beer. It was an easy enough night for the bartender, though Troy noticed there was no jar where the attendees could leave him a tip.

There were less than two dozen guests in the room. Here in Prague, the cholera disaster was much closer. But even so, while some people were wearing masks, most were not. Most of the bidders were white, coupled-up, Euro elites. A few were single men, including one east Asian, who was all in red leather. Another man, an Arab, wore a long black robe, lined in yellow, with a white headdress ringed in black. His dark beard was trimmed close to his face.

Another 20 or 30 men, many of them large, many with bulges under their jackets, waited out in the rotunda. It would be impolite to carry weapons into the auction. Probably, it would also be a *faux pas* to bring your hired goons in with you, whether they were packing or not.

In the far, darkened corner of the room was a white grand piano. It was enormous. No one was playing it. The piano was not part of the entertainment tonight. Soft music itself would be a distraction. It was a quiet room.

Troy and Dubois sipped wine, Troy white, Dubois red.

The man with the monocle moved to the center of the room, and stood next to the table obscured by the white cloth.

"Dear friends," he said, raising his voice only the slightest amount. Everyone came to attention at once.

"Thank you for assembling here on such short notice. Some of you know me, some do not. Everyone is welcome. For the purpose of these sales, I call myself Ambroz, derived from the Greek, and which means immortal. No, I don't expect to live forever. But I believe these pieces, which we all adore and we all covet, will do exactly that - their beauty will last until the end of time."

Around the room, the guests clapped at Ambroz's cleverness.

He raised a hand.

"Tonight we have one item for sale, and only one. It is an exquisite six-carat blue diamond, set tonight in gold, though you can easily present it any way you like. For two centuries, it was known by its German name, Tiefsee Diamant, or in English, Deep Sea Diamond. It went missing in 1939 and was thought to be lost forever. As far as most authorities are concerned, it is still lost, but those of us in this room know better."

A ripple of nervous laughter went through the room.

"After the second world war, this incredible piece was recovered intact and in exceptional condition. It has been in a private collection since the early 1970s, and at this moment, we can reveal it for our special friends."

Ambroz's chubby hand had sneaked across to the white cloth. With a flourish, he whipped the cloth away, uncovering a dazzling blue diamond sitting on a square of black velvet. Troy noticed for the first time that a narrow overhead spotlight beamed directly on the diamond, making its various curves and cuts sparkle.

A new ripple went through the crowd, this one more inarticulate than before. It sounded like "Ooooohhh."

It was not the Star of Versailles. The man had been saying that for the past couple of minutes, but you never knew. He could claim it was one thing, and it could be something else entirely. He could say it went missing in 1939, when it fact it was just stolen. Troy didn't feel anything in particular about it being a different diamond. This trip to Prague had seemed like a bit of a long shot.

Ambroz kept speaking.

"The color blue is associated with open spaces, freedom, intuition, imagination, inspiration and sensitivity. It can also represent trust, loyalty, sincerity, wisdom, confidence, faith and stability. Celebrated for its striking blue color, the Deep Sea Diamond will captivate the hearts of gem aficionados and collectors alike."

Ambroz was silent for a long moment, letting the diamond do the talking for him.

"The intense hue of this diamond, akin to the deep color of the vast ocean, is a sight to behold and evokes a sense of wonder in all who see it. Paired with unparalleled clarity, this gem is nothing short of a masterpiece. I think you'll agree the Deep Sea Diamond is a testament to the artistry of nature."

People circled around the diamond, moving in and out, speaking in hushed voices, as if someone might overhear.

"Imagine this treasure as the centerpiece of your collection, something you share with only the closest confidantes. Or, if you are more daring, imagine it adorning the finger of that one and only love."

No doubt the diamond was incredible. But Troy wasn't here to look at an amazing gem, likely stolen by the Nazis from someone they murdered, possibly in the Holocaust. He was here to find the Star of Versailles.

"I'm going to start the bidding at seven million euros," Ambroz said. "When you are ready to make a bid, simply raise your hand and I will acknowledge you."

The bidding went above ten million, but Troy tuned it out. Ambroz spoke slowly and carefully, not at all the fast-talking backcountry auctioneer. Eventually, the diamond went to the Asian man in red. When it was over, Troy and Dubois stood near the windows again, sipping wine and gazing out at the lights of the snow-covered city.

The place was emptying out quickly. As each person or group left, a few more bodyguards in suits peeled off and left with them. Soon there would be no one, both in the auction room, and the foyer.

Troy glanced at the bartender. He didn't seem to be packing up.

Ambroz came out of a side room and walked directly to Troy and Dubois. He smiled and extended a hand. Troy shook it. It was soft, almost like a cushion.

"The auction was not to your liking, officers?" Ambroz said.

Troy and Dubois looked at him without answering right away. They both sipped their wine instead.

"Is that what we are?" Dubois said.

Troy might never have answered at all.

"Oh, come now," Ambroz said. "I know all the buyers in this part of the world. People don't just suddenly turn up, people that I've never heard of."

"We live in Singapore," Troy said, finding his voice.

"Of course you do."

"If you thought we were the police, why did you hold the sale?"

Ambroz shrugged. "There was nothing illegal about this sale. It was just as I described. A private seller, who wishes to remain anonymous, put an exquisite diamond on sale, which has been in his family since the 1970s. Between you and I, he has experienced some embarrassing financial concerns just recently. A temporary glitch, I assure you, which this sale will help alleviate."

"If it was a legal sale," Troy said, "then why not hold it at a well-known auction house? You could publicize it in the newspapers, or in those little flyers they mail out to rich people. You'd get more money that way, wouldn't you?"

Ambroz smiled, but it was a painful smile. "The ownership of the diamond was in a gray area, and my seller preferred to keep it that way. The buyer can of course do whatever he chooses."

"The owners who lost it in 1939?" Dubois said. "What became of them?"

"Long dead, of course."

Troy smiled darkly. "They probably died in 1939, or maybe the early 40s. I'm just guessing. And the thieves died by 1945, unless they slipped away to South America before the hammer came down."

Ambroz shrugged. "Perhaps all of that is true. History is filled with tragedy."

It was a friendly enough conversation, so Troy decided to take it another step.

"What do you know about the Star of Versailles?" he said.

Ambroz shrugged. "What you know. It's a mysterious gemstone, exceptionally rare not necessarily for its beauty, but because it's made of more than one precious stone at the same time. No one knows for certain where it came from or who the original owners were. It's housed at the Musee Poitier in Paris."

"We've heard differently," Dubois said. "We're trying to track it down. We think it was in the south of France as recently as two nights ago. We thought it might have come here."

The man's breath seemed to catch in his throat.

"Are you saying it's been stolen?"

"Maybe it has," Dubois said. "Maybe it hasn't. Maybe it was never at the Musee Poitier in the first place. Or maybe what I'm saying is just a rumor that we heard."

"I can tell you this," Ambroz said. "It didn't come here."

"Any guesses where it might have gone?" Troy said. "If in fact it went anywhere?"

This, in the end, was why they had come here. Ambroz knew where missing things were, things with incredible value. But he was also a man who made his living from being discreet.

Ambroz looked at Troy. One of Ambroz's eyes was normal. The other seemed to swim like a fish behind the monocle.

"Aren't you the arms dealer, Mr…"

For a second, Troy nearly forgot his cover story. "Elon," he said. "I'm an investor. Those weapon sales were just rumors, nasty ones at that."

He smiled broadly.

Ambroz smirked. "No one who comes here has ever committed a crime. But if you were an arms dealer, then you would know more about the Star of Versailles than I."

"Oh? Why is that?"

Ambroz shook his head. "Don't you already know? It's not really a gemstone at all. Or, it's not just a gem."

“You just said it was,” Dubois said.

"I was being polite. If you'll both excuse me, I have a transaction to finalize. By now our buyer, who I know well, has moved the necessary funds."

Troy grabbed Ambroz by the arm. They were the last people in the room, except for the bartender. There weren't even any guards left. This man might as well walk around naked.

Ambroz stared at Troy's hand on his upper arm. The grip there was iron.

"You don't get to walk away," Troy said. "You couldn't run far enough, hide deep enough, or put enough layers of security around you that I won't find you. I'm not your typical cop."

Ambroz’s eyes were wary. He nodded. "I believe that."

“Then tell me what’s going on, and we don’t have to meet again.”

“It’s a weapon,” Ambroz said. "Don't ask me to explain it because I don't know. Weapons are not my field. Supposedly, they're yours."

Troy nodded. That was fair enough. "Weapons are my field."

“Well, then you tell me.”

"The Poitier Family Trust had the gem. They never explained to anyone where they got it, how much they paid for it, or how long they've had it. It's never even been appraised, at least not in a public way."

Ambroz shrugged. "The Poitier family is as corrupt as anyone on the continent. They were probably holding it for the real owners. This is what I've always understood. Perhaps the real owners, or someone like them, have taken it back."

“You haven’t heard anything about it being for sale?”

Suddenly, Ambroz tried to wrench his arm free. Troy let him go.

“It’s not for sale,” Ambroz said. "If it were for sale, I assure you that I would know. But if they wanted to sell it, I wouldn't deal with animals like that anyway."

That was a big statement, coming from a man who had just brokered the sale of a diamond stolen by the Nazis in World War II.

"Had I known it went missing, I would have already left for my rural home in Slovakia. This sale wouldn't have happened tonight because I wouldn't be here. I was told years ago that if the Star of Versailles ever changed hands again, get away from the cities, especially an important city like Prague. Go to the country, someplace no one cares about, and which has no chance of being targeted."

“Targeted by whom?” Dubois said.

“Am I under arrest?”

“Would you like to be?” Troy said.

“Am I under arrest?” Ambroz said again.

Troy just shrugged. "For what?"

He wasn't going to bother telling this man that they were Interpol investigators, and technically they didn't have the power to arrest anyone. There was also no sense mentioning they already had a pretty good idea who took the stone.

Ambroz nodded. "Right. I've done nothing wrong." He gestured around the room. "Please stay as long as you like. Have another glass of wine. Enjoy the view of the city. It was very lovely to meet you both, and I hope you'll keep us in mind if we can meet your needs in the future."

He stalked off. A few seconds later, he passed through a doorway and was gone.

Troy looked at the bartender. The man was balding. He was smartly dressed in a white shirt, blue pants and suspenders. The clothes fit him well.

He held up a chilled bottle of white wine, shrugged and smiled.

"Why not?" Troy said. "One more for the road."

CHAPTER TWENTY SIX

11:20 pm Central European Time
Inside a car
Near Prague-Kbely Airport
Prague, Czech Republic

"It's clear he's expecting something to happen," Jan said.

Troy and Dubois sat in the nondescript sedan they had driven from Berlin. They were parked on a dark side road a few miles from a tiny airport - barely more than a paved airstrip - on the outskirts of Prague.

The airport served as a stopping point for military planes, mostly cargo and passenger. Czech politicians also used the airport. Miquel had obtained the use of the runway and the refueling station for the El Grupo airplane. It was just less than a two-and-a-half-hour flight from here to Istanbul.

They were listening to Jan Bakker report on the activities of Hassan Celik during the past couple of days. "He has a five-year-old daughter named Aysegul. He has a 28-year-old wife named Afet. Our files indicate that Celik and Afet are estranged, possibly because of his work with and proximity to prostitutes. Regardless, in the past 72-hours, Celik purchased plane tickets for his wife and daughter to leave Turkey and go to the United States. They arrived in Akron, Ohio, a little more than 24 hours ago."

"Round-trip or one-way?" Dubois said.

"Round-trip," Jan said. "But that's unlikely to matter. The return passage is three weeks from now. Afet and Aysegul are not American citizens. The tickets were booked suddenly, with little apparent planning beforehand. Many people with the means to do so book round-trip tickets, regardless of their intentions, because one-way tickets arouse suspicion."

"You think he evacuated them before the storm comes?" Troy said.

"Yes, I do," Jan said. "Something along those lines. He has also left Istanbul. As of earlier this evening, he has gone west to a country estate he owns on the European side of the Bosporous Strait. It is located several kilometers outside of the Black Sea beach town known as

Yalikoy, in the foothills of the Strandzha mountain massif. It's a sparsely populated area, two hours drive outside of the city."

"If he's so worried, why not leave Turkey entirely?"

"Celik's international travel is restricted. This appears to be because of his previous imprisonment, his suspected continuing criminal activities, and his ties to human trafficking. The only way he can leave is to smuggle himself out, and he doesn't seem ready to risk that."

"I thought he was a Turkish intelligence asset?"

"I believe he is," Jan said. "That doesn't mean his participation is voluntary, and it doesn't mean they want him to go abroad."

"We need to talk to him," Troy said. "Maybe bring him in if we can."

"Yes. Celik probably organized the theft of the Star of Versailles, and he seems to have knowingly sent Hermann Ranker to his death. Although Celik denied it to Ranker, he might know something about the killings in the South of France, and may even have ordered them. He evacuated his family from Istanbul and left there himself. This suggests that he knows the Star of Versailles in a weapon, or that something dangerous is about to happen."

"In what way could it be a weapon?" Dubois said.

"I misspoke," Jan said. "I doubt very much that it's the weapon all by itself. But it could be part of a weapon or weapon system. Could be its unique composition is a triggering mechanism of some kind. That's unusual, but quite possible, and there are many ways it might work. For example, it is a one-of-a-kind item, and its presence in a certain environment might drive a chain reaction of chemicals that interact with it, causing an explosion."

For Troy, that was a lot to digest, and maybe beside the point.

"Describe Celik's estate if you don't mind," he said.

"I am looking at satellite imagery of it right now," Jan said. "The house is small as estate homes go, five bedrooms, three bathrooms. The land is 10 hectares, or about 25 acres. Most of it is hilly and heavily wooded. There is currently some snow on the ground."

"Do the trees keep their leaves in winter?" Troy said.

"Yes."

That was good. The trees might afford cover to someone trying to approach the house without being noticed.

"I also have specs for the property," Jan said. "The land is surrounded on three sides by a large stone wall, five meters high. There are shards of glass embedded in the stone at the top. There is one gate in or out, and it is an electronic gate controlled from inside the house and protected by security cameras."

“What’s the situation with the part where there’s no wall?”

Dubois glanced at Troy. Even in the dark, he could see that she didn't like the idea of trespassing on this land.

"There's no wall on the south side of the property because the land there is so steep coming down from the mountain, and so densely forested. The house was built in the 1890s, has had numerous owners over more than a century, and no one has seen fit to cut down the forest simply to extend the wall. That includes Celik. The truth is, the property climbs well up the hillside and then fades into the surrounding forestland. If someone extended the wall, it would make it that much clearer where the property ends and public lands begin. With no wall on the forest side, it is easier to imagine you are the master of all you survey."

“Are there security cameras facing the forest?” Troy said.

"Hard to say," Jan said. "I would think so, though if there are, they don't appear to be connected to any outside networks. I can't find their controllers, in other words."

“If a person came in from the air, say a skydiver?” Troy said.

"The person would be exposed. Close to the house, the property is wide open with a few small outbuildings. One is an old carriage house with a trail that connects to the road leading to the front gate. One is a pool house. There is a large in-ground pool, obviously closed this time of year. The other may be a small guest house."

"Does he have protection? Bodyguards?"

“Yes,” Miquel said. "Celik is known to keep a stable of violent, well-armed and extremely dangerous guards around him. The leader of his guards is a 45-year-old Russian fugitive named Stanislaus Prokov. He spent 16 years in a Siberian prison for a Moscow murder he committed in 1999. He was a hitman for hire, working for rising businessmen in the era of lawlessness the Russians call the Wild '90s. He is thought to have committed several other murders for which he was never charged."

“Tell me more,” Troy said.

“The rest of Celik’s security team are Turks," Jan said. "There are three more men, all younger than Prokov, and all of whom were in Turkey’s armed forces during the Turkish invasion of Syria in 2019. All of them were in units implicated in the extensive war crimes and human rights violations the Turks were accused of during that incursion."

Syria raises its ugly head again.

Even worse than Syria reappearing in Troy's life, was the fact that these guys were among the same Turk invasion force who wanted to massacre the Kurdish civilians who were under Troy's protection.

"I don't like these people already."

"It makes sense not to like them," Miquel said. "It makes sense to fear them and be careful about what they might do."

Miquel seemed to be giving Troy free rein here to attack Celik's people and kill them preemptively. "Are you saying what I think you're saying?"

"I'm saying do what needs to be done," Miquel said. "You've done it before. These men are killers. We must reach Celik and find out what he knows. They stand between you and that goal."

"I can't drop straight into their midst, can I?"

"No," Jan said. "There is a better option. About five kilometers up the mountain from the estate, there is a broad meadow. Five kilometers is about three of your miles."

Troy nearly laughed. When talking to Troy, Jan Bakker always referred to miles as *your miles,* as if Troy had invented miles and was the only one on Earth who used them.

"They're not mine, Jan. Hundreds of millions of people use miles."

"The meadow is to the south and the west of the house," Jan said, ignoring that point. "The terrain below there is very steep woods."

Troy was beginning to see how it could be done. "You're saying a person could land in that meadow, then hike downhill to the house?"

"It would be challenging," Jan said. "But a person could do it."

Troy thought about it a long moment.

"I need a sniper rifle," he said. "Bolt action is fine, like an M24. It has to have a telescopic sight, bipod, a large sound suppressor and flash suppressor. That stuff is non-negotiable guys. If I have to shoot to get in there and find Celik, I don't want to get too close, and I don't want the guards to know where the shots are coming from."

Throughout his time with El Grupo, the Europeans had been consistently funny (in the sense of odd, not in the sense of ha-ha) about providing Troy with weapons. If he had to get through four hardened killers, three of whom were combat vets, he couldn't afford to mess around.

They said nothing in response, so Troy continued. "I need an MP5 machine gun, with three or four 30-round magazines. I need at least three incendiary grenades. I need a hunting knife with a sheath I can strap to my ankle. I need a small, concealable pistol that still packs a punch, like a Glock 29. If there's snow on the ground and on the trees, I need a white jumpsuit to help me blend in."

There was a long pause. In his mind, Troy could almost see Miquel and Jan trading looks of exasperation. But it turned out he was wrong.

“Done,” Miquel said. "Jan has typed up all of this. There is an Interpol safe house in Istanbul. Everything you need will be there, exactly as you've ordered it."

“What am I supposed to do,” Dubois said, “while the American hero attacks Celik’s house with this arsenal you’re providing him?”

Troy looked at Dubois and smiled.

"You're going to fly the jump plane," he said. "Miquel, did I mention we need an airplane?”

CHAPTER TWENTY SEVEN

February 17
4:45 am Istanbul Time (3:45 am Central European Time)
The Skies near Yalikoy
The Strandzha Mountains / The Black Sea Coast
Istanbul Province, Turkey

"I don't care if you're a double agent," Dubois said. "You know that, right?"

Troy didn't know what to make of that statement.

"Thank you," he said.

He was sitting in the front passenger seat of a single-engine, propeller-driven De Havilland DHC-2 Beaver. It was a tiny plane, built sometime between 1947 and 1967. Something about that was both reassuring and deeply concerning.

They were pressed shoulder to shoulder in the cockpit. Dubois guided the plane toward the jump site. The sky around them was dark, with auras of light from distant towns. The closest one was probably Yalikoy.

In the small hold behind them, Troy had piled his gear. Parachute, guns (including the requested sniper rifle in its padded case), lights, and a knife. It was open question what Dubois was going to do when he jumped - in planes this small, changes in weight made a big difference to flight characteristics.

"I've known for months," Dubois said. "Well, I suspected. But I gave you a pass because you were cute."

At the Istanbul safe house, Troy had made another call to Missing Persons in front of her. He didn't care at this point. He was tired of keeping secrets, at least from Dubois. While Dubois stood in the same room, Troy had told Persons that the Star of Versailles might be a weapon of some kind. Their efforts to track it down had come to nothing. He was going to Turkey to talk to the man who might have organized the theft.

He told Persons that the gemstone, the weapon, whatever it was, might be in the hands of some dead-enders from ISIS.

He told Persons he was concerned the thing might be in Syria.

“I was afraid of that myself,” Persons said.

“You forgot to mention it,” Troy said.

"Not everything can be shared right away. Believe me when I say that you haven't been the only person out there looking."

“I don’t want to go back to Syria,” Troy said.

Persons said nothing in response to that.

"We still have assets there, yeah? Special Forces, Delta?"

"Some," Persons said. "They don't have a lot of freedom of movement. The place is sliced up between warring parties like a patchwork quilt."

“We might need them to retrieve something for us.”

"It's hard to move around over there," Persons said. "Everything is bogged down. It's not straightforward, like driving from Buffalo to Pittsburgh."

"What about Assad?" Troy said. "Maybe we should tell him."

"Assad has the upper hand, but he doesn't like us very much. He tends not to listen to the things we say."

Troy sighed. "That's what we get for lying all the time. People stop believing us."

"Assad is a ruthless dictator who murders civilians," Persons said. "He's an ally of Russia and Iran." In his world, showing sympathy for the point of view of Bashar al-Assad must be like showing sympathy for the devil himself.

"Haven't seen much of Alex these days," Troy said, changing the subject. There was no sense talking about all the wonderful things allies of America did.

"Alex isn't far. He's been busy. It might surprise you to know we have friends in Romania and Moldova. There's a refugee crisis. Some of our people got trapped inside the quarantine zone. Alex has been bringing them out."

“This might be more important,” Troy said.

"It might be," Persons allowed. "But it's also the first we're hearing of it."

"Colonel, if you'll excuse me," Troy said. "I have to go fall out of an airplane."

"Good luck," Persons said. "Let me know how it goes."

Troy hung up.

Now, in the airplane, Dubois was watching her instruments carefully. The night was nearly black outside of the windscreen. Her hands were small and light on the controls.

“What made you suspect?”

"Alex," Dubois said. "The helicopter pilot. He just kept turning up. New York City. The Austrian Alps. Hong Kong. Albania. Belgrade."

"I barely know the guy," Troy said. "I don't even like him."

Dubois nodded. "He told me."

“He works for them,” Troy said.

She glanced at Troy. "Who are they?"

Troy shook his head. "I don't even know. I'm kind of glad I don't."

“Who is Colonel Persons?”

"He was one of my first commanders in the Navy SEALs. Then he was at Joint Special Operations Command, and brought me there."

“Metal Shop?” Dubois said.

Troy shrugged. "There's no such thing as Metal Shop. Anyway, Persons is a civilian now. He supposedly works for the NYPD."

“Like you did when we first met.”

Troy nodded. "That's right."

“Do they pay you?” Dubois said.

Troy looked at her and grunted. "Does who pay me?"

“Whoever. Are you drawing two paychecks for the work that we do?”

Troy shook his head and smiled. That was one secret he wasn't quite ready to share.

"Three paychecks?" Dubois said. "Money drops to a numbered bank account on the Isle of Man?"

“Agent Dubois, I have to go get ready.”

She let the issue go.

"Be careful, Agent Stark. I don't have a good feeling about any of this."

“Neither do I," Troy said. "Neither do I.”

***

“Over the site in twenty seconds,” Dubois shouted.

Troy waddled to the jump door and slid it open. A burst of cold wind tore in. Everything – the wind, the propeller of the engine – suddenly became LOUD.

The ceiling in this plane was very low. Troy was crouched near the opening. The rifle case was strapped across his legs. The MP5 was strapped to his left arm. The Glock was in one of his jumpsuit pockets. Everything was heavy and cumbersome.

The wind was in his face. Above him, there was the sweep of a billion stars. Below him, there was darkness interrupted by fast-moving clouds. Below that, far below and to the north, perhaps he could see the lights of the beach town, and the vast dark of the Black Sea.

"Ready?" Dubois shouted.

"Yes!"

"Then go!"

Troy half-dove, half-fell out into the void. An instant later, the plane was gone.

He felt the adrenaline rush through his body as he fell. There was a rush of pure speed, the wind howling past her ears. He sensed his heart pounding in his chest. He plummeted toward a cloud bank below. He dropped into them, and the world around him was a blur of black and gray. The cold mist enveloped him like a thick blanket, and the turbulent air churned as he fell through it.

Suddenly, the clouds parted, revealing the white surface far below. Troy twisted his body, angling himself towards the earth. The wind rushed past, tugging at his clothes and hair. Snow and ice pelted him. The wind was deafening now, filling his senses with a constant roar that seemed to drown out all other sound.

The white surface of the ground rushed upward toward him. Everything was white. White on white. The speed was dizzying and increasing every second.

His hand found the cord and pulled.

A second passed, then another. With a sudden jolt, the parachute pulled his upper body backward, kicking his legs out in front of him. He looked up and the chute was open, white against the dark of the sky.

The broad white expanse of the meadow was close below him. All around it, the forests marched off in every direction. The trees were dark, frosted with white, a different look from that of the meadow.

He touched down with a thump. It was a hard impact because the rifle case made it impossible for him to run. He landed and fell backwards onto his butt, the chute drifting down behind him. Thankfully, the snow was soft and deep enough. He looked back as the chute settled on the ground.

His breathing was fast. Great plumes of white steam came from his mouth.

"Stuck the landing," he said.

He untied the heavy rifle case from his legs, shrugged out of his harness, bundled up the chute, and buried it in the snow.

The night air was chilly, and he was sweating. To the east, he fancied he could just see the lights of the plane disappearing back toward Istanbul.

He stared out into the darkness from the high mountain meadow. The wind whipped along the peak above him, the trees rustling and shaking. Far below, straight down through the forest, there was the aura of lights in the sky.

He checked his compass, although he had a good sense of the direction just by feel. The lights were north of here, north and a little bit east. Probably it was the house.

He shifted his gear. Now, the big rifle case and the MP5 were both strapped high on his back. He had grenades in his front pockets. His Glock was at his waist, easy to reach in an emergency. His hands were free.

He went to the edge of the meadow. The woods dropped off, not as steep as a cliff, but not much better. He was three of his miles out, so he risked a quick sweep with a flashlight. There were a few small animal tracks, a fox maybe, but no obvious path down from here.

He took a first tentative step into the snow and found his footing. He pushed between trees, and began the plunge downward. He blundered forward and ever downwards between trees, through snow and dense underbrush. At times the snow was above his calves, almost to his knees. Here and there he passed areas where the ground was bare, where the canopy above was thick, or where wind had brushed the snow off. High above him, the wind shook the trees, bringing a gentle snowfall.

He went on like this for what seemed like a long time. It was hard work. It occurred to him that el Grupo was not the best job to keep you fit, certainly not like the SEALs. The training was not constant in el Grupo. There were no mandates or tests to pass. How strong you were was up to you.

Eventually, he came to the end of it. The forest here was not as dense as above. He pressed himself against a thick tree, and looked around it. Perhaps thirty yards from here, and a full story below him, there was a full break in the trees.

Steam rose from his mouth.

It was the estate. He'd made it without tripping any motion detector lights or alarms. In these woods, motion detector lights would probably go on and off all night long.

He scanned the open area. He could see one of the high walls from here, off to his left. There was a light dusting of snow on the grounds, so there was no telling where the pool was. That might be it off to the right - there was a small, one-story building over there. The main house was diagonally across from him.

The place was lit up. There were double doors leading to a wide stone staircase down to the grounds, maybe three or four stairs. The house was big, not gigantic, two stories high, with lights on in practically every room. Notably dark were a few windows upstairs and on the left side of the house.

If I was Celik, that's where I'd be.

Three men stood around on the back stone steps, talking and smoking cigarettes. They wore heavy coats and had rifles slung on their backs.

Celik had them up late, and he was probably sleeping. Maybe in the daytime, when Celik felt safest, that's when these guys slept. Maybe they never slept.

Troy took a long breath and hunkered behind the tree. He took the rifle carry case off his back, quietly undid the latches and opened it. The pieces of the sniper rifle, along with the accessories, were all snug in their compartments.

Slowly, in something close to absolute silence, he put the rifle together and loaded it. He had a magazine with five rounds. The gun was exactly what he had ordered - telescopic sight, flash and sound suppressors, and a bipod to steady his shot.

He glanced around the tree. The men were still there. They were talking in low voices. It sounded like a murmuring brook to him. Now and then, one of them laughed at what another had said. Plumes of steam came out of their mouths.

Below him a little way was a large rock. There seemed to be a space between trees there. He slid down toward it, staying low, moving slowly. He was white against the snow, but the trees were dark. If he gave himself away, this could be a long night.

When he reached the rock, he lay alongside it for a little while. The MP5 was digging into his back. He breathed carefully through his nose.

He poked his head up. He was still above the men, still back in the woods, but the shot from here was very good.

He brought the rifle up and planed the feet of the bipod onto the rock. He crouched behind it. This was going to happen fast. Three men, and Jan had told him Celik was here with four bodyguards. If he took all three of them, the fight was mostly over.

What if one of these guys is Celik?

No. No way. With a gun strapped on his back?

Troy pointed the sniper rifle in that direction. The three men stood together. Smoke rose between them. Troy got low, looking through the sight. His right hand moved to grip. His finger slipped onto the trigger. His left hand held the barrel.

He put one of the men in the circle. The man's face seemed inches away. The man put a cigarette to his mouth. Troy brought the muzzle down just a bit, centering on the man's chest. The guy was wearing a jacket. No body armor or heavy vest was apparent.

"Old Macdonald had a farm," Troy whispered. "And on that farm he shot some Turks."

Are you an assassin?

That's what Mikey had asked him over the phone.

"No," Troy said now. "I'm not."

Everything slowed down. He took a breath and squeezed the trigger.

The gun kicked.

Chngk!

It barely made a sound.

The man's body jerked, and he fell to the ground.

Troy ejected the spent cartridge, and moved the gun. The two remaining men stared down at the man who had just been shot. Troy put another man's chest in the circle.

Chngk!

The second man dropped. This was like shooting ducks in an arcade.

He moved the rifle, but the third man was gone. Troy peered over the top, but that guy had gotten the message. No sound, no muzzle flash, if he stuck around he was going to die. Troy caught a glimpse of the man bolting up the stairs and into the house.

"Dammit!"

Troy pushed the sniper gun away and went over the top of the rock. He slid over the top and down the other side. He pulled the MP5 down.

The opening in the trees was ahead and below. He dropped down, taking giant sliding steps through the snow.

Two men lay on the steps, writhing like snakes.

Troy's breathing was loud in his own ears. He ran across the open ground, machine gun in front of him.

He dove and slid in the snow at the bottom of the steps.

One of the men he shot lay there, looking at him. He seemed to be trying to dig something out of his coat.

"Don't do it," Troy said. He pointed the MP5 at the guy. "Stop that or I'll kill you right now." If this were combat, a war zone, he would kill the guy without talking to him.

“Don’t you make me regret this?"

The man held up his empty hands. His eyes were flat and resigned, not scared, not angry. His chest rose and fell.

The other man, lying behind him, had stopped moving at all.

Troy crept to the top of the stairs. He took one of the incendiary grenades from his chest pocket. The double doors here were heavy wood with glass windows at the top. It was impossible to guess how thick that glass was. With his foot, Troy opened the door the slightest amount.

TUNK! TUNK! TUNK!

Shots were fired from inside, hitting the door, but not blowing holes right through it. Troy pulled the pin from the grenade, let the compressor fly, then pushed the door hard. It swung open a foot, maybe eighteen inches. He tossed the grenade in, then rolled down the stairs over the two men he'd just shot.

TUNK! TUNK! TUNK! TUNK!

More shots hit the door.

BOOOM!

Light flashed, and the two windows shattered. Flames blasted out. Troy covered his head as shards of glass and chunks of wood from the window frames flew.

Someone inside was screaming, shrieking.

The sound was unreal, like an alarm.

The doors had held. Troy climbed the stairs again, staying low. Then he popped up and ripped the inside with the MP5.

DUH-DUH-DUH-DUH-DUH.

He fired into the flames. All he could see was fire and shadow.

The screaming stopped.

He ducked down again. His breath was LOUD in his ears. He waited. Nothing. No return fire.

"Three men down," he croaked. "Probably three down."

He looked at the two guys on the stairs. The one who was still alive had brought out a pistol from inside his coat. He was facing the wrong way, though.

"Don't do that," Troy said. He drew a bead on the guy.

The man pushed himself and rolled down the last two steps. The gun was in the man's right hand. He brought it up and…

DUH-DUH-DUH.

Troy gave him a quick burst.

"I told you not to do that."

***

"What is it?" the girl Salma said. "What's going on?"

Hassan Celik went to the top drawer of his bureau and pulled the black pistol out of there. It was Czech made, CZUB, a good gun so he understood. He didn't spend a lot of time thinking about weapons. The Czechs made high-quality stuff in general. That was enough to know.

Hassan looked at her. She was a lovely young Syrian. She was still under the covers, pulling them up to her chin as if that was going to protect her.

She was a refugee from the civil war who had been attempting to make it to Europe. She made it as far as Hassan Celik. It wasn't a terrible result, all things considered.

Until now.

Downstairs, there was gunfire.

Hassan flinched. Salma made a squeak like a frightened mouse.

A moment ago, there had been an explosion.

"Put some clothes on," Hassan said. He pointed at the large walk-in closet. "Go in the closet and take the light bulb out. Pull the doors shut behind you. All the way in the back there are some boxes piled on the floor. Squeeze in behind them and pull a few coats down on top of you. Be very quiet. No one has any reason to look in there."

Her big, pretty eyes stared at him. She was indeed beautiful. She deserved a life of some kind, not because of her beauty, but just because of the fact of her. All things, beautiful or not, deserve some kind of life.

An image of his daughter flashed in his mind, a bow in her dark hair.

His little flower. Aysegul.

Hassan regretted everything now. He had made a terrible mess. Even so, if he had it to do over, he would probably do all the same things again, not because they were the right things to do, but because that's who he was.

We are determined from birth. Genes, parents, circumstances, everything.

"Do it! Once you get back there, don't make a sound."

“What about you?” Salma said.

Hassan shook his head. "Don't worry about me. This has been coming."

He was already dressed. He had dressed in seconds as soon as the shooting started. He went to the door to the bedroom and listened. There was a sound of crackling flames. Something was burning. Much of the house was wood.

He glanced back at Salma. She was putting on a sweater. He watched as she pulled on a pair of jeans and went to the closet doors. A second later, she was gone. He watched the light under the doors. Then it went out.

Good enough.

He unlocked the wide door to the bedroom and peeked out.

Stanislaus Prokov was here in the hallway, on the floor, leaning against the wall. Big Stan Prokov, the enforcer, a man who was impossible to kill. He was a tall, broad-shouldered man who began murdering for hire on the streets of Moscow when he was a teenager. He had come of age in the Russian gang wars of the 1990s. He had survived the Siberian prisons. And here he was.

It looked like he had been set on fire. His jacket and shirt were burned away. Bits of the clothes still clung to his arms. His skin was seared both on his upper body and his head. Fine tendrils of smoke were still rising from him. His blue eyes rolled in their sockets and found Hassan.

“Where are the others?” Hassan said.

Prokov’s mouth barely moved. "Dead."

“Oh God.”

“Kill me,” Prokov said. "I can't go to hospital. I am wanted man."

It was amazing that he could even speak.

Hassan shook his head. He moved down the hall. Prokov reached weakly for his leg, but Hassan stepped past quickly.

Red and orange shadows danced at the far end of the hall. A man appeared there. a silhouette. He was tall and well built, all in white. He carried a small rifle, maybe a machine gun, like an Uzi. It was pointed forward in Hassan's direction.

“Don’t move,” the man said.

Hassan pointed his own gun. "Who are you?"

"Police," the man said. "Interpol."

A surge of relief swept through Hassan's body. He nearly fell to his knees. The police! There were so many worse people who could have come.

But if he was the police, why would he kill Hassan’s men?

“What do you want?” Hassan said.

"The Diamond Dogs. You're the leader, right?"

Hassan shook his head. "There's no such thing. It's just a name. It's a fake, designed to throw off computer searches. Something happens, and people think it's the Diamond Dogs. Who are they? No one knows."

The man took a step closer.

"Very clever," he said. "It worked."

“You’re guilty of murder here,” Hassan said.

The man didn’t touch that idea.

“You organized the theft of the Star of Versailles.”

Hassan shrugged. "Yes."

“Who hired you?” the man said.

“They’ll kill me if I tell you.”

“I’m going to kill you if you don’t tell me.”

"You're a cop," Hassan said. "You can't kill me."

“Did someone tell you I was a cop?”

Hassan looked at him. The things he was saying, Hassan couldn't follow.

“You did.”

"I lied. I'm black ops. I work for American intelligence. No one even knows I'm here. There are three dead men downstairs, and the guy behind you doesn't look like he's doing too good. If I kill one more, who could blame me? I need to retrieve the Star of Versailles before something bad happens. They told me to do whatever is necessary."

Hassan was at the end of the line. He recognized that. He was a walking dead man. If it was possible to stop what was coming, that would be a worthwhile thing.

The man stepped further up the hall. He was close now. Tall, very white, he spoke English with some sort of American accent, maybe New York City. Many Turks spoke English, but when they did, they spoke it elegantly, like the better-educated British. The Americans spoke it like they were trying to kill it.

“The Star of Versailles went to Syria,” Hassan said.

The American’s body jerked as if Hassan had shot him.

"There's an archaeological site in Syria. I don't know which one. In the desert, outside Idlib. There's a bomb. It's underground, inside a vault."

“What kind of bomb?” the American said.

Hassan choked back the urge to cry.

"There's a woman in the closet in the bedroom. Don't hurt her. Don't let the house burn down with her inside. She's a good person. She has nothing to do with any of this."

“What kind of bomb is it?” the man said again.

Hassan gritted his teeth. "They took my daughter. I had no choice."

“What kind of bomb?”

Hassan almost couldn’t believe the words coming out of his own mouth.

"It's a radioactive dirty bomb. It's very large, possibly like a doomsday bomb. They made it with stockpiles of the missing Soviet uranium that was stolen in the 1990s, and cobalt which they were mining, in Africa I think. They use large amounts of RDX, which will make the explosion larger and more intense and spread the cobalt further. The cobalt is poison when it's blasted into dust and goes into the air. Obviously, so is the uranium. The idea is that the two poisons will spread over a wide region, carried by the wind."

"Who?" the man said. "Who made it?"

“Al Qaeda.”

“That’s who has the diamond?”

Hassan shook his head. "A man called al Shabah has the Star of Versailles, or soon will. He was in Al Qaeda, but later joined ISIS. There's almost nothing left of ISIS. He survived the war that destroyed the Islamic State. He survived the Russians, the Iranians, the Assad regime, the Kurds and the Americans. He is still alive, and he wants to use the bomb. He has a small militia that fights on. He will finally die this time, and if he gets his way, he will take millions of people with him."

"What does the Star of Versailles have to do with it?"

"It's the trigger. The bomb doesn't work without it. Al Qaeda built the bomb, and they decided not to use it. But you can't just get rid of a bomb like that. So they put the key to using it somewhere safe. Now, the last holdouts of ISIS have the key. They hired me to get it. They took my daughter from me. They left me no choice."

"But how?" the man said. "How does the diamond trigger the bomb?"

Hassan shook his head. "I didn't build the bomb, my friend."

"But you know about it."

"I do," Hassan admitted. "Some."

"Talk or I kill you, and then I'll kill the woman in the closet."

Hassan still had the gun in his hand. He could point it and pull the trigger, but he had no doubt that this man would shoot first. He would see Hassan's hand about to move. He would spot a change in Hassan's face.

The man's eyes gave Hassan nothing. There was no sympathy, pity, remorse, or any human emotion in there at all. Governments created men like this to burn through resistance like flamethrowers. He could kill Hassan and not think about it again.

"You'll never stop them now," Hassan said.

"Why don't you let me worry about that?"

"All right," Hassan said. "Suit yourself. A laser beam. It looks almost like a pen, hand-held, easy to obtain in any advanced country. The kind university professors use to point at the blackboard, only more powerful. It needs a focused beam, about 425 or 450 nanometers in wavelength, which often shows as indigo in photographs. Directed into the Star of Versailles, it will destabilize the cobalt in the diamond, causing a chain reaction. Combined with the explosive power of the RDX…"

He stopped and sighed, partially because talking about it was futile, and partially because he didn't care anymore. "To be honest, I could explain the science to you, but I doubt you would understand it. A huge amount of RDX, a lot of uranium and cobalt, and something to trigger it correctly. You can grasp the potential, I suppose."

"Where is the bomb?" the American said.

Hassan spoke truthfully. "I told you, I don't know. In the desert somewhere. At an archaeology dig. It's been closed because of the civil war. There are many archaeological sites in Syria. If I knew which one it was, they would have killed me."

“You’re lucky they didn’t kill you anyway.”

Hassan shrugged. "Am I? Am I lucky?"

Hassan thought of the wreckage of his life. At least his wife and daughter were safe and far away from here.

“Was the diamond ever in your possession?” the man said.

"Please spare the woman in the closet. She's done nothing wrong."

“Did you ever have the diamond?”

Hassan slumped. There was nothing left inside of him. He was a shell.

"It passed through Istanbul. I gave cover to the men who were transporting it. They went as aid workers in a truck to the frontier at Bab al-Hawa, north of Idlib. I don't know if they made it across or not."

Now he was lying. Of course, they made it across. They took the diamond from the thieves, crossed Europe and entered Turkey with it. They were resourceful. If they couldn't simply drive through the checkpoint, they could use the food, water and first aid supplies to bribe their way across into Syria.

The American was staring at him now. He reminded Hassan of a scientist looking in wonder and horror at an unusually disgusting insect.

"How will you live with yourself if the bomb goes off?"

Hassan shook his head.

“I won’t.”

He raised the pistol.

The American pointed his machinegun.

“Drop that gun.”

Hassan jammed the muzzle of his pistol under his own jaw, pointing it upward into his skull. He had read about this in recent days and even looked at diagrams. This was the best, most effective way to do it. If you were brave and didn't jerk away, the chances of success were about 100%.

“Celik!”

Hassan pulled the trigger.

CHAPTER TWENTY EIGHT

6:00 am Syria Time (5:00 am Central European Time)
A ruined building
Idlib, Syria

“I expected you before now.”

The Ghost was in his blasted and pockmarked private room, in the darkness and shadows of the wasted city. They couldn't risk so much as a candle now.

The young man named Yasser stood before him. Even in the bleak half-light, the Ghost could see that Yasser was covered in grit and soot, his eyes were tired, his body was slumped in near-total exhaustion.

Ali Talib hovered just inside the doorway. Ali moved like a cat, which is why he was still alive. He could cover the distance from there easily.

"The way was difficult," Yasser said. "Nothing prepared us for it. Everything is destroyed north of here. Everything is rubble. We could not bring the truck across the frontier. We traded food and supplies with the border guards for entry into the country. We had to walk through the devastation and the fighting. France to Istanbul, and then to Bab al-Hawa was easier than Bab al-Hawa to here.”

“You have the gifts?” the Ghost said.

“Yes.”

“Let me see them.”

From the front pocket of his torn and dirty jeans, Yasser took out something wrapped in a cloth. He undid the cloth, and held out to the Ghost the thing that had been revealed.

It glowed green, with blue highlights, even in the dark. It seemed almost as if it had a light source inside of it. The Ghost took it in his hand. It felt heavy. He knew it couldn't be true, but it seemed heavier than a brick.

"My God," he said. "It's so beautiful."

Yasser sighed. "I hope I never see it again."

The Ghost wrenched his eyes away from the glowing stone and looked at Yasser.

“And the pens?”

Yasser nodded. "I have them."

He reached into his jacket pocket and came out with two small, colorful cardboard boxes. They were identical, with pictures on each one of what looked like a dark fountain pen, firing a purple beam. There was large white lettering in English on the boxes, and another European language in a smaller font below that.

The boxes were crumpled a bit, but even by themselves, they were almost magical. It had been a long time since the Ghost had seen consumer goods. For a split second, an image of stores filled with bright and colorful products flashed across his mind. He shook that away. It existed, he knew. But it was in another world and on a different path from the one he walked.

“They work?” he said.

"Yes. We tested them. They have small batteries inside. Everything is new and perfectly functional. Do not shine them in your own eyes. The instructions are clear about that."

The Ghost took the boxes and examined them. The gifts almost took his breath away. He was a man steeped in complete faith. He never doubted, not for a moment. But even he was astounded by these things that had come to him.

“No true follower of Allah has ever held more powerful weapons,” he said.

The responsibility was staggering. His body was beginning to tremble.

"Ismail is dead," Yasser said. "He died after we crossed the border."

The Ghost looked at Yasser again.

"I know. I'm sorry. But you may rejoice because your friend is with Allah. Allah laid your path before you."

Yasser nodded. He spoke mechanically, as if his body was still here, but his animating spirit had gone elsewhere.

"He stepped on a mine inside the ruins of a building. We were trying to stay out of sight by passing through open ruins. He did not know how to avoid a mine. It was concealed beneath a metal plate. He was maybe ten meters ahead of me. I saw… it. We are soldiers, but not in the sense of a war like this."

Yasser stared at the floor. The Ghost could see that he was crying now.

"You've done the task that God commanded," the Ghost said. "The honor bestowed upon you is immense."

Yasser said nothing.

Ali Talib was there now, looming just behind Yasser. Quietly, without speaking again, the Ghost took two steps to the side. Ali stepped up, gun in hand, and shot Yasser in the back of the head.

CRACK!

It was a small pistol, and not very loud. In an environment like this, it made almost no impression at all. The bullet hit a wall and whined off into the night.

Yasser jerked, then instantly slumped to the floor. He never knew what was coming for him. If he felt anything, it was for less than a second.

For a long moment, they stared down at the corpse.

"He did great work in the shadows," the Ghost said. "But he would have been a weight, tied around our waists, for us to drag. And he would have suffered. He was suffering already. This was a merciful death."

Ali nodded. "Yes."

The Ghost looked up at Ali. "How many are left?"

"We have a dozen in the streets, holding the line. We have six good men we can take with us. The rest, very few, are sick or wounded."

The Ghost nodded, but the count was grim. They had lost nearly everyone, many of them exceptional fighters, men who gave everything and feared nothing.

"Tell your men," he said. "Rest today, stay in the shade and out of sight, sleep if they can. Eat whatever is left, drink water if they have it. In the early evening, as soon as the cover of darkness comes, we will leave here."

“Very good,” Ali said.

The Ghost gestured at the body of Yasser.

“And get rid of that for me.”

CHAPTER TWENTY NINE

6:35 am Turkey Time (5:35 am Central European Time)
An unnamed road
Istanbul Province, Turkey

“Where are you now?” Miquel said.

Troy had to give him and Jan Bakker credit. They were always in the office. He had them on the encrypted mobile phone, which was riding on his knee. Ahead of him was a narrow road with tracks through the thin crust of snow. There were no lights except the headlights of the black SUV he was driving.

"I don't know. I'm on a back road, headed toward Istanbul. I took our friend's car. He didn't need it anymore."

“Will you go back to our place?”

Troy thought of the Interpol safe house in Istanbul, where he and Dubois had stayed briefly last night. It was a threadbare and underwhelming place. But the thought of laying his head on a pillow, even for a little while, seemed like almost impossible luxury.

"Yeah," Troy said. "I'm tired. This night has taken a bite out of me. First, I need to drop the girl at a hospital. She seems traumatized."

"Girl? What girl?"

Troy glanced at the young woman in the passenger seat. She was wearing a sweater and blue jeans. He made her bring sneakers, and those were on her feet now. She had pretty brown eyes and dark hair. She leaned back and stared into space. She hadn't so much as looked at Troy since they got in the car.

“Woman,” Troy said, correcting himself and Miquel at the same time. "She's Celik’s girlfriend, I guess. He hid her in the closet. She's having a bad night. She saw what was left of him on our way out. Also, the Russian or whoever was still sizzling. There was no way to go around all that. It was right in the hallway. Plus, the house caught fire."

“Jesus,” Miquel said.

"I don't think they have a fire department out there. The place is just going to burn until it stops on its own."

“This is very bad news,” Jan said.

“About the house?” Troy said.

"No," Jan said. "About the bomb."

“Tell me about it.”

"A uranium and cobalt dirty bomb, if successfully detonated, will lead to catastrophe. Winds shift direction in that region all the time. If the wind blows south and west, it will blow radiation into Damascus, Lebanon, and Israel. If it blows east, it will blow radiation into the Kurdish regions, Iraq and eventually Iran. North, and it will blow back into Turkey. If the winds blow directly south, Damascus again, as well as Jordan and Saudi Arabia. There's no easy way to predict which way it would go."

“Sounds great,” Troy said.

"A nightmare scenario is the wind keeps shifting direction, and radiation gets blown gets blown back and forth, all over the place. A bomb like that, assuming it works, will cause widespread death and misery, not to mention confusion and distrust. It could precipitate a war between hostile and heavily armed actors in that region. It is also possible that such a radiation cloud could go around the entire world."

He paused.

"The repercussions would be enormous. Even if the crime was pinned on ISIS, keep in mind that many factions believe ISIS was deliberately created by the CIA to destabilize Syria and the broader Middle East."

Troy thought he'd heard it all. He honestly didn't think he'd heard that one before.

"Like who?" he said. "Who believes that?"

“Oh, no one that important,” Miquel said. "Russia. China. Iran. Hezbollah. Shiite tribes and militias in Iraq. The Assad government. Roughly three-quarters of all Muslims polled worldwide."

“He told me it’s buried at an archaeological site,” Troy said.

“There are hundreds of archaeological sites in Idlib province alone," Jan said. "They are in a state of chaos and disruption since the war started. They've been bombed and looted repeatedly."

"Okay, so we're going to need help," Troy said. "We need an entire army to scour that place."

“It’s not that simple,” Miquel said. "Even if we had the manpower, the war never ended. The country is divided up by factions. Some of the factions are just remnants of previous factions that disintegrated, with no allegiance to anyone. Entire cities are destroyed and full of refugees. The recent earthquakes have made the entire northwestern portion of the country impassable."

Troy shook his head and rolled his eyes.

“I’m aware of that, Miquel. I did a combat tour in that funhouse country."

"There is a possible way to save time," Jan said. "Uranium dust gives off a chemical signal in the air. It can be detected with a laser. There is a tiny, measurable background amount of uranium in the air, everywhere, all the time. Obviously, there is some variability. But suppose there was a much larger amount around a particular antiquities site. It might suggest that area is where the bomb is located."

“How would we measure that?” Troy said.

"Drones," Jan said. "If I can put ten drones with underbelly-mounted lasers in the air, I'll have them search an expanding perimeter from the Bab al-Hawa crossing, outward. They'll have to fly low, but…"

“They’ll get shot down.”

"A few will," Jan said. "Certainly. But maybe not all."

Troy had to admit, it was a good idea. If it would work or not was an open question.

“Are you going to go there?” Miquel said.

Troy looked at the phone.

Aren't you the boss? Don't you assign me places to go?

Not in this case. No boss in their right mind, even the Director of El Grupo Especial, could reasonably say, “Oh by the way, you’re going to Syria.”

On the other hand, Miquel was the one who said, “Oh by the way, you’re going to cholera-infested Romania.”

"I don't want to go," Troy said. "I'm tired. I need some sleep. I don't enjoy Syria. But what else am I supposed to do?"

"You can sleep for a while," Jan said. "It will take me a couple of hours to acquire these drones and get them in the air. It could take hours to detect an unusual uranium fingerprint."

“What if the bomb goes off before then?” Troy said.

"There's nothing you can do," Jan said. "Syria, even northwestern Syria, is too large to simply go there hoping to get lucky."

Troy nodded. He could see the wisdom in that.

“Agent Dubois has the propeller airplane,” Miquel said. "It will save you a lot of time if she…"

"Agent Dubois cannot come," Troy said. "This is an active war zone we're talking about. It is beyond Agent Dubois's training."

"She can fly you to…"

Troy didn't even wait for Miquel to finish. "Miquel, Dubois can't come. I don't know how much clearer I can be about this."

"…an airfield near the border, where you can cross on your own."

Troy sighed. "Okay. I get it. That's fine. As long as being close to the border doesn't give her any crazy ideas."

He hung up the call. He looked at the girl.

"Do you believe these people?"

She stared at him, eyes lost and blank. She really was a very pretty girl. Not much for talking, though. Dubois was a chatterbox compared to her. Troy didn't even know if the girl spoke English or any other language. He had communicated with her in the house entirely by shouting and pointing at things. The pointing, she understood.

"I have one more call to make," he told her.

If she knew what he said, she showed no sign.

He pressed the button for Missing Persons.

"My favorite person," Persons said when he answered the phone.

"I talked to the Turk," Troy said.

"Where is he now?" Persons said.

"He shot himself in the head."

"Why?"

"He did bad things. I guess he felt sorry."

Troy told Persons the entire deal, as he remembered it. Now was not the time to omit anything. After Troy finished, Persons spoke.

"None of the available options are good," he said. "There is no way to enforce a ceasefire, even temporarily. There is no way to get Assad to cooperate. There is no way to evacuate millions of people from an entire region. It'll be very hard for Special Forces to move west through hostile territory, and it would be hard to get their orders changed on the fly anyway. I can work on that, but I can't promise anything."

"I need help," Troy said. "I can't do this by myself."

Then he said something he hadn't thought about saying before. Usually, the person in question just appeared suddenly and mysteriously, like a phantom. Troy had never considered asking for him.

"I need Alex here."

"That I can do," Persons said.

CHAPTER THIRTY

5:55 pm Turkey Time (4:55 Central European Time)
The skies over Southeastern Anatolia
Approaching an unnamed airstrip
Near the Turkey / Syria border

“Would it kill you to appreciate the view?”

The single engine of the tiny De Havilland DHC-2 Beaver droned steadily. Dubois's hands were steady on the controls, guiding the plane through the open skies. The late afternoon sun was beginning to set in a burst of gold against the waning blue.

Stark stared at the horizon ahead.

“I didn't come here for sightseeing.”

Dubois sighed, feeling the weight of the tension in this relationship. She could barely bring herself to look at him, so she focused on the task at hand instead.

“You could be a little more sensitive to other people’s concerns,” she said.

Stark shifted in his seat. "In what sense?"

"You keep blocking me from participating in missions. And then Miquel goes right along with you. It’s all very macho, isn’t it?”

She heard the bitter edge of resentment creeping into her voice.

“What are you talking about, Dubois?”

Tawkin’. Doo-BWAA.

His New York accent became stronger when he was irritated or defensive. She had noticed that before.

"Do you know how it feels to be discarded as not good enough again and again? I bet you don't. You think I can't contribute? Who is flying this airplane right now?"

Stark fell silent. Dubois held her breath, waiting for an answer. Instead, there was only the wide-open sky and fading light, beautiful and indifferent to their bickering.

"I never said you can't contribute," Stark said finally. "I'm going into a combat zone. I don't want you there."

The isolated airfield they were headed for was about ten minutes away. It would be closing in on full dark when they arrived. There were no lights and no air traffic control at this landing spot. They were entirely on their own.

Even so, Dubois felt supremely confident. The Beaver was very forgiving when it came to landing and takeoff. It was a great, great airplane. She had been flying planes like this since she was a teenager.

"All of the violent and dangerous missions we've been on," she said. "They don't count as combat?"

Stark shook his head, the motion barely perceptible in the waning daylight.

“No.”

The brevity of his response hung there in the cramped space between them. His one-word dismissal of everything they had done until now was somehow more biting than if he had tried to mount a detailed argument.

“Well Dubois, you see, in war it’s like this…”

He didn't even bother. He had been to war, she hadn't. In his mind, that was all that needed to be said. It was so arrogant that if she didn't have to fly the plane, she would probably strangle him.

She didn’t say another word.

In a short while, the airstrip appeared, surrounded by scrubland. Dubois brought the plane down in semi-darkness, though she had been dropping the elevation for a while.

She watched the instruments. The plane touched down with a light BANG, and then it was rolling along a pitted and bumpy runway. She pulled it to a quick stop, in case the runway got worse up ahead. Better not to hurt the plane.

Once stationary, she killed the engine, plunging them into total silence.

“How was that?” she said.

Stark shrugged. "Smooth. You're a good pilot. I never said you weren't."

“I’m a great pilot.”

Now he grinned, but he didn't answer. She could picture him comparing her unfavorably to pilots he had known before, fighter pilots, pilots who flew the giant cargo planes, all of them probably men. Even the mysterious Alex, from what she had seen of his helicopter piloting skills, was crazy good.

“Let’s go,” Stark said.

They disembarked, their boots crunching against the gravelly ground. Stark slid open the jump door and grabbed a gear bag. Dubois took in their barren surroundings.

There was the runway itself, long enough to accommodate much larger planes. Maybe fifty meters away, there was a square of beaten earth with windsocks at the corners, which qualified as a helipad. Near the helipad, there was a fenced-in area with a large tank that might be a refueling station. There was no hangar or building of any kind. There were no other planes parked anywhere, not even derelict ones.

"We're ten kilometers from the border," she said.

Stark nodded. He was distant again, as if he had already crossed over that border. He was gone from her.

Come back, Stark.

"I know," he said.

Dubois took the satellite phone from her bag. She punched in a combination of numbers. The static hiss of a connecting call was an oddly comforting sound in the desolate landscape. She glanced at Stark, who stood a short distance away, his eyes scanning the horizon.

"Hello?" a voice said.

"Jan? It's Agent Dubois."

"Ah, Dubois, glad you made it." Jan Bakker's voice crackled through. He sounded fatigued from long hours spent in front of computer monitors.

"I've got news, not all of it good. Is Agent Stark with you?"

"He's here," she said. "Go ahead. We're listening."

Stark drifted back to her, but still didn't speak.

"I've had drones over the target area all day," Jan said, the clatter of keyboard keys punctuating his words. "We lost five to rocket fire from the ground, and one went down from a system malfunction."

"Did you pick up anything?" Stark said.

"Yes. The drones recorded abnormal uranium radiation levels across several archaeological sites. That's troubling on its own, although it could be normal variability. But one site, in particular, was much higher than the others. It's an ancient subterranean bathhouse which dates back to the Roman Empire. It made use of an underground river. The Romans called it Salona Augusta. It's at the heart of a larger excavation site, long abandoned. I obtained high ambient radiation counts with one drone, then confirmed it by doing close passes with two others. The uranium counts there are thirty to fifty times above normal."

"Thirty to fifty?" Dubois said. She didn't like the sound of that. A chill went along her spine.

"It seems that something is there, which doesn't belong," Jan said. "I will send you the coordinates for it."

Stark smiled, but there was nothing cheerful in it. "Thank you."

After they hung up, she and Stark stood together in total darkness. Her feelings for him were a dull ache inside her chest. She didn't want to say the L word. She didn't even want to think it.

"You don't have to do this," she said. "No one is forcing you."

"Circumstances are forcing me," he said. "I don't have a choice."

Dubois chose not to answer that.

In the distance, the thrum of rotor blades grew steadily. Dubois glanced towards the horizon. There were no lights in the sky, and it was too dark to see anything approaching.

As it drew closer, right before it arrived, the helicopter's navigation lights blinked to life, in flashes of red and green. With deft control, the pilot eased the aircraft to the helipad, then onto the ground, its landing stirring a cloud of dust that veiled its descent like a shroud. The chopper powered down, its rotors slowing.

The cockpit door swung open, and a compact figure emerged. She could barely see the details of him in this light. But she knew who it was and what he looked like. He was handsome and somewhat short for a man, probably six inches shorter than Stark, with café-au-lait skin and a dark beard neatly trimmed.

He usually dressed casually, and she pictured him tonight in loose pants and a light jacket, with soft suede boots on his feet. She pictured him reading a book with a nice cup of coffee. He was the farthest thing from the soldier type. Her own father was a French paratrooper, and he had been big and broad, almost as big as Stark.

"Has Alex been in combat?" she said.

Stark shrugged. "I would say Alex has been in just about every situation imaginable."

"So you don't know?"

Stark shook his head. "I don't know anything about him. I don't even know if Alex is his real name. I tend to doubt it."

Without wasting a moment, Alex walked to the nearby fenced enclosure adjacent to the helipad. He carried a pair of heavy bolt cutters in one hand. He lifted them and snapped the lock on the gate with practiced ease. The metal gave way with a bell-like clink that echoed faintly in the open air.

Alex worked quickly yet methodically.

Dubois watched, arms crossed, as Alex lifted the steel lid from its resting place atop the fuel tank inside the enclosure. He reached in and extracted a hose, its length snaking out behind him as he maneuvered it towards the idling helicopter.

The hose connected with a snap, and in a moment, there came the sound of fuel coursing into the aircraft's tanks.

Dubois leaned against the cool metal of the plane.

"I don't like this."

Stark met her eyes, but he didn't speak. He moved closer to her, and they stood facing one another.

Dubois shook her head. "I'm afraid," she said. "I feel like you're going to die this time, and I'm not going to be there to help you."

Her hands clenched into fists at her sides.

Don't cry. Don't do that here.

Before Stark could respond, Alex's voice cut through their little huddle.

"Hey lovebirds!" he shouted. "We're on the clock here, and it's getting late."

"I'm not going to die," Stark said. "You'll see me again."

He turned away and headed toward the waiting chopper. She watched him go, her heart pounding in her chest. Then, without another word, without even looking back, he climbed aboard. Alex followed suit, sealing the cabin door behind them.

The engines came to life as Dubois stood alone on the deserted airstrip, the wind from the rotors whipping her hair and her clothes. Tears blurred her vision now, hot against her cheeks, as the helicopter lifted off the ground.

In a minute, the chopper became nothing more than a speck against the dark sky. Dubois stood alone a moment longer. To fly back to Istanbul, she would need to stop to refuel at a legitimate airport along the way.

Or maybe you can refuel here.

She stared at the fenced-in enclosure and noticed something strange. Alex had made no attempt to close it again. He had cut the lock, but he didn't even try to pretend the thing was closed.

Wiping her tears on the sleeve of her jacket, she walked over to investigate.

Inside the fence, she found the pumps as Alex had left them: one for kerosene-based jet fuel, still reeking from its recent use, and another for aviation gas - avgas, the kind her plane used. She thought of it as "her plane" now.

Her hand reached out, fingers tracing the familiar contours of the avgas pump. She pulled the handle and the pump came to life.

"I'll see you again, you big dummy," she said, speaking out loud, practically shouting. It didn't matter because there was no one here to listen. Not only did she have all the fuel she needed, Jan had sent the coordinates of the uranium-rich archaeology site to both Stark and her.

“I’ll see you in Syria.”

CHAPTER THIRTY ONE

6:10 pm Syria Time (5:10 am Central European Time)
A footpath
On the outskirts of the city of Idlib
Syria

They passed like shadows.

The moon, a thin crescent barely visible in the evening sky, cast an eerie light over the ruins of Idlib. The Ghost and his men walked in single file, a silent procession.

The Ghost walked fourth, in the middle of the group. The lieutenant, Ali Talib, was there just ahead of him, his presence as steady and reliable as always. Six more men, three in front and three in back, shrouded in black and armed to the teeth, made no noise as they stepped deliberately along the footpath leading eastward.

As they weaved between the skeletal remains of buildings, the distant sounds of battle reached their ears. Gunfire erupted intermittently, playing a staccato rhythm. The heavy WHUMP of Assad's artillery resonated through the night, shaking the very ground beneath their feet.

The Ghost felt an odd sense of detachment. He was aware of the violence unraveling mere kilometers away, where his remaining fighters engaged with the enemy. The men had made a frontal attack to the west.

At the level of tactics, it must seem insane, desperate, even suicidal. At the level of strategy, it was a diversion which allowed this smaller group to escape the city. Well, behind them, something large blew up. The Ghost didn't even turn to look.

Ali Talib glanced back at him, nothing of his face showing except his eyes. There seemed to be a silent question in his gaze. The Ghost nodded, acknowledging the sacrifice of their brothers-in-arms.

"Do not lose hope," he said, his voice just above a whisper, but loud enough for everyone in the line to hear him. "The bravest heart is the one that stays close to Allah."

The Ghost knew that whatever lay ahead, his men would go on without hesitation. He spoke as much for himself, and for the men fighting and dying right now in the city streets, as he spoke for these men here.

They moved like spirits in the night, and left the dying city of Idlib behind. Within the folds of the Ghost's black tunic rested the Star of Versailles, its weight light but its burden immense.

His fingers brushed against the fabric, feeling the outline of the diamond. Alongside it, concealed in another pocket, were the laser pointers. In the quiet moments between the distant sounds of gunfire and artillery, the Ghost summoned silent prayers to Allah.

He prayed not just for victory or survival, but for the moral strength to wield the power he had been given, and the wisdom to understand the intricate machinations of the lasers when their time came.

The sound of fighting faded into the distance, replaced by the crunch of gravel as they crossed the desolate Syrian countryside. A slight breeze whispered across the barren landscape as a seed of doubt took root in The Ghost's mind.

The existence of the dirty bomb had been a specter haunting his thoughts ever since he first heard of it in the damp and fetid concrete cell blocks of Camp Bucca. Among the screams of torture right nearby, there were whispers among the prisoners - a mix of fear, awe, and the siren call of ultimate power. Knowledge of the bomb became embedded in his mind at that time.

But did he dare believe in it? After all, the men in this prison were undergoing horrors that would make them say anything, accuse anyone, reject and offer their own children in exchange, then beg for death itself, if only to make it stop. Why wouldn't they tell of the bomb?

"It exists," an elder with a white beard and weathered face told him. The man had been beaten severely, and his closed right eye was a mass of swollen flesh and pus. "But we must never use it."

"Why? Look at what these devils are doing to us."

The old man shook his head. "We are not out to destroy the world," he said, his voice echoing across the years. "We are not out to exact revenge for these crimes. We are out to save this wicked world from itself."

Perhaps that was true. But perhaps this world was beyond saving. Would Allah have given them the weapon, if the world was worth saving? Would Allah have placed the tools to detonate the weapon in the Ghost's hands, if he was not to use them? The Ghost had survived countless battles. Yet here he was, alive, healthy and uninjured, when so many others, on all sides, were gone.

Why?

As if in answer, the dark sky split open with the rage of conflict. A formation of jet fighters streaked overhead, their engines a horrible roar. The Ghost paused, his gaze lifting to follow their trail. There was beauty everywhere, a terrible beauty even in these weapons of the enemy.

They flew so fast that they were gone in mere seconds. A moment later came the ground-shaking roar of an explosion on the horizon, its flames a monstrous bloom against the night.

He spares you to perform the appointed task.

"The fighting is close," Ali said, his voice utterly calm. "Some of our brothers fight on in the desert, and Assad will root them out if he can. We know that Assad's forces have taken positions in the hillsides above the ancient site."

"We will slip through under their noses," the Ghost said. "We have Allah's protection."

They walked on. In time, the moon cast its pale shadow over a field of demolished stonework, a landscape of ancient ruins, now utterly destroyed. To the north lay the dark shadow of the hills where Assad's men crouched like cowards.

"Spread out," the Ghost commanded in a subdued tone. "Find the entrance. Do not risk a light." His men dispersed silently among the debris.

The large expanse, once a testament to human achievement, lay desecrated, several hundred meters of history turned to rubble. The Ghost approached what remained of an ancient amphitheatre, Ali Talib by his side. The curved rows of stone seats were now fractured and jagged, like fingers of the dead reaching to the sky.

The Ghost grunted. It was incredible, this theatre. Two thousand years had passed, and still it was here.

“They were unbelievers, the ones who built this place,” he said, his voice low, as he traced his fingers along a cracked stone.

"Yes," Ali said. "The Prophet had not yet come."

For a fleeting moment, the Ghost allowed himself the indulgence of imagination. He pictured the amphitheatre as it might have been: vibrant with color and movement, resonating with the voices of actors and the applause of an audience. It was a stark contrast to the ruin before him - a cultural memory destroyed by endless war.

He thought of the Taliban in Afghanistan - extremists who had dynamited giant, ancient statues of the Buddha erected by a previous culture. The Ghost was not that rigid type of believer.

His interpretation of the Quran rejected modern Western degeneracy, of course. And he had murdered many enemies of Allah, including apostates who had turned their backs on the true teachings. But he would never try to erase the past. He accepted that cultures existed before the wisdom of the Great Prophet was offered, and that those cultures, however misguided, were part of the endowment that Allah bestowed.

He laughed, very quietly, and only for a second. He liked history.

A call went out, echoing off the ruins. It was too loud, perhaps, but it was also a sound the Ghost longed to hear.

"They found the entryway," Ali said.

The Ghost felt a jolt, as if the words had turned his blood to ice. He stood motionless, absorbing the weight of the discovery. Everything had led him here, to this precise moment.

"Let's see it," he said.

They crossed the terrain to where the other men had gathered. There was a vertical fissure in a wall, a crack that led downwards. With deliberate care, they descended through it one by one. Rocks were kicked loose by their feet and pulled down by their hands as they went. The structure was fragile.

As they lowered themselves, one of the men in the front lit a flashlight. A few seconds later, another man did the same. The Ghost did not forbid it. They were underground now, out of sight of any watchers on the surface. The walls opened up around them. They picked their way down to a broad stone staircase, worn by the ages, but as wide and grand as the stairs in a palace.

They made two turns, each stairway long, passing deeper into the earth. Suddenly, they reached the bottom, and the subterranean bathhouse unveiled itself. The men murmured among themselves in a sort of wonder. The arched ceilings soared above their heads. The stone baths were still here, and their flashlights cast quivering reflections on the dark water. There was water, even now, after the passage of millennia. The place was an engineering marvel.

The Ghost's gaze landed on the object of their quest - the bomb. It loomed large, like a whale resting on a thick wooden table that seemed dwarfed by its enormity. Its metal skin glinted dully under the beam of their lights. The marks of the welding that constructed it were clearly visible.

Above the bomb, a funnel-like hole in the ground stretched upwards toward the surface. Instinctively, the Ghost knew that the hole would concentrate the blast and drive it upwards into the sky.

But it was the bomb itself that commanded his attention. He approached it with reverence as he retrieved the Star of Versailles from its hiding place inside his clothes. There was a sort of alcove or indentation in the front of the bomb, with a small hole leading inside that would absorb and direct the energy of the diamond and its other components.

The Star, revealed now, flashed green and blue as it caught stray beams of light.

The Ghost's hands trembled - just slightly - as he held out the gem, manipulating it, coaxing it gently into the spot designed to receive it. When it settled perfectly into place with a soft click, a hush fell over the assembled men.

There was no sound at all for a long moment.

“Mashallah,” Ali Talib said.

God has willed it.

CHAPTER THIRTY TWO

6:45 pm Syria Time (5:45 pm Central European Time)
Approaching the Roman baths at Salona Augusta
Idlib Province
Syria

“Watch it!” Troy said.

His knuckles were white on the grips of his seat, his eyes locked on the rocky terrain flashing beneath them. The hills rose like the backs of slumbering beasts on either side of them, as the helicopter hugged the ground, weaving through a serpentine valley. Sudden outcroppings of stone seem to leap out of the shadows like aggressive animals. They were going fast.

"Relax," Alex said. "I know what I'm doing."

The rotors sliced through the air mere feet from the steeply sloping ground, setting loose cascades of pebbles that rattled down the hillsides.

Nap-of-the-earth flying, a technique to avoid enemy radar detection. Troy hadn't missed this kind of thing.

They emerged from the confines of the valley, and the world spread out into open land beneath the cloak of night. They stayed low, nearly skimming the tips of wild grasses brushing against the underbelly of the craft. Being out of the gorge offered some relief, but the openness brought a sense of vulnerability as well.

They were visible out here, and Troy didn’t like that feeling either.

The radio crackled to life inside their headsets, a voice speaking in rapid Arabic cutting through the chops of the rotors. Alex didn't respond, and flicked a switch instead, silencing the call.

"I don't really speak Arabic," he said with a shrug, though his eyes never left the dark horizon. "Anyway, it's probably Assad's people. I doubt I could tell them something they want to hear."

The desert stretched out ahead of them.

“How long?” Troy said.

Alex glanced at his instruments. "Five minutes."

Alex was almost certainly NOT the man's name. The two were not friends. They were not partners. They were thrown together, again and again, because the skills of one fit the skills of the other, like a hand inside a glove. Troy wasn't even sure he liked Alex. Alex worked for Missing Persons, and Troy was fed up with Missing Persons.

The chopper was slowing.

“We’re here,” Alex said.

The ancient ruins stood like specters in the moonlight, the remnants of a civilization long crumbled to dust. Alex skirted the edge of the debris, looking for a place to put the chopper down.

"Look alive," Troy said, his eyes scanning for any sign of people on the ground. If this was the right place, the ISIS fighters were probably already here.

"You look alive," Alex said. "I need a place to land."

A sudden flash split the darkness, followed by the high whine of artillery. A rocket streaked past, missing the chopper by maybe ten meters.

"Oh man," Troy said. "Here we go again."

In the distance, back the way they had come, a barrage of rocket fire let loose. There were hills back there, but Alex had crossed them deep inside a ravine.

“Damn it to hell,” Alex said, although his voice was as calm as before.

He banked hard to the right, and the chopper lurched violently upward. The rockets rained down on the archaeology dig. A line of explosions marched from left to right, further obliterating things that were already ruined.

"Drop this thing!" Troy said. His voice was raised almost to a shout. Alex's calmness was starting to freak him out. "We're on someone's radar. We need to get out of this thing and away from it. Drop it now!"

"It's a nice bird," Alex said. "I hate to lose it."

“Put it down!”

Alex brought the chopper straight down with an expert touch. He hovered above the ground, but only for a few seconds. As soon as it touched the ground, both men were in motion. Troy grabbed his MP5 and his gear bag and blasted the door open. He dropped to the ground, ducked low so the spinning rotors wouldn't decapitate him, and ran.

"Move! Move! Move!"

Alex was shouting as they sprinted in opposite directions away from the chopper. Troy could hear him from here. It was a terrible idea to shout.

“Shut up!” Troy hissed at him.

WHUMP.

The sound was deafening - a concussive wave of heat and force. Troy hit the dirt. He glanced back for half a second, just in time to watch the bird burst into a fireball, shards of metal hurtling through the air.

Troy wedged himself into some crack in the earth and curled into a tight ball.

A moment later, the worst of it was over. Now, the chopper was just a burning husk of its former self. It looked a bit like a Halloween jack-o-lantern.

“Stark!”

"Here!" Troy hissed. "Stop shouting like that!"

It was too late. From somewhere across the strange landscape, a burst of machine gun fire rang out. Troy didn't see the muzzle flashes. He was on the other side of some mound or hillock of stone from it.

They were just probing. They had seen the chopper get hit. They heard the voices calling to each other. They knew that Troy and Alex were here.

“So much for the element of surprise.”

Troy's ears rang, and the acrid smell of burning fuel stung his nostrils. Men were shouting to each other somewhere nearby, rough guttural voices in a language Troy did not understand.

A shadow moved to his right. He turned the MP5 on it. He waited… waited…

The shadow took the form of Alex running along the side of the mound. He dove, sliding on the sharp stones, just as more gunfire broke out from across the way. They must have seen the moving shadow. Bullets whined off the ruins.

Now Alex was next to him, on the ground, breathing hard.

“I think we’re in trouble,” he said.

“I’m going to have to kill those guys,” Troy said flatly.

“You do you,” Alex said.

He climbed to a sitting position next to Troy.

“You ready to move?” Troy said.

Alex looked at him. "Do I have to?"

Troy shrugged. "No. But they know where we are. No doubt they're working their way around, looking to get an angle on us. If you stay here, you're going to die."

"Let's go," Alex said.

"You have a gun?"

Alex held it up. Troy recognized it right away. It was a Glock 17, with an extended double-stack magazine sticking grotesquely out the bottom. It was matte black, so it wouldn't reflect light. It was a very good gun, maybe not a war zone gun, but good nevertheless. Troy had the MP5, two more grenades, and his own Glock.

He might borrow the 17 if things got sticky around here.

"How many rounds in the magazine?" he said.

"Thirty-three."

Troy nodded. "Good man. Do you have any extras?"

"Extra what?"

Troy nearly laughed. "Bubble gum."

"I don't have any gum."

Troy shook his head. "Never mind. Let's move it."

They started out, moving to the left, staying low. Troy's breath came in ragged gasps as he and Alex maneuvered around the jagged stones, the shadows of the ancient ruins looming like sentinels. Now and then, they stopped, and Troy peered through cracks in the stone, scanning for their opponents.

The sky briefly turned to day as a flare arced overhead, bathing the desolate landscape in a stark, eerie light.

"Get down!"

Troy shoved Alex to the ground just as machine gun fire shredded the silence, bullets chipping stone and kicking up clouds of dust.

DUH-DUH-DUH-DUH-DUH.

Alex screamed - a shrill sound that cut through everything and made Troy's heart skip wildly.

"Shut up!" he barked. "Stay down!"

"I'm hit!" Alex said.

"I know that," Troy said.

He moved like a snake, whipsawing along, belly to the ground. Those guys were close, on the other side of this mound, and maybe twenty meters on. Trading tit for tat machine gun fire wasn't going to clear them out of there.

His hand found the weight of a grenade in the front pocket of his vest. Troy hadn't used these grenades before last night. They had been waiting for him at the safe house in Istanbul before he and Dubois had flown up to Celik's place.

Miquel had promised him grenades. These were grenades and a half.

Troy pulled the pin on the grenade, let the compressor fly, and gave the thing a good hard toss over the side. He heard it bounced across the stones.

BOOOM!

He hit the ground again, the explosion raining tiny pellets and heavier chunks down on him. Flames lit up the sky.

Someone started shrieking over there.

Then Troy was running back along the mound as bullets strafed where he'd been only seconds ago.

WHUMP!

Another rocket hit the ground near the burning helicopter. It sent tremors through the ground.

"Come on!" Troy grabbed Alex by the jacket and dragged him along, Alex's movements stiff and clumsy.

"I'm hit!" Alex said, his voice edged with pain, as if that earned him the right to relax in one spot for the rest of the night. It wasn't going to work that way.

“I know!”

They stumbled and scrambled across the battered rocks.

A concussion grenade detonated right where Troy had just been. The impact threw jagged shards of stone like lethal confetti. The shockwave hit them, knocking them off their feet, stealing the air from their lungs.

Troy lay on the ground, spitting dust as he tried to regain his bearings. Every instinct told him they had to keep moving. But he had to look at Alex's wounds first. Alex might not be able to run in another minute.

“It was a mistake coming here,” Alex said.

Troy nodded. "Yeah." Coming to Syria was always a mistake.

The machine guns opened up again, a bunch of them at once. This time, Troy could see the muzzle flashes. Across the way, a group of men were firing into the air.

DUH-DUH-DUH-DUH-DUH.

Troy's head snapped up. Behind them was another sound. He listened closely.

DUH-DUH-DUH-DUH-DUH-DUH.

The men were firing at something.

There was a brief window of silence. The sound was there again, the unmistakable drone of a piston-fired propeller engine in the sky.

His eyes narrowed as he spotted the silhouette of a very small, very slow plane careening toward the ground. They were shooting at an airplane.

“Tell me she didn’t,” he said.

He watched, heart in his throat, as the aircraft descended rapidly, chased by the angry staccato of gunfire. The plane hit the desert with a brutal impact, sparks and flame streaking into the darkness like a dying comet. It skidded along the ground and came to rest fifty meters from the burning helicopter.

“Is that Dubois?” Alex said.

“I hope not.”

“I left the gate to the fuel station open for her.”

Troy looked at him. He almost couldn't comprehend what Alex had just said. He could have just as easily said, "I flew in from Mars on a giant pig."

“Why would you do that?” Troy said.

Alex shrugged. "I thought we might need her."

Treachery everywhere. Troy wasn't sure how much more betrayal he could take. He pulled out a penlight with trembling fingers, flicking it on to assess the damage done to Alex. The pale beam revealed gashes ripped deep into Alex's skin.

Troy sighed in something like relief.

"It's not terrible," he said. "It's your lower arm, and it's your calf. I can tie them both off. I've seen a lot worse. You're not going to bleed to death."

“Am I going to lose the limbs?”

"I don't know," Troy said, answering in all honesty. "I guess it depends on how long we're stuck here."

“Oh God,” Alex said.

WHUMP!

A shell exploded nearby, the force hurling fragments of stone through the air. They pelted Troy's back and Alex's prone figure.

"It hurts! I'm going to lose my leg. I know it."

"Okay, shut up," Troy said. "I don't want to hear about that."

Alex's teeth gritted against the pain, his breaths shallow and rapid. "I hate combat. I hate bleeding!"

Dubois emerged from the darkness like a specter, her form barely distinguishable against the darkness. She hit the ground with a roll that kicked up dust and debris, coming to a stop inches away from where Troy knelt beside Alex.

Machine gun fire tore up the night again. Bullets chipped stone apart just above their heads. A landslide of dust and tiny rocks fell down on them.

“How did you find us?” Alex said.

She gestured at the penlight in Troy's hand. "That thing lights the place up like the Eiffel Tower at night."

Troy snapped it off, plunging them into darkness again. Coronas of light were stitched onto his retinas.

"Didn't I tell you not to come here?" he said to Dubois. "What did I say? I said don't come here. It's a war zone."

Dubois ignored him. She gestured at Alex.

“What’s wrong with him?”

"He got shot," Troy said. "It's probably not fatal."

“I’m going to lose my leg,” Alex said.

Dubois didn’t hesitate, shrugging off her pack and pulling out a first aid kit.

"Why don't you let me deal with that, and you go deal with them?" She nodded toward the mound of rubble and the unseen assailants beyond it.

“They shot my plane down.”

Troy shook his head. "I told you not to come here."

Somewhere up the line, another concussion grenade detonated. They were probing again, trying to anticipate where Troy was going next. That decided him. The bad guys were looking. Eventually, they were going to find.

"All right," he said. "You kids have fun."

He moved right this time, instead of left. Slithering over the uneven ground, Troy crept towards the edge of the rubble, his movements deliberate and silent. Every sense was heightened. It was almost like he was an insect with antennae, and he was feeling for the enemy's vibrations.

He peered cautiously over a chunk of ancient stone.

And saw them.

Three men were over there, three silhouettes hunkered down, scanning the darkness. But they were looking the wrong way. Troy was on their left flank, and even a little bit behind them.

It was a gift, one that wouldn't last. Now was the time.

RIGHT NOW.

He brought the MP5 around. He breathed deeply.

He popped up, firing instantly.

DUH-DUH-DUH-DUH-DUH.

He hosed them with gunfire. They didn't even get the chance to turn. Two bodies went down immediately. The third man lurched away.

Adrenaline pumping, Troy went over the stonework. He sprinted toward the two downed men. Both were writhing and squirming.

He ran up to them and pulled the Glock.

BANG! BANG!

Two shots into one head, finishing him.

BANG! BANG!

Two shots into the other.

He ran on. The limping figure stumbled ahead, leaning heavily on the ancient stones to keep himself upright.

Troy followed, hanging back just a bit, every muscle coiled tight as he stalked his prey. He could take the guy now, but he wanted to see where he was going.

As Troy watched, the man vanished into a narrow fissure in a stone wall. A faint glow came from there, as if there were lights on inside.

The man squeezed himself through, in obvious agony, and then was gone.

Troy crept to the opening.

He paused at the edge, his entire body tingling.

CHAPTER THIRTY THREE

7:25 pm Syria Time (6:25 pm Central European Time)
The Roman baths at Salona Augusta
Idlib Province
Syria

"Fools rush in…" Troy said quietly.

He crouched near the opening, unwilling to go inside. That would be a good way to get shot to ribbons. The fissure seemed to lead downwards into the earth, rather than horizontally into the wall.

It made sense. There were supposed to be underground baths here.

He held his third and final grenade in his hand. He had a moment of hesitation. If there was a nuclear weapon down there, a radioactive dirty bomb, what would this grenade do to it?

Nah, that's silly.

The thing needed a trigger. That's why they went to the trouble of stealing the Star of Versailles in the first place.

He held the grenade up to his mouth and kissed its metal surface.

"That's for luck," he told it.

Combat would drive anyone insane. And quickly, too.

He pulled the pin. It came out with a soft click. He let the compressor go and lobbed the grenade through the fissure. For a second, he watched it go tumbling down, disappearing into the earth.

Then he dove backward and crawled for cover.

The explosion was a monstrous roar, shaking the ground beneath him. Rocks and debris hailed down around him.

As the dust settled, Troy felt the presence before he saw it. Dubois was in a deep squat near him, using some tall rocks for cover. Her shadow seemed to dance in the flames that were surging up from underground.

He wasn't remotely surprised to see her there.

"How's Alex?" he said.

He looked back at where the fissure had been. Now it was a wide, smoldering gash, like the entrance to a cave with a ring of fire around it.

"He's fine," Dubois said. "He's in pain, but he's not going to lose any limbs. He's a bit of a crybaby, to be honest. I haven't seen that side of him before."

Troy nearly smiled. Now wasn't the time.

He gestured at the opening. "Want to go down there?"

She shrugged. "After you."

Troy's boots crunched on the scorched earth as he took point, descending into the gaping maw that had once been a solid wall of stone. Dubois followed, maintaining some distance behind him.

The once-hidden stairwell carved by ancient Romans appeared below them, its wide stone steps beckoning them deeper into the earth. The air grew cooler and more humid. Troy took the steps lightly but slowly, the snout of the MP5 poking out in front of him.

Halfway down, three dead bodies lay sprawled across the steps. Their limbs were contorted unnaturally, halos of blood around them.

Troy stepped over the corpses, and behind him, Dubois did the same. In a few more moments, they reached the bottom. The space was vast and open. Archways disappeared into the darkness. The stone baths were at their feet. Some of them still held water. In fact, somewhere down here was the sound of water trickling.

The only light was from a single lantern, the old-school kind, with an open flame at the end of a wick. Figures cast by the flame danced on the walls like an eerie performance of shadow puppets.

A man was there, dressed head to toe in black, his back to them. He was far enough away from, and below, where the grenade exploded, that it didn't seem to have impacted him. He stood in front of a large metal object that bore an uncanny resemblance to a giant, welded football. He could have been a priest of sorts, and the metal ball his god.

The man fidgeted with a small device in his hands.

Troy looked again. The thing was a lot like a penlight, or a laser pointer. He grunted. The incredible story that Hassan Celik had told him was true. At the very least, these people believed it was true.

Troy lifted the MP5 and sighted. He stepped a bit closer, moving like a cat.

A thin, piercing beam of light suddenly shot from the device in the man's hand. In a strange way, the light was dark, barely brighter than the darkness in this chamber.

Indigo. He said it would be indigo.

For some reason, or no reason, Troy was distracted by that laser beam. The beam hit the surface of the metallic football, skimming over it.

"Hey!" Troy shouted. "Put that thing down."

The man ignored him.

Just shoot him. Get this over with.

The beam found its target. The diamond. The Star of Versailles was on the bomb, seemingly embedded in its side. When the dark beam hit it, the diamond began to glow, green yes, but also a strange and magnificent shade of blue.

"All right," Troy said. "I'll shoot him."

He sighted again.

BOOM!

Something hit him from behind with terrible force. Troy went sprawling to the bath deck. His gun skittered away, across the stone floor, and came to rest inches from the water's edge. Troy rolled over, and a large silhouette loomed over him. Then the weight of the man crashed onto his chest, driving the air from his lungs.

"Dubois!" he gasped. "Stop that guy! Don't let him shine that light!"

Dubois sprang into action, sprinting madly toward the man in black. As she closed the distance, she launched herself into the air, legs extended in a perfect arc. Her boots connected with a solid thud against the man's back. The impact sent him stumbling forward, the beam of the laser flying from his hand then flickering out.

Troy had a split second to think:

Way to go, Dubois!

The man who had jumped Troy pushed himself to his feet. He was also dressed in black. He took a step back, then fished inside his tunic for a few seconds and came out with a small gun. Before he could point it, Troy launched himself across the ground. Then he was at the man's legs. He gripped the man behind the knees and lifted him.

The guy was big and heavy. He fell backward, landing on his back on the stone floor. His gun bounced away and then slid into one of the baths with a splash.

Troy climbed on top of him, but the man was strong. He tossed Troy off, and scrabbled backwards and away on his hands and feet.

He was crawling like a crab toward Troy's MP5.

Troy jumped up, took two steps, leapt, and landed on the man. Their arms locked up. They wrestled on the ground, arms and legs grasping and clawing. They grunted and gasped in each other's ears.

The man shoved Troy off again. Troy landed on his back. This might be the strongest man Troy had ever fought.

The man climbed heavily to his feet. His dark eyes stared down at Troy.

With a surge of adrenaline, Troy rolled over to one knee and then launched himself. He hooked his arms around the man's knees again. He screamed as he lifted the man one last time, as high as he could. The man fell backward, at a steeper angle this time.

His head cracked against the stone floor.

Troy was on him then, delivering a rapid succession of punches. There was no style, there was no one-two. He just pummeled the guy, shot after shot. The man's big hands reached for Troy. Troy slapped one down. The other grabbed Troy's neck from the back. The hand there was like a savage claw, digging into the flesh. It felt like it might tear Troy's spine out.

Troy nearly screamed. He wrenched the hand away with both of his own hands.

BAM! He punched the guy again, a hard right to the face.

The man's eyes were going blank. Troy grabbed the guy by the hair, leaned his head back and punched him in the throat. Once, twice, three times.

The final punch landed with a dull crunch.

The eyes were looking at nothing.

Troy collapsed on top of the guy. Troy's heart pounded, his breaths came in sharp rasps. He lay on the guy's chest, straddling him. The guy didn't move at all.

Troy put two fingers to the artery in the guy's neck. Nothing.

Get up! Get up! This isn't over.

He turned just in time to see the other man had recovered. He had a new laser pointer in his hand. A cold dread settled in Troy's stomach as he watched the man aim the dark light at the diamond. The gemstone responded instantly, beginning to glow and pulse ominously.

Dubois was nowhere in sight.

"Damn it."

The glow intensified, spreading across the entire bomb. It bathed the subterranean chamber in an otherworldly light, revealing that the baths went on and on underground, into an uncertain distance.

Troy rolled off the big man's body and pulled the Glock.

He put the man with the laser pointer in his sights, and squeezed the trigger. He fired again and again, the shots echoing deep into the subterranean chamber.

BANG! BANG! BANG! BANG!

The man staggered but remained upright.

He kept the beam focused on the diamond.

BANG!

The man jerked, but did not go down. He was single-minded in his focus. The entire chamber was filled with light in a cascade of colors. Orange, green, blue.

The bomb seemed to be trembling now.

Dubois burst back into view. She hauled herself out of one of the ancient stone baths. Water cascaded off her.

The room seemed to shake, vibrating with a sinister energy as everything took on the glow of the bomb.

Dubois charged at the man, her body a blur. She hit him low and drove him to the ground, then slithered up his body like a snake. She pinned both him and the laser pointer beneath her weight.

She was as light as a feather, but Troy had shot the man five times. He shouldn't have much strength left.

The chamber's trembling stopped almost instantly, and the unnatural luminescence dimmed. It retreated through the endless chambers and seemed to coalesce around the diamond again. It pooled there for several seconds, and then it was gone.

Troy pushed himself to his feet, gun trained on the laser man's head. Troy stumbled toward them as the light in the man's eyes went out.

"Is he dead?" Troy croaked.

Dubois felt for a pulse. "Yes."

Troy went to the bomb. The Star of Versailles was there, no longer glowing. It was very pretty though, flickering green and blue in the flame of the lantern. Troy reached out and touched it. It was perfectly cool. He plucked it off the bomb and slipped it into his pocket.

"What are you going to do with that?" Dubois said.

"Do with what?"

"The Star of Versailles."

He shook his head. "The Star of Versailles is at a museum in Paris."

They made their way above ground again. The stairs were easy, but it took some time to climb the collapsed walls of stone. As they climbed, they became aware that the earth was still trembling. When they reached the surface, they understood why.

Assad's people hadn't let up. They were bombing the ruins back to the…

The ground shook with each impact.

WHUMP! WHUMP! WHUMP!

They moved across the shattered landscape. Alex was where Dubois left him. They slumped down onto the dirt and rubble on either side of him.

"Thanks for abandoning me," he said.

"We're done," Troy said. "It's time to go home. We'll get you to a hospital. If gangrene hasn't set in yet, you should be fine."

"That's terrific," Alex said. "But how are we supposed to get out of here?"

Troy pulled out the satellite phone and dialed Colonel Missing Persons. There was a delay as the call bounced across the world.

"Stark? How's it going?"

"It's done," Troy said.

"All of it?"

Troy shrugged. "Well, someone should probably come and collect the bomb. I don't think that's our skill set."

"Very nice," Persons said. "We'll send the right people." He sounded almost as if he had expected this result the entire time.

"We have Syrians bombing our location," Troy said. "Our helicopter is cooked. It would be nice if we could be relieved here."

"I'll use the nuclear option," Persons said.

"It might be nice if you did that more often," Troy said, watching the skies.

As if summoned by his words, a trio of fighter planes roared overhead. They flew toward the distant hillside with impossible speed. A series of explosions erupted over there. In the aftermath, the hills were quiet. No more rockets came their way.

"Colonel?" Troy said, but the phone call had gone dead.

The three of them lay there, fires burning and ruins smoldering around them. For a pleasant change of pace, no one was shooting.

After a time, Troy couldn't say how long, dark silhouettes appeared in the sky. Their searchlights probed the ground.

"Black Hawks," Alex said. "The profile is unmistakable."

One of the Black Hawks hovered nearby, drawn by the guttering ruin of Alex's chopper. A group of soldiers fast-roped from the helicopter. They hit the ground, lights shining everywhere at once, and then advanced rapidly toward Troy, Alex and Dubois.

"Americans!" Troy screamed.

He tossed his gun aside and put his hands in the air. Next to him, Alex and Dubois did the same.

"Americans here!"

CHAPTER THIRTY FOUR

February 23
7:05 am Eastern European Time
Aboard the mega-yacht *Cristina*
Open water southwest of Crete
The Mediterranean Sea

"Nico! We have problems."

Nico Allesandro opened his eyes. He was on his king-sized bed in his stateroom, looking over the sky and sea of the Mediterranean. The curtains were pulled aside. It was just after sunrise, and the sky outside his windows a mix of pale yellow and blue, fading into darkness to the far right.

He looked at the cabin doorway. A young man named Silvio stood there, cradling a machine gun.

"What is it?" Nico said.

"Helicopters."

"Are they for us?"

Nico tried to piece that together. They were in the middle of the wide open sea between Greece and North Africa. The nearest African country was probably Libya. Would the Libyans come all the way out here to bother them?

"Police?" he said.

Silvio shook his head. "I don't think so. They came out of the rising sun, blinding us, like military helicopters would do. They passed over, circled, and it looks like they will come in for another run."

"God," Nico said. "Libyans?"

The Libyan government had collapsed years ago. Whoever controlled the remnants of that country now were lunatics, religious fanatics, and highway robbers. If they were flying Libyan military helicopters, this was trouble indeed.

"I don't know," Silvio said. "They don't answer the radio."

Nico swung out of bed. He pulled a pair of slacks on over his boxers and pulled a loose-fitting shirt from his open bureau closet. He was painfully aware of his large belly. He looked around the floor. All he had was sandals for his feet. He was woefully unprepared for something like this.

"Should we wake Antonio?" Silvio said.

Nico looked at him sharply. The question answered itself.

"No. Not until we understand what is happening."

Nico was the personal assistant to Antonio Di Napoli DeLorenzo, who for many years was one of the most powerful men on Earth. Antonio DeLorenzo, boss of the Calabrian 'Ndrangheta. In the past, Nico had imagined himself to be Antonio's *consigliere*. But those days were fading away.

Antonio was old, and wasn't himself anymore. He was reduced to vagabond status, a fugitive from justice in a dozen countries. They had been on this voyage to nowhere for more than a year now.

When they first left Italy, it had seemed like a good idea. Antonio could stay out of prison until his indictments blew over, or were fixed through payoffs or threats to the judges. But it hadn't worked like that. There were more than 60 individual indictments, in four different jurisdictions, in Italy alone. These things weren't going to go away. And all this time at sea had made Antonio confused. His mental state seemed to fall off a cliff in just the past two or three months.

"Show me these helicopters."

Nico followed Silvio down a long carpeted hallway with cabins on either side. This ship once belonged to a Saudi Arabian prince, who had a penchant for hosting wild parties at sea. At one time, all of these cabins would have been filled with the prince's guests, indulging in drugs, alcohol and orgies with prostitutes.

Now the rooms were empty, except for a few used by the chef and the household servants, and others where Antonio's remaining bodyguards slept. Since no one was here, Nico felt it would be wrong to force the help to sleep in the barracks-like servant quarters. The captain and his small crew always had decent rooms of their own, but Nico might as well let the lower workers enjoy a little bit of luxury while it lasted.

They reached the wide main deck and passed through the glass double doors to the outside. Helicopters. Nico shook his head. The prince used to park his personal helicopter on the deck just above here.

Nico stood on the deck, just outside the doors and in the shadow of the lip of the top deck. It was a cold morning, but the sky was a pale blue. It looked like it would warm up a bit into a lovely day. In front of him were four or five men in dark windbreaker jackets holding machine guns and watching the sky to the east. There were others on the deck below.

"Silvio, how many men do we have?"

Silvio didn't hesitate. "Ten gunmen."

"If it's the police, we see what they want. If it's someone else, pirates, or some military, we fight. Ten good men should be enough to hold them off."

Silvio nodded "Understood."

He reached to the collar of his jacket, pulled it up a couple of centimeters, and murmured something into a tiny microphone there.

"Maybe we will teach them a little lesson," Nico said.

It was a very large boat, but there wasn't room to land more than one or two helicopters at a time. If they tried to land without answering the radio, the men on board would put holes in them.

"Helicopters!" a man shouted from the deck below. Nico saw a dark arm point at the sky in the east. The rising sun was bright over there. Nico shielded his eyes. There was a group of dark specs there, quickly growing larger. It was hard to say how many there were. They were coming fast.

Silvio walked further out onto the deck and raised his gun toward them.

Unconsciously, Nico took a step backwards toward the doors.

A few of the men yelled.

A burst of heavy gunfire rang out from the first helicopter. Nico barely glimpsed the thing before the shooting started. It was black, small, egg-shaped, it's cockpit like a tiny glass dome. The firing came from two guns mounted in the front.

DUH-DUH-DUH-DUH-DUH-DUH-DUH-DUH.

It sounded metallic, like the grinding of steel treads. There was no time to respond. The gunfire strafed the lower deck. Nico wasn't sure if the men down there were hit or not. Silvio and the handful of men on the main deck returned fire, the sounds of their guns like children's toys compared to the guns from the helicopter.

The helicopter zoomed overhead and was already gone, almost before they began firing. Another was right behind it.

"Get down!" Nico screamed.

He dove to the decking in the corner near the doors.

Silvio and his men opened fire.

The second helicopter opened fire.

DUH-DUH-DUH-DUH-DUH-DUH.

Nico felt his heart pounding, about to give out. He covered his ears and rolled onto his side. He saw Silvio get shot, the rounds so powerful they nearly cut the young man in half. It wasn't just Silvio. All the men on the main deck, all of them except Nico himself, were chopped down and cut apart.

They made strange jerking gestures, they fell sideways, blood splattered, and parts of their bodies flew off. They fell like rag dolls.

Nico couldn't breathe.

A new group of black helicopters arrived. These were fatter than the first two, and they moved slower. Now that he could make them out clearly, Nico could see they had no markings on them of any kind. It was impossible to know who they were or where they had come from. There were four, five, maybe half a dozen of them, in a swarm around and above the ship.

Directly in front of him, a fat helicopter came down and hovered maybe ten meters above the deck. Ropes depended from either side, and men in black uniforms jumped out, sliding down the ropes to the main deck. They had rifles slung over their shoulders. Nico counted four men drop on each side.

The helicopter pulled up and away, as another one moved into position. No shots were fired from the ship, not even one. Were none of the men still alive?

There were eight enemy gunmen on the ship, and eight more coming. The men moved in a crouch, all in black like movie ninjas, snouts of their rifles sticking out ahead of them. Nico pushed himself to a standing position.

He raised a hand to them, as if to say STOP.

"You cannot enter," he said.

The lead man stood tall. He kept his rifle pointed at Nico's chest. The other men fell into a formation of some kind behind him.

The man's black uniform seemed thick and bulky. He must be wearing body armor underneath. It made him look like a superhero. He wore a black hood. The only thing showing was his dark eyes. Even his hands were covered in black gloves.

"We're here to see Antonio DeLorenzo," he said in very good Italian. His speech was unaccented, as if he had come from nowhere. He didn't sound like a foreigner speaking Italian. He didn't sound like an Italian from any particular region speaking Italian. He sounded like no one at all.

He learned to speak in language school.

"He's sleeping," Nico said. "He's an old man and needs his rest. I can speak to you for him."

Was it an absurd thing to say, given the massacre that had just taken place? Maybe, but Nico had seen just this kind of approach work before. Sometimes a massacre was just a message. It might not need to go any further.

"Who are you?" the man said.

"I am Nico Allesandro, don DeLorenzo's close aide and confidante."

The man nodded slowly, but the gun never wavered. Nico was mindful of the muzzle looming there. It was not the most alarming part of this experience. Nico had been held at gunpoint before.

"Antonio needs to understand, and whoever succeeds him needs to know, that the problem with Mateos Baruti is over. Baruti is dead, and that's that. The American policeman, and his family, cannot be targeted anymore."

Nico thought about that. The name came to him.

"Troy Stark."

"Stark," the masked man said. "Yes. He is to be left alone from now on." The man gestured at the ship all around them. "Or there will be more of this."

Nico nodded. It was hard to kill Stark and his family anyway. The two men who had gone to New York had failed in an attempt to kill the eldest brother. The next morning, their bodies were found dumped in the snow on the back porch of a private mafia social club in Queens.

"I can pass that message," Nico said. "Both to Antonio, and to the powers in Calabria." There was no sense pretending Antonio was in charge anymore. Even these men - American commandos, Nico supposed - knew that Antonio was too old to continue.

BANG! BANG! BANG!

Nico saw all three muzzle flashes before he heard the first gunshot. It was strange how light and sound seemed to bend time. His body jerked involuntarily.

Behind him, one of the glass doors shattered.

The pain was not immediate. There was more a sense that he could not breathe at all, and that he could not speak, and never would again.

He looked down and saw the blood beginning to flow down his chest and stomach. He hadn't even had time to button his shirt when he got out of bed. The bullet holes were not as bad as he would have imagined.

These are the entries. The exit wounds must be worse.

Yes, of course. That was true.

Nico's legs became weak. He felt like he couldn't stand anymore. His vision began to dim, becoming dark at the edges. The light was going out. He looked at the man in black, nothing there but eyes now, cold and without remorse.

"Don't worry about it," the man said. "We'll tell them ourselves."

CHAPTER THIRTY FIVE

February 26
4:30 pm Eastern Standard Time
Casey Key
Osprey, Florida

"Are you ready to do this?"

Troy and Dubois were parked in a blue Chrysler convertible along a beach road that fronted the Gulf of Mexico. To their left, the sea was a deep blue, a darker tone than the sky, which was pale blue. There wasn't a cloud in the sky anywhere.

It was a beautiful day, just the right kind of hot. The sun bathed them with bright warmth. Troy could feel it searing his skin. He'd had plenty of winter just recently, more than enough.

Straight ahead was a modern white mansion built on a rocky outcropping sticking out into the ocean. The house was barely visible behind the white walls that surrounded it. Troy happened to know that there were two nearly identical houses inside those walls, one on either side of a sparkling in-ground pool.

The house once belonged to Manuel Ocho Rios, the Mexican drug lord, often known by the nickname "El Maximo." Ocho Rios had built the house for maximum security. The island road was narrow and winding. This far north, an old one-lane bridge was the only way on or off the island by car. There was no way to make a fast approach by land.

If you did make that approach, you were confronted by the high walls, ringed with razor wire, and outfitted with cameras. If somehow you beat the walls, you then had to guess which of the two nearly identical houses was where Ocho Rios was hiding.

Better to come by sea. If you approached that way, the property towered above your head. All you needed to do was anchor your boat and climb the jagged rocks, while El Maximo's gunmen pelted you with machinegun fire.

It was a difficult place to attack.

When El Maximo became a permanent guest of the United States government and moved to more modest accommodations, the house was seized. It made the perfect safe house for large groups of people who needed to be hidden and protected all at once, and preferably in the same place.

Troy had it on pretty good authority that his family would be moving out of here pretty soon. The threat from the Calabrian mob appeared to have subsided. The violent deaths of Antonio DeLorenzo, his *consigliere*, and all of their bodyguards had something to do with it. The so-called nuclear option had worked its magic, at least for now.

No one seemed to have been elevated to the top spot in the southern Italy gangster world yet. It would probably be a little while. But the consensus was that the next man up wouldn't have an appetite for war against the US intelligence networks, the Joint Special Operations Command, and the clandestine special operators who lived their lives in a hazy gray area outside the normal rules of engagement.

Troy had no feelings about that, except relief. DeLorenzo's crew had put a hit on Troy for something that happened in the course of doing his job. When that hit didn't work, they put a hit on Troy's family members.

Play stupid games, win stupid prizes.

"I don't know," Dubois said. "I'm nervous."

Troy shrugged. "So am I."

"I'm a nervous wreck," Dubois said. "Maybe we should go back to the hotel."

He turned to her. She was wearing giant sunflower shades on her eyes. They looked ridiculous. She wore jeans shorts and a yellow t-shirt. The sash in her hair was pale blue like the jeans. She had yellow checkerboard sneakers on her feet. She looked great, just the right amount of homespun sexy.

She would never be the all-American girl, of course. Was there an all-Senegalese / French girl? Did such a thing exist?

Did it matter?

"I told them we were coming."

"I'm going to be the raisin in the milkshake here."

"Let's just do it," Troy said.

"All right," she said, but she seemed to be trying to swallow something large. It was like Dubois had a tennis ball lodged in her throat.

Troy put the car in gear. "We've faced worse before."

Less than a week ago, they'd been in Syria, where terrorists nearly set off a radioactive dirty bomb. A week before that, they'd been in Romania, in the heart of a weaponized cholera outbreak. In between, Dubois had been kidnapped by a Serbian criminal gang in Belgrade.

"No, we haven't," Dubois said.

He drove toward the high white walls of the house. The road made a hard right and wrapped around the property. Further on, there was a break in the wall. Incredibly, the gate was open. Troy made a left and pulled into the round driveway behind a dark blue classic Mustang and a gold Toyota sedan.

"Foolish to leave the gate open," Troy said.

"I thought the threat was over," Dubois said.

Troy shook his head. "It's never over. Nothing is ever over."

They got out of the car and walked up a sort of whitewashed alley between the houses, which loomed above them. A few yards ahead, the space opened up. Here was the glimmering turquoise pool, currently filled with shouting Stark family children. They were playing an imaginary sport that involved a missile made of Nerf-like material. At first glance, Troy couldn't tell if it was a team sport or every man for him or herself.

To the right, Donnie stood over a giant two-tier gas barbecue. The lid was up. He had a spatula in one hand, tongs in the other, and he was turning and flipping and in general messing around with what looked like three dozen hotdogs, burgers, and sausages. He was wearing a chef's hat, long colorful shorts, and no shirt.

At the far end of the pool, Mikey and Pat stood and chatted with beers in their hands. Behind them, the wives sat drinking wine on a patio overlooking the ocean.

"Man, oh man," Troy said.

No one had noticed them yet. That was a good thing, because if they were quick about it, they could still retreat back to the car. It was a bad thing because these people were supposed to be hiding after a murder attempt. They weren't paying any attention to who came in.

Suddenly, Troy's mother was there. She was deeply tanned, her blue eyes shining behind her glasses. She wore a white t-shirt with a cartoon depiction of a Florida license plate on it. It was a personalized vanity plate.

It read: MAFIA.

"Hi, ma," Troy said.

She turned, looked at Troy and Dubois, and smiled. She was carrying a wooden tray with cheese, meats, crackers and olives on it.

"Troy! We've been waiting for you."

She looked at Dubois. "And you! Welcome to our house. Well, we found out this morning that we're getting kicked out of here, but it's still ours for a couple more days. I guess the threat level is back down to zero, huh? That's what we're hearing."

"I don't know anything about it," Troy said.

She looked at Troy, eyes full of mischief. "If you assassinate another mob boss, maybe we can get this place again next winter. Hint, hint, hint. But you have to time it right. We don't want to be here in July."

There it was, the famous Stark humor. Dark, very dark.

Troy didn't try to deny anything. What would be the point? Half the time, his mom didn't even believe the things she said herself. She just said them to be funny, and try to get a rise out of people. So he didn't touch her comment at all.

Instead, he put a hand on Dubois's tiny back.

"Mom, this is Agent Dubois."

"Mariem," Dubois said.

It was crazy. Troy still thought of her as Dubois. The name Mariem didn't seem to fit. Maybe there was a nickname he could come up with.

La Maxima, perhaps.

Now everyone had spotted them. Mikey and Pat were coming along the pool. Donnie was rubbing his hands on a small towel. He picked up his beer can in his giant hand and made a beeline to get to them before his brothers.

"I've never been happier to almost get murdered," he said. "This place is awesome. The kids love it."

"Can we stay?" one of the kids shouted from the pool.

"Uncle Troy doesn't have control of that," Donnie said.

"He could kill somebody, couldn't he?"

"That's your grandmother planting silly ideas in your head. Your uncle Troy doesn't kill people. Not on demand."

The entire family was coming in for hugs now. They were already hugging Dubois, although they didn't even know here. It was a family of huggers.

"Everybody," Troy said. "This is my girlfriend Mariem."

NOW AVAILABLE!

ROGUE ATTACK
(A Troy Stark Thriller—Book #8)

"Thriller writing at its best."
--Midwest Book Review (*Any Means Necessary*)

From #1 bestselling and USA Today bestselling author Jack Mars, author of the critically-acclaimed *Luke Stone* and *Agent Zero* series (with over 5,000 five-star reviews), comes an explosive new, action-packed thriller series that takes readers on a wild-ride across Europe, America, and the world.

After elite Navy Seal Troy Stark is forced into retirement for his dubious respect for authority, his work in stopping a major terrorist threat to New York is noticed. Invited to join a secretive new international terrorist-fighting organization, Troy must hunt down all threats to the U.S. that originate from overseas—and pre-empt them by any means possible.

In ROGUE ATTACK (Book #8), Troy Stark plunges into the heart of darkness to sabotage a submarine-borne drug ring with ambitions as deep as the ocean. His only allies: his wits and his team. Can this clandestine operative outwit the masterminds of an international drug empire before their latest product floods the streets?

"Thriller enthusiasts who relish the precise execution of an international thriller, but who seek the psychological depth and believability of a protagonist who simultaneously fields professional and personal life challenges, will find this a gripping story that's hard to put down."
--Midwest Book Review, Diane Donovan (regarding Any Means Necessary)

"One of the best thrillers I have read this year. The plot is intelligent and will keep you hooked from the beginning. The author did a superb

job creating a set of characters who are fully developed and very much enjoyable. I can hardly wait for the sequel."
--Books and Movie Reviews, Roberto Mattos (re Any Means Necessary)

An unputdownable action thriller with heart-pounding suspense and unforeseen twists, ROGUE ATTACK is the eighth novel in an exhilarating new series by a #1 bestselling author that will have you fall in love with a brand new action hero—and turn pages late into the night.

Future books in the series are also available!

Jack Mars

Jack Mars is the USA Today bestselling author of the LUKE STONE thriller series, which includes seven books. He is also the author of the new FORGING OF LUKE STONE prequel series, comprising six books; of the AGENT ZERO spy thriller series, comprising twelve books; of the TROY STARK thriller series, comprising eight books; of the SPY GAME thriller series, comprising ten books; of the JAKE MERCER thriller series, comprising seven books (and counting); of the TYLER WOLF thriller series, comprising seven books (and counting); and of the new LARA KING thriller series, comprising seven books (and counting).

Jack loves to hear from you, so please feel free to visit www.Jackmarsauthor.com to join the email list, receive a free book, receive free giveaways, connect on Facebook and Twitter, and stay in touch!

BOOKS BY JACK MARS

LARA KING THRILLER SERIES
ASSET ONE (Book #1)
ASSET TWO (Book #2)
ASSET THREE (Book #3)
ASSET FOUR (Book #4)
ASSET FIVE (Book #5)
ASSET SIX (Book #6)
ASSET SEVEN (Book #7)

TYLER WOLF THRILLER SERIES
DOUBLE AGENT (Book #1)
DOUBLE CROSS (Book #2)
DOUBLE ASSET (Book #3)
DOUBLE DOCTRINE (Book #4)
DOUBLE JEOPARDY (Book #5)
DOUBLE THREAT (Book #6)
DOUBLE TARGET (Book #7)

JAKE MERCER THRILLER SERIES
ABSOLUTE THREAT (Book #1)
ABSOLUTE DAMAGE (Book #2)
ABSOLUTE FORCE (Book #3)
ABSOLUTE PERIL (Book #4)
ABSOLUTE TREASON (Book #5)
ABSOLUTE VENGEANCE (Book #6)
ABSOLUTE TARGET (Book #7)

THE SPY GAME
TARGET ONE (Book #1)
TARGET TWO (Book #2)
TARGET THREE (Book #3)
TARGET FOUR (Book #4)
TARGET FIVE (Book #5)
TARGET SIX (Book #6)
TARGET SEVEN (Book #7)
TARGET EIGHT (Book #8)

TARGET NINE (Book #9)
TARGET TEN (Book #10)

TROY STARK THRILLER SERIES

ROGUE FORCE (Book #1)
ROGUE COMMAND (Book #2)
ROGUE TARGET (Book #3)
ROGUE MISSION (Book #4)
ROGUE SHOT (Book #5)
ROGUE STRIKE (Book #6)
ROGUE ORDER (Book #7)
ROGUE ATTACK (Book #8)

LUKE STONE THRILLER SERIES

ANY MEANS NECESSARY (Book #1)
OATH OF OFFICE (Book #2)
SITUATION ROOM (Book #3)
OPPOSE ANY FOE (Book #4)
PRESIDENT ELECT (Book #5)
OUR SACRED HONOR (Book #6)
HOUSE DIVIDED (Book #7)

FORGING OF LUKE STONE PREQUEL SERIES

PRIMARY TARGET (Book #1)
PRIMARY COMMAND (Book #2)
PRIMARY THREAT (Book #3)
PRIMARY GLORY (Book #4)
PRIMARY VALOR (Book #5)
PRIMARY DUTY (Book #6)

AN AGENT ZERO SPY THRILLER SERIES

AGENT ZERO (Book #1)
TARGET ZERO (Book #2)
HUNTING ZERO (Book #3)
TRAPPING ZERO (Book #4)
FILE ZERO (Book #5)
RECALL ZERO (Book #6)
ASSASSIN ZERO (Book #7)
DECOY ZERO (Book #8)
CHASING ZERO (Book #9)

VENGEANCE ZERO (Book #10)
ZERO ZERO (Book #11)
ABSOLUTE ZERO (Book #12)

Made in United States
Troutdale, OR
07/09/2025

32748755R00142